Also by Vanessa Gray Bartal:

The Paradise Montana Chronicles:

Bumpy Road to Paradise
Purgatory in Paradise
Reunited in Paradise
Growing Pains in Paradise
Enchanted Cottage in Paradise
Road Trip from Paradise
Christmas in Paradise

The Lacy Steele Series:

Morning Cup of Murder
Building Blocks of Murder
A Family Case of Murder
Arch Enemy of Murder
Class Reunion of Murder
Wedding Day of Murder
Icy Grip of Murder
Ladies' Circle of Murder
Last Resort of Murder
Fowl Friend of Murder
Temp Job of Murder

The Kings of Montana Series:

Cowboy Down
Cowboy Lost
Cowboy Found
Cowboy Proud
Christmas with the Kings

The Bun and the Gun

Vanessa Gray Bartal

Chapter 1

Maggie stared at the muffin on her desk. It was pumpkin, not as tempting as blueberry, but still respectable.

"Later," she whispered to the muffin. "I'm working."

Now, the muffin seemed to be saying. Two crumbles of streusel on top made it look as if the muffin had eyes, judgmental eyes that commanded to be eaten.

"I'm not supposed to eat you at all. I'm on a diet," Maggie whispered.

The diet's a joke, and you know it, the persistent muffin responded.

"Shut up," Maggie whispered. She pushed the muffin away, which turned out to be a tactical error when some of the streusel stuck to her hand and demanded to be licked off. The muffin was smarter than she gave it credit for.

"Maggie Eldridge?"

It was unfortunate timing for Maggie that she was licking streusel off her palm like a cat bathing itself when the beautiful man showed up.

"Guh," she replied, her tongue still out of her mouth and now feeling five times fatter than usual. She reeled her tongue back inside her lips and hid her streusel-licked fingers under her desk.

"Hi, my name is Ridge Colton, and someone gave me your name. I'm planning a trip overseas, and I was hoping you might help," he said.

"Really?" she blurted.

"You're Maggie Eldridge, a reference librarian, correct?"

"Yes, but, I mean, you're not in college are you?" If he was in college, she should be in an old age home. He looked closer to thirty, but Maggie couldn't figure out why else he would have tracked her down for help at the university where she worked.

He smiled and, have mercy, he looked even better when that happened, like tiny face angels were on standby waiting to pose him in the most alluring position. "I'm not in college, but this is my first business trip to the Middle East, and a friend of a friend gave me your name as a potential contact."

"That makes more sense," Maggie said. "Where are you traveling?"

"Jordan, Saudi Arabia, and Dubai," he said.

Her face lit. "Three of my favorites. I'd love to talk to you and offer any help I can, but I have a day full of meetings. Does another day work for you?"

"How about tonight? We could meet for coffee," he suggested.

"Um," Maggie stalled while her sluggish brain tried to offer an answer. Was it safe to meet with a strange man for coffee, even if he looked as good as this man looked? Or maybe that made him more dangerous. Maybe he used his looks to lure unsuspecting, chubby librarians to their doom. "Coffee's good." If he were a serial killer, he'd better also be a bodybuilder. She would not easily be lifted into any sort of getaway car. Her eyes fell to the muffin. Now she needed to eat it, if only to aid in her defense.

"Great. Here's my card with all my contact information. Does six work for you?"

"Six works," Maggie said. "Do you know the coffee shop on Bodega?" It was the same coffee shop she'd visited this morning, the one where she'd procured the muffin.

"No, but I'll find it. Cheers." He gave her the smile again, the one that blazed out of his face like the time Harrison Ford opened the Ark of the Covenant and killed all the Nazis.

Maggie nodded stupidly at his retreating backside. It was wrong that some men should be so naturally handsome while others should be so naturally…not. She wasn't a socialist when it came to money, but looks were another matter. If only there were a way to give some of Ridge Colton's handsomeness to some of the average men she'd known, the world would be a more equitable place.

Shaking her head, she returned to work and, before she knew it, one hand was on the muffin and she had devoured half of it. "Stop making me eat you," she whispered. In reply she imagined the muffin laughing, a twisted, evil laugh of triumph.

Ridge returned to his car, sat inside, and closed his eyes. What were his first impressions of the librarian? *Genial.* The word popped into his head and wouldn't be dissuaded until he gave it full consideration. Throw a white wig on her, and Maggie Eldridge would make an excellent Mrs. Claus. She exuded warm friendliness and good cheer. Those were nice qualities to have, but not necessarily the qualities he was looking for. He needed quick intelligence and a strong drive to get the job finished, no matter the obstacles. Was she the sort of woman who would persevere through any difficulty? Or would she turn tail and run at the first hint of trouble? He couldn't yet say and decided to reserve judgment until later. Hopefully the meeting tonight would give him more information. He checked his watch and sighed. Six hours until their next meeting. With nothing left to do until then, he headed for the nearest gym and grabbed his duffle, glad for the chance to slip a workout into what had been a hectic few days.

When six rolled around, he arrived at the coffee shop and saw the librarian already there. *Punctual.* He liked that about her. Her head was down and bent over a few books that were spread open in front of her. Her clothes were different, meaning she had probably gone home to change. Now she wore a faded sweatshirt that read "Bookmarks Are For Quitters," and her hair was piled loosely on top of her head, instead of the tight bun she'd worn earlier. Ridge found himself smiling a little at the sight of her. There was something warm and welcoming about her. He felt drawn to her warmth, but that was a danger signal. He had to think rationally, like a boss and not like a man looking to make a new friend.

In front of her sat a mug of hot chocolate and plate with two cookies on it. The Mrs. Santa image of her intensified and he had to shoo it away. She was not his grandmother; in fact, she was four years his junior.

"Miss Eldridge," he said. Her head popped up. She was wearing reading glasses that magnified her eyes. She squinted in confusion, remembered she was wearing the glasses, and whipped them off.

"Hi," she said, offering up a friendly smile. He searched the smile for any hints of attraction and found none. One thing he did not want on his team was a fawning female or any budding romances. He had purposely chosen her as one of his potential candidates because she was not a femme fatale. But sometimes it was the plainer ones you had to watch out for. Throw them a little attention and they tended to hang on for life with an undying hope. This one didn't appear to be that sort and, if he were being honest, she was prettier than he had been expecting. Not his type, but he could see the appeal for some other men.

"Cookie?" she asked, sliding the plate nearer to him.

"No, thanks," he said. After spending nearly ninety minutes working out, the last thing he wanted was to pour sugar into his body. She had no such compunctions. He watched as she broke off a large chunk of a cookie, ate it, and washed it down with a sip of hot chocolate.

"When is your trip?" she asked after he had returned from placing his order for a plain, black coffee.

"Two weeks," he said. "I'm heading up a new team, and everything has to be perfect. I've been studying language and etiquette, but I wanted to speak to an American who's been there to see what more I could learn. I understand you lived abroad for a semester."

"I did, and I've traveled back and forth many other times," she said.

"Did you ever feel unsafe?" he asked.

"No, but I observed local custom and donned a hijab. And I was with friends who kept me from wandering places I shouldn't have gone," she said. "As long as you're conservative in your dress and behavior, you shouldn't have any problems." His coffee arrived. She eyed it and gave a wry smile.

"You don't like black coffee," he guessed.

"I like all coffee," she said.

"You smiled when my coffee arrived," he pointed out.

"I was thinking something," she said, waving her hand as if to push away the conversation, but now his curiosity was piqued.

"What were you thinking?" he asked.

She looked him in the eye. "That they did a study on psychopaths and their preferred mode of coffee was black."

He leaned in slightly and smiled because sometimes flirting came so naturally to him he didn't realize he was doing it. "Do you think I'm a psychopath?"

She leaned in slightly and rested her chin in her hand. "That's a quandary. If I say yes, you might kill me to keep me from telling others. If I say no, you might kill me because you believe I've been lulled into complacency by your friendly demeanor."

"Which one is your answer?" he asked.

"I would say it needs further study, but the fact that you refused a warm chocolate chip cookie and eyed my hot chocolate like it's poison tells me you don't approve of sugar. And anyone who doesn't approve of cocoa and cookies must automatically be labeled psychotic," she said and, to his surprise, he laughed out loud.

"What if I avoid those things because I'm diabetic?" he asked.

She shook her head.

"What do you mean no?" he asked.

"You're not type 2 diabetic because there's no fat on your body and, generally, type 2 is brought on by lifestyle. You might be type 1, but type 1 can still eat sugary treats, they simply have to adjust their insulin. And an active guy like you would have an insulin pump, which you don't. Therefore, you do not have diabetes, and your dislike of sugar is a personal choice because you view your body as a temple."

Ridge was having fun, and that was unexpected. "What's wrong with viewing one's body as a temple?"

"Nothing. I do it, too. And I offer it routine cookie sacrifices to keep it pleased," she said, and he laughed again.

"All right, you've convinced me. I'll try a cookie." He reached for the plate in front of her, and she smacked his hand.

"That offer was only on the table when I thought you were a nice guy. Now that I know you're a psychopath, you're going to have to get your own."

He blinked at her, shocked. He was used to a certain amount of deference from women, and not one of them had ever smacked his fingers. "Okay," he said at last. "Be right back." He returned to the table and, a few minutes later, a waitress arrived carrying an entire tray of warm cookies.

Maggie put her hands to her mouth. "It's like Christmas."

Now it was Ridge's turn to smile, but he didn't dare explain why. He wasn't stupid enough to tell any woman she reminded him of Mrs. Claus. "What makes you think any of these are for you?" he asked.

"You're really going to eat," she paused to do a quick count, "eighteen cookies?"

"I'm saving some to mail as Christmas presents to my friends and family," he said, and it was her turn to laugh. She had a nice laugh, as warm and infectious as everything about her.

"Hey, big spender, that must be some Christmas list," she said.

"I'm going to give two to my mom because moms are special," he said.

"She's lucky to have you, and she'll be thrilled to receive her Christmas present in September."

"I'm going to save them until December," he said.

"They'll be nice and green then. Festive," she said.

All of a sudden he remembered he was supposed to be working. With effort, he pulled himself back to an objective standpoint and began to ask her questions.

"Why does a college reference librarian have so much interest in the Middle East?" he asked.

"My undergrad is in Middle East studies, and I had a close friend from Jordan," she said.

"Had?"

She blinked and took a sip of her cocoa before answering. "He died."

"I'm sorry," Ridge said.

"It was a long time ago," she said, but her hand shook slightly when she set the cocoa down.

Wisely, he moved on to other topics. They talked for a long time and, when the conversation was over, he walked her to her car and shoved the bag of leftover cookies into her hands.

"I couldn't possibly," she said as she opened her car door and tossed the bag of cookies inside.

Ridge laughed, something he had been doing the whole evening. "Thank you so much for meeting with me. I really appreciate it."

"The pleasure is mine. I use my undergrad far too little these days. It's almost like picking an obscure major as a clueless eighteen year old was a bad thing," she said.

"Well, it certainly came in handy tonight."

"Have a great trip. If you can ignore all the political and religious wrangling, Jordan is a wonderful country full of warm, friendly people."

"I'm looking forward to it," he said. He took her hand and shook it, holding it a second longer than necessary. "You've washed this since you licked it today, right?"

"Of course," she said, tugging it free. "Then I licked it again later. There's no known cure for my mental illness, but I'm on medication for it."

He laughed. "After spending an entire evening with you, that part's not hard to believe. Have a good night, and enjoy those cookies."

"What cookies? They're already gone." She gave him a little wave and drove off. He stood in the street staring after her, smiling. He liked her. She reminded him of the girls back home in small town Texas—warm, friendly, and real. After being away so long and incessantly surrounded by people dying to get ahead, Maggie Eldridge was a breath of fresh air. But he couldn't hire people based on whether or not he liked them. He would go home and review the information he had on her. Then, after some distance, he would be unbiased enough to render a decision. At least that was his hope. The stakes were too high to mess up.

Chapter 2

Maggie had forgotten all about the coffee meeting she'd had with the handsome stranger. It wasn't the commonness of such an occurrence that made it forgettable. In fact, it was the first time in her memory a man who looked like Ridge Colton hunted her down and asked for her help. But it was that sort of dramatic un-ordinariness that made it forgetful. How could she possibly dwell on something so spectacularly odd? Literally the nicest looking man she had ever encountered in real life had come looking for her and bought her a tray of her favorite cookies. If she were a different sort of woman, she would have fallen in love with him right there, and then she would spend the rest of her life dwelling on her memories. Someday she would be in a nursing home telling the other residents about the fun evening she'd spent with the man with blindingly perfect teeth.

But, being Maggie, she instead forgot all about it. It had been an anomaly and, in her experience, anomalies were best forgotten. So she froze the cookies he'd given her and, occasionally when she took one out and popped it in the microwave, he passed through her brain. Mostly she wondered if he was having fun on his trip. She hoped so. She felt an almost personal interest whenever anyone ventured to Jordan, a country she loved. If he didn't also love it, it would feel like a slap in the face to her. But the truth was that she would never know how it turned out because she would never see him again. Men like that, men who could be the star of their own television show, did not come calling on Maggie Eldridge and, truth be told, Maggie Eldridge was thankful. She was a low-maintenance woman, and she preferred low-maintenance men. Give her an average-looking accountant any day of the week, someone who worked hard, enjoyed binge watching Netflix on the weekends, and always remembered to put the toilet seat down. High-maintenance men who spent a mortgage payment on shoes and needed to be constantly entertained and adored were of no interest to her.

Now it was Saturday two weeks after the meeting and past time for Maggie to clean up her yard. Her mother, an avid gardener, had tried since Maggie's birth to get her interested in the hobby with no luck. But today, as September waned, it was time to clean up her flowerbeds. So she dressed head to toe in the expensive gardening gear her mother had bought her, looking like a *Plow & Hearth* catalogue threw up on her. On her head was a giant straw hat. On her body were denim overalls embroidered with daisies. Her feet wore giant rubber clogs printed with shovels, and her hands were enrobed in leather-tipped gloves, printed in ducks for reasons Maggie had yet to discern. So far the gloves were the only functional part of the mortifying ensemble. The problem, she realized, was that with the blooms gone, she had no idea what was a weed and what was a flower. For the last twenty minutes she had been staring at the dirt wondering if the things with prickers were friend or foe.

"Hello."

Maggie whirled so fast she toppled over backwards. The man who spoke reached down to help her up, but she scrambled crablike away from him.

"What are you doing here?"

"I need to talk to you," Ridge Colton said.

"No, no, no," Maggie said. She scrambled backwards until she bumped the house and used it to pull herself up. "I never told you where I live. How did you find me? *Are* you psychotic?"

"No."

"Is this about the cookies? Because, okay, I ate them, but I can get you some more."

"Maggie," he said, taking a step closer.

"Aa, Aa, Aa," she said, scolding him as she would a naughty puppy. "Stop. Stay or I'll…" she scanned for a usable weapon. "Why didn't I take that ninja class in college?"

He put his hands up, palms out in surrender. "Easy there. You don't need ninja classes and, even if you had them, I could still disable you."

"I'm going to scream now," she warned him.

"I was stating a fact, not making a threat. Look, I'm standing right here with my hands up, in full view of your neighbors. I'm not here to hurt you. All I want to do is have a little conversation, and then I'm on my way, okay?"

She nodded slowly, her eyes still casting about for an escape.

"My name, my real name, is Cameron Ridge and I'm from the government."

Her eyes bugged. "I said I'd pay you back for the cookies."

"Will you forget about the cookies?" he said, exasperated.

"Then what? I don't understand. I don't speed, I've never pirated movies or music, I'm current on my taxes. What could someone from the government want from me?"

"I want to offer you a job."

She blinked. "A job?"

"I'm assembling a new team, something elite with a precise focus. Your experience and language skills are exactly

12

what I'm looking for." She was smiling now. "What's the smile for?"

"This feels a lot like when Tony Stark was asked to join the Avengers. Am I being pranked? Did my little brother put you up to this?"

"No." He opened his jacket to reveal a gun in its holster. She flattened herself against the house again and opened her mouth to scream. He closed the distance between them and pressed his palm over her lips.

"Maggie, please. I'm telling you the truth. I'm going to give you some information and you can call it in to verify it when I'm done, okay? Nod yes, and I'll lower my hand."

She nodded yes. They were toe-to-toe and his sheer size was intimidating. "Are you FBI?"

He shook his head.

"CIA?"

He shook his head.

"MI-6?" her tone turned hopeful.

"Definitely not," he said, smiling. "I'm part of an organization whose letters you've probably never heard before. After 9-11 and the Patriot Act, intelligence splintered into multiple offshoots. Most, like ours, have the sole task of focusing on one terror cell at a time."

"And you want me, a chubby college librarian, as part of your elite task force. Will Santa and Elvis be there? Will I get a gun so I might singlehandedly take down bad guys, like Bruce Willis in *Die Hard*?"

"No word yet on Santa or Elvis. You will get a gun, but nothing will be singlehanded, and Bruce Willis didn't need a gun. As for being chubby, that's a matter of opinion." He touched his finger to the tip of her nose and winked.

"You're good. You didn't break character once and you got the prop gun and everything. I almost believed you were a spy. Are you by chance also a stripper? Because it's not my thing, but a lady I work with is looking for someone to do a bridal shower soon."

"Tell you what—you take this." He folded a business card into her fingers. "Call the number and ask all the questions you want. Tomorrow I'll be at the coffee shop at noon. Meet me if you're interested." He took a step back and paused. "By the way, nice outfit. My grandma has that same hat. And Samson hasn't barked once. You should have gotten a little yappy dog—better burglar deterrent."

"The hat was a gift, and how did you know my dog's name?" she called. In answer, he tossed her a backwards wave.

Maggie gave up on weeding. She went inside, sat beside her sleeping Great Dane, Samson, and stared at the card. On it was a phone number in bold, black print. With shaking fingers, she picked up her phone and dialed.

Chapter 3

"So you're actually a…" Maggie stood beside the table, unable to finish the sentence. She had shown up early to the coffee shop, but Cameron Ridge was already there.

"A spy? Yes," he said.

"Are you allowed to say that?" she asked.

"It's all right, I'm going to self-destruct in five seconds," he said.

She was in too much shock to laugh. She sank into the chair across from him. "Tell me again why you want a reference librarian on your team."

"People have this misconception about the intelligence community, that we're TV characters who constantly have to defuse bombs. The truth is that about 95 percent of our work is gathering and compiling information."

"That does sound up my alley," she agreed.

"Your training as a librarian makes you an asset. But your knowledge of the Middle East and ability to speak Arabic make you invaluable. You had to know you've been on our radar for some time."

"I get excited if more than ten people on social media remember my birthday, and you're telling me I've been on the spy network's radar?" she said, aghast.

He nodded.

"Where would I work?" she asked.

"Washington, DC."

She winced. Currently she lived in Washington State in a small college town whose main industry was cherry orchards. Could she give that up for the hustle and bustle of the capitol?

"Let me make sure I understand what you're saying: I say yes to you, move to DC, and, just like that, I'm a spy?"

"Not quite. You'd have to train at Quantico."

"You said you're not FBI."

"We're under the same umbrella and we share training," he said.

"What's the training like?"

"Twenty weeks, part classroom, part physical."

She squirmed. "How physical?"

"Running, climbing, pushups, sit ups, hand-to-hand combat. And we'll teach you how to handle a gun."

"See, this is the awkward part of things for me. It's all well and good when we're talking academics and research. But physical fitness is a whole other can of worms. If my high school had observed senior superlatives, I would have been voted most likely to fall down a flight of stairs while eating a caramel apple. Because that actually happened to me once. And now you're telling me I have to become Chuck Norris."

"Not Chuck Norris. Just not Chuck E. Cheese," he said. "It's a requirement for everyone, but not because you're going to be in the field using the skills you'll be learning. Think of it as basic training."

"The job sounds intriguing, Mr. Ridge."

"There's no mister. It's either Ridge or Cam," he interjected.

"I know I can do what you want and be good at it. But the sad truth is that I'm pathetically out of shape, unless you consider round a shape. I have never successfully run a mile, done a pushup, sit up, or pull up. And rope climbing? They had to put up a special net to catch me."

"Those things are a matter of will," he said.

"Says the Adonis with abs that can crush walnuts," she said, and he laughed.

"Maggie, what it comes down to is wanting. If you want to do it badly enough, then you'll find a way. Ask a fit friend to train you or hire a personal trainer. You don't have to run a marathon; you only have to run a couple of miles."

"What if I try and I fail?" she asked.

He shrugged. "Then you fail. You wouldn't be the first. There are no guarantees."

"You're suggesting I give up my job, house, friends, town, and even my dog temporarily, and for what? The off chance that I might be able to pass training that right now seems completely impossible? What if I hate it?"

"What if you love it?" he said softly, and Maggie's heart started to thunder. All at once she knew she was going to give up everything and take a chance on an adventure she didn't know she'd been missing.

"Yes," she whispered and then mashed both of her hands over her mouth.

He smiled a cocksure smile that said he knew she would cave. Maggie took a moment to swallow down the bile that had risen to the back of her throat. Had she really committed to such a crazy prospect? She couldn't think about it now or she might genuinely flip out. Her mind flailed about for a subject change.

"What part of Texas are you from, Ridge?" she asked.

He froze. "How did you know I'm from Texas?" He had worked hard to eradicate his accent, if only to protect his family back home. The more of a bland everyman he became, the better for all involved.

"Lucky guess," she said. He carried himself like a Texan, as if he still had Manifest Destiny flowing through his veins. And then there were his manners. She'd heard him call more than one woman ma'am, and he had held every door for her.

17

And there was the way he kept twisting his right ring finger. "Are you missing your Aggie ring?"

"Now that's spooky," he said, a hint of a twang creeping back into his words. "What else can you tell me about myself?"

She studied him intently a moment before speaking again. "You wear reflective aviator shades because you want to read people without them reading you. You're former military, probably something elite like a ranger or SEAL, and you still order your life as such. You only date women who have reached a certain level of physical perfection, but then feel perpetually disappointed when the rest of them is lacking. You're a youngest child and there's a large age gap, probably at least six years. And right now you're craving Mexican food."

It took a lot to shock him, but Cameron Ridge was shocked. "Everything was exactly spot on. Are you a profiler in your spare time? How did you do that?"

She tapped her temple, pleased with his praise. "Intuition. Except the Mexican food thing. You probably smell the restaurant next door and it's making you hungry."

"True. Let's go next door and get lunch. I'll answer any questions you might have."

"Why are so many stupid people famous?" she asked.

"Questions about the job," he clarified, though he was relieved to see she was regaining her equilibrium. He placed his hand on the small of her back and used it to usher her out of the coffee shop and into the restaurant next door, holding the doors for her each time. When they walked in, several female heads turned to look at them, first Ridge, with his astounding good looks, and then Maggie. She could practically hear what they were thinking. *She must be his cousin; there's no way they're together.* She felt like grabbing a microphone and assuring everyone she knew he was out of her league and she had no interest in him anyway.

They were seated quickly. She picked up a menu, set it down, and picked it up again but it was hard to concentrate when her brain was abuzz.

"I guess you're kind of my boss now," she said.

"It's not official yet," he said. "Besides, I'm not exactly your boss. We're part of the same team and will report to the same person."

"But you're in charge," she said.

"Kind of. I'll be doing the legwork, and you'll be my support," he said.

"Like a girdle," she added and he choked on a sip of water.

Ridge intended to spend the time talking about work, but somehow they never got around to it. Instead conversation varied from books to movies to college to—briefly—his time in the military. If he were being honest, he would admit it was the most fun he'd had in ages, and he liked Maggie. A lot. There was no pretense with her, and it had been a long time since he felt such an instant connection with anyone, male or female. He had become so accustomed to the fast-paced, intense world of government espionage that he had forgotten what it was like to be with someone real, someone untouched by the things he knew and saw. There was a part of him that was tempted to un-invite her to Washington because he didn't want her fresh-faced innocence to change or go away. Though not his type, she was the kind of woman who, if he had more brothers, would make him attempt to play matchmaker.

When they could linger over lunch no longer, they eventually wandered back to the coffee shop for drinks and, to Maggie's delight, another tray of cookies. Finally when Ridge could no longer hold off the inevitability of his return flight he walked her to her car. They paused and faced each other.

"Thank you for lunch and yet another bag of cookies," she said, holding the bag aloft.

"Technically it goes on my expense account, but you're welcome."

"I should have held out for a pony," she said, causing him to laugh again. His cheeks were beginning to hurt from so much unusual repetitive motion. "Can I tell you something and not have you take it the wrong way?"

"Try," he said, feeling a bit wary now.

"You're the kind of man a lot of women hit on, so I want to be clear this isn't what I'm doing. But it feels like I've known you longer than a few days, and I like you. You're a good guy."

"Thank you."

"But wait, there's more. Thank you for giving me this opportunity. I have the feeling it's going to be life changing."

"Hopefully in a good way," he said.

"Fingers crossed."

They stood smiling at each other. The moment stretched and began to feel awkward as neither knew how to make a polite escape. If it were a date, they would kiss goodbye. But it wasn't a date, they were both clear on that. At last Maggie opened her arms and hugged him. It was probably not the best way to say goodbye to one's new boss, but it was heartfelt, and she hoped that would convey.

It did, and Ridge returned her hug, giving her an enveloping embrace of his own.

"See you in six months," she said. "I hope."

"See you in six months, for sure." He pulled back and looked her in the eye. "You can do this, Maggie. If I didn't have full confidence, I wouldn't have hired you."

20

She nodded. "I'll give it my all, Boss." After hailing him a little three-fingered salute, she got in her car and drove away. For the second time, Ridge stood in the street and watched her drive off, a feeling of warmth spreading through him. Being near Maggie felt like coming home, and he had no desire to stop and analyze why.

Chapter 4

Maggie put her hand on the front door, twisted the knob, then turned and ran back to the bathroom. After losing her breakfast, she brushed her teeth, touched up her makeup and stared at herself in the mirror. *I can't do this.*

"You can do this." Her little sister, Amelia, stood in the doorway, disheveled and still half asleep. Her sister, on a break from college, had come to help Maggie settle in to her new home. She would also be taking care of Maggie's dog, Samson, until the new dog sitter could begin the next day.

"Do you honestly think so?" It was a sign of her desperation that she was now relying on a college junior for encouragement, but her baby sister had been the most enthusiastic member of her family by far when it came to Maggie's new job. She had even gone so far as to pick out new clothes for Maggie to wear. And Maggie had let her because she was kind of a mess when it came to finding things to wear and her sister was a budding fashionista.

"Maggie, come on. Look at you." She put her arm around Maggie's shoulders and stared at their joint reflection in the mirror. "You made it through twenty weeks at Quantico, you learned to run not one but five miles, you lost twenty pounds. You have never looked better."

"Looks aren't everything," Maggie felt obliged to remind her.

Amelia rolled her eyes. "Maybe not, but they'll take you pretty far, and you look hot."

"I'm not supposed to look hot; I'm supposed to look professional."

"That, too," Amelia said, pulling out her phone and beginning to scroll. "You've got this," she reiterated as she yawned.

"I have to ride the train for an hour. What was I thinking buying a house so far away from work?"

"That it was all you could afford unless you wanted to hock a kidney?" Amelia said.

"There's that," Maggie said. It was either buy a tiny, two-bedroom house in the suburbs far away from the city or share an even tinier apartment in downtown DC. Maggie opted for privacy and a break from city life. As a bonus, the house had come with a fenced yard for Samson. All she'd had to do was install a doggy door with a sensor so he could let himself in and out at will while she was at work. She would be working crazy hours and would have a long commute, something she felt terrible about. One of her first tasks after her move had been to find a dedicated dog sitter who would check on Samson every afternoon and at a moment's notice on the days Maggie couldn't make it home. Still, she felt guilty about leaving him alone so much. The only tradeoff was that she now ran with him every morning, a bonus he seemed more than happy to accept.

"Okay, okay, I can do this," Maggie said, trying hard to feel the hollow words. She wasn't at all certain she meant them. So far she had survived the transition because so many things had required her attention: find a house, move her belongings, unpack, find a dog sitter, change her address, connect the utilities. The tedious list had taken all of her focus and provided a handy distraction from homesickness, uncertainty, loneliness and fear. Now they were hitting hard. She was really in a new city, about to start her first day on a new job, as a spy, no less. She knew no one besides her boss, a man she hadn't seen in six months.

"You can totally do this. What's the big deal? You're going to be a librarian, same as before," Amelia said. Maggie had fudged her job description a bit, telling her family she was going to be a librarian for an obscure government office. They had no idea she was actually going to be working in covert ops because she wasn't allowed to tell anyone, not even her parents. They had thought her training at Quantico was standard procedure for everyone. Maggie didn't dare tell them the truth, that she'd had to withstand tear gas, spend three days in wilderness survival training with no food, been physically forced to fight with other cadets, learned the basics of how best to disable and kill an enemy, and had extensive training with multiple different types of weapons. It was more, a thousand times more, than she ever thought herself capable of. And the fact that she had done it gave her a new sense of pride about herself she had never felt before.

She straightened and brushed a hand down the skirt her sister had picked out for her. New clothes hadn't been simply for vanity, they'd been a necessity. Since losing twenty pounds, nothing fit anymore.

"I can do this," she said with more certainty. She kissed her sister's cheek, scratched her dog's ears, grabbed her bag, walked to her car, drove to the train station, boarded the train, and sat down, clutching her bag to her chest like a lifeline. She had brought a book, intending to read during the long commute. Instead she sat stock-still and counted the stops until it was her turn, suddenly feeling very much like a little girl lost once again.

At last it was her turn. She stood and disembarked with a mass of other suburbanite straphangers. The new company was five blocks from her Metro stop. Today the weather was nice, but she was already dreading the walk during torrential downpours or snowstorms. Since it was now March, there were bound to be many such downpours. To her surprise, several of the people from the Metro also went into her building with her. She tried not to gawk. The building itself was a ubiquitous brown brick monstrosity, built sometime during the age when any sort of pleasing aesthetic was considered a luxury. The sign out front read, "Landwood Consolidated." To the outside observer, it was any other boring corporation. Only those who worked there knew it was actually a highly classified government agency. Of the three classification levels, top secret, secret, and confidential, Maggie now qualified for secret clearance. A big part of her still couldn't believe it, so she tried not to think about it.

She pulled out her badge—the one she had checked for seven times before leaving home—and fumbled a little as she slid it through the door. The badge was the first level, the innocuous one posted for strangers. After that came the retina scan and armed guards. Maggie smiled nervously at them, but they were like palace beefeaters—neither made eye contact or acknowledged her in any way. Her bag went through the scan with no beeps, and she was at last on her way to the elevator that would take her to the floor that housed her new office.

She stepped off the elevator once again feeling nauseated. Absolutely no one looked up to acknowledge the newcomer, and that was fine by her. She made her way to her cubicle, set down her bag, and faced her computer. And that was when she saw it—a chocolate chip cookie with a bow on top. The sight of it made tears spring to her eyes and she fought hard to push them away. Someone in this swarming mass of humanity knew her, at least a little bit. Someone was glad she was here. To Cameron Ridge, she was slightly more than badge number 53709.

Smiling now, she logged on to her computer and read the daily briefing, the listing of intelligence reports that detailed exactly what was going on in the world. It was the same report the president received every morning. With a jolt, Maggie realized she might one day be adding to it.

It was Maggie's first such briefing, and she read it with all the shock and horror one might imagine. How was the world not currently at war with so much going on? And how was everyone able to keep it out of the evening news? Suddenly every conspiracy theory she had ever heard seemed much more believable. After an hour, which she spent learning to navigate the computer programs she would be using daily, her phone buzzed. She jumped, startled by the unusual sound.

"Mr. Ridge would like to see you in his office," a woman said and immediately disconnected while Maggie flailed for a response.

Maggie stood, righted her skirt, and pressed a hand to her hair. It had grown overly long while she was in training. Most days, today included, she wore it all up in a tidy knot. As she walked down the long trail to Ridge's office, she could feel multiple pairs of eyes on her. It felt a little like the last walk to a guillotine, but she had no idea why. There was no sign of a secretary outside Ridge's office. Maggie would later learn she worked on a different floor and was shared between three people. Without a secretary as a buffer, nothing stood between Maggie and her new boss but a heavy wooden door. She took a breath, opened the door, and stepped inside.

She had wondered how she would feel upon seeing him again. Their last meeting had felt so natural, so fluid. It was as if they had known each other forever and could say anything. Had that been a fluke? Would the fact that he was now officially her boss change everything?

She took a tentative step inside and stopped short. His head was down, bent over something she couldn't see, and he seemed to be reading intently. When he at last looked up, there was no smile of welcome. They regarded each other in silence, his eyes scanning her from head to toe. And *then* he smiled.

"You made it."

She beamed. "I really did, and I only blacked out and threatened to quit eighteen times."

He chuckled. "Congratulations, Maggie."

"Thanks, Ridge. Still Ridge?"

"Still Ridge," he said.

"Thank you for the cookie," she said.

"What cookie?" he asked, looking so innocent she almost believed him.

"The one I showed to all the other employees when I ran through the office yelling, 'The boss gave me a cookie. Where's yours?'"

"See? I knew you would make friends easily and keep the drama to a minimum," he said.

"I haven't actually talked to anyone yet. Is that weird?"

"It hasn't been the warmest environment. I don't know why," he said, frowning. "Do you need anything, do you have questions?"

"How are some people able to solve a Rubik's Cube in mere seconds?" she asked.

"Any questions about the job," he clarified, smiling.

"Oh, not so far. Just trying to learn how to navigate the computer systems, so far, so good."

"Great. Well, if you need anything, my door is open. Hey, let's plan a time to grab coffee. You can catch me up on your adventures in Quantico."

"Sounds great. Also, you should know that 'Adventures in Quantico' is officially going to be the title of the movie I'm writing," she said.

"You're writing a movie?" he said.

"Yes, in fact this job is a clever ruse to get me closer to several noted Hollywood producers."

"Hollywood is on the other coast," he informed her.

"I knew I shouldn't have taken that mail-order geography class from the discount club. There's three dollars I'll never see again."

He chuckled. She gave him a little wave and let herself out of the office. The long walk back to her cubicle felt no less conspicuous. She tried to make eye contact and smile, but every time she caught someone's eye, he or she looked furtively away. *Weird,* she thought.

At lunch she made her way to the break room with trepidation. It felt like being in middle school all over again. She was tempted to eat at her desk, but that wouldn't do. This was her life now; she needed to meet people and make friends. Tentatively, she entered the room, filled her bottle with water, and sat down at a long table with a few other people. No one said a word. A minute later, a man with blue, spikey hair sat down across from her.

"You're the token librarian," he announced.

"I am," she said. "Are you the token Smurf?"

The room seemed to hold its breath, but the guy laughed, as Maggie hoped he would. "Baby, I am way too mighty to be tiny," he said.

"That's going to be a wordy tattoo you'll someday regret," she said. He laughed again and held out a hand to shake.

"Name's Blue."

"Real name?" she asked. "Because if we're calling ourselves by our attributes, my name is 'Likes Dessert.'" She shook his hand and a couple of other people in the room chuckled.

"Believe it or not, it's my real name," he said. "And it gets worse."

"Your wife is yellow and your children are green?" she guessed. "Not that there's anything wrong with that."

"Wrong. My middle name is Indigo," he admitted.

"Blue Indigo. That's pretty cool," Maggie said. "If I name my first kid that, it's a total coincidence that has nothing to do with you, so don't get cocky."

A round-faced woman with a short brunette bob sat down beside Maggie. "Okay, I like you. I'm Babs, short for Babette. Never call me that."

"I'm Maggie, short for Margaret, never call me that," Maggie said, smiling hello at Babs.

"Where'd you move from?" Babs asked.

"Washington, the state. How about you?"

"Another government agency, same as Blue," she nodded at the blue-haired man. "He's a hacker, and I do data entry, snore, snore."

"I saw you got called up into the dragon's lair," Blue said, and Maggie was confused.

"Huh?"

"The boss's office," Babs translated. "Was it horrible? Did he yell at you?"

Smiling, she looked between them to see if they were joking. "What are you talking about?"

"Cameron Ridge, AKA Satan," Babs said.

"Are you kidding? He's one of the nicest guys I've ever met," she said.

Blue laughed and then instantly sobered. "Wait, are you being sarcastic or do you actually think that?"

"I'm serious, I like him a lot. He's super sweet," Maggie said. "Are you guys joking?"

Babs and Blue looked at each other. "I've cried three times since I transferred here," Babs said.

"Me, too," Blue agreed.

"Are you for real?" Maggie asked.

"Are you?" Blue said, but Babs nodded in a knowing fashion.

"It's because he's ultra hot, right? Believe me, eventually you start to see past that, usually right about the time you spend your lunch break bawling in the bathroom and searching your phone for other job openings," Babs said.

"Wait a minute, are you actually saying you think Ridge is mean?" Maggie said. "What has he done that's so bad?"

"If you don't do something the way he wants, the minute he wants, he will scream at you and make you feel like the stupidest creature that's ever inhabited the earth," Babs said.

"Or worse, he won't scream at you. He'll sit there and stare while you try to maintain eye contact and bladder control. Eventually you lose both and turn to crawl back to your desk in utter shame."

Maggie sat back, flabbergasted. "I don't believe this."

Babs and Blue nodded together. "Wait until it happens to you. You're going to want to go crying back to your cherry orchard."

"But what about the actual job? Do you like the work?" Maggie asked.

"The work's cool. I mean, it's stressful and a total overload, but it's doable. It's Cameron Adolf Ridge who makes life unbearable," Blue said. "Be careful, I'm serious."

"All right," Maggie said, still sounding puzzled. How could she possibly reconcile the man she had met with the man they were describing? He had left her a welcome cookie, for goodness sake.

"Hey, let us take you out tonight, sort of a welcome wagon type thing," Babs said.

"That sounds amazing, really, but my little sister is in town for one more day, so I kind of need to be with her tonight. Rain check?" Maggie said.

"For sure," Blue said. He held his fist over the table, and she bumped it.

By the time lunch was over, she felt like she was on her way to making some friends. Later, as Ridge passed her desk and gave her a sly wink, she felt more than a little confused over her new friends' description of him. Was he the sweetheart who had recruited her or the monster they believed him to be? Time would tell.

Chapter 5

By the time a month passed, Maggie felt all settled in. She had her commute down pat, and she had almost started to enjoy it. She was reading so much she could barely keep enough books in stock. Her dog seemed slightly morose, but it helped that he adored his dog walker. And the fact that the days were getting longer meant Maggie could take him on a walk in the evenings, in addition to a run in the mornings. She was trying to buy his love and forgiveness with exercise, and it seemed to be working.

Work was going well, better than well; it was great. After Babs and Blue extended their welcome, it was as if she had passed some sort of test and the other inhabitants of the office began to creep closer and make themselves known. In addition to Babs and Blue, she had also become friends with two women named LuAnn and Ellen, both data entry specialists. As for her actual work, it was fast paced and challenging, but she was loving it. The only fly in the ointment was Ridge.

He was predictably busy and seemed to be under an enormous strain. He and Maggie had yet to get together outside of work, and they barely saw each other at work. Twice he had asked her to accompany him to meetings because they would be listening to audio in Arabic and he wanted his own translator—her.

The second audio had been hard to listen to because it had depicted an operative's torture and eventual murder. Maggie made it through dry-eyed and even managed to take notes, but it left her shaken. Miraculously, she and Ridge had the elevator to themselves on the way back to their floor. He rested his hand on her arm.

"Are you all right? That was brutal."

She nodded, not trusting herself to speak much. Did she want to cry or throw up? Maybe both. "Does it ever get any easier to hear that kind of stuff?" she croaked.

"Easier, no. More commonplace? Yes," he said. He gave her shoulder a squeeze. The elevator dinged, and they went their separate ways. "Ellen, my office," he said, tapping the desk of a woman who looked around the room, panicked and forsaken. Maggie watched as the two of them disappeared into his office. When Ellen emerged sometime later, she headed for the bathroom and didn't come out the rest of the day.

"Another one bites the dust," Blue whispered as he eased by her office later. Maggie didn't understand it. What was the problem? She *knew* Ridge was a nice guy. Why didn't that convey to the rest of the team?

The next week, she tapped gently on his door. "It's open," he barked, sounding like the last thing he wanted was a visitor. Maggie took a tentative step inside and held a plate aloft.

"It's Ellen's birthday," she explained. "We're having a party. Want to come?"

"Can't," he said, his eyes never leaving his computer.

"I thought you might say that, so I brought you some cake."

"Thanks. Leave it on my desk."

She took a step forward. "You can tell it's delicious because it's lumpy and half falling over. That's how you know it's made with love."

When it became obvious that she wasn't going to leave until he acknowledged her, he peeled his eyes away from the screen and looked at the cake. "That's the ugliest cake I've ever seen. Whoever bought it should get their money back."

"I made it, thank you very much. And then I dragged it all the way here on the train, carried it five blocks in the rain, and lovingly presented it to Ellen. And now to you." She held out the plate and set it purposefully on his desk. "Happy Ellen's birthday to you."

"Thank you, Maggie." He turned back to his computer.

"I can't leave until you taste it. Otherwise I know you're going to dump it in the trash as soon as I'm gone," she said.

He sighed. "How do you do that?"

She tapped her temple. "Intuition."

"I'm beginning to think psychic would be a more apt descriptor." Nonetheless, he picked up the fork and took a large bite of the cake. And then quickly wolfed the rest down in two more bites.

"Would you like me to bring you a turkey leg and a flagon of ale, King Henry?" Maggie asked.

"Sorry. I skipped lunch and I guess I didn't realize how hungry I was," he said. He sighed heavily.

"Ridge, are you okay? You seem incredibly tense."

He gave her a wry smile.

"Okay, I know you're the head of this team and that's an immense amount of pressure, but we're all behind you, ready to help with whatever you need. So, you know you're not exactly alone, is what I'm saying."

He blew out another breath and a little of the weight seemed to leave his shoulders. "Thank you."

"Are you sure you don't want to come to the party?" she asked.

"I really can't, but thanks. Hey, what are you doing tonight?"

"I'm going to take my dog for a walk and then, um…I was trying to think of something that makes me sound like I have a life outside of work, but I came up dry. I'll probably watch reruns of *The Great British Baking Show* and fall asleep on the couch. Again."

"Let's go out. We haven't had a chance to celebrate since you came to town, and I'm miraculously free tonight. Sound good?"

"Sounds superlative," she said. "Do you want me to bring you more cake or a barrel of mead?"

"Thanks, but I should probably call it quits on sugar for today."

"Yeah, you're looking kind of flabby in that one cell of yours that has body fat. It's good you're attempting to be disciplined for once," she said.

He made a flicking motion with his fingers. "Away with you, pest."

She curtsied. "Yes sir, I'm sorry sir. Please don't beats me again," she said in her best cockney accent. He shook his head, but he was smiling when she closed the door.

They met at a trendy cocktail bar in downtown DC. Maggie could tell immediately it wasn't her type of place. She stood outside waiting for Ridge and watched all the beautiful people stream by. She had visited a lot of large cities, but DC was unlike anywhere else. Nowhere had ever felt as competitive or driven. She felt judged as she stood outside alone, but maybe it was her imagination. Maybe no one cared about the lone librarian trying hard to blend in to the bricks behind her.

"Hey, sorry I'm late," Ridge said, approaching from her left. He looked exactly like every other young professional around them, well-cut suit, tie, and expensive shoes. Maggie felt dowdy, even though she was wearing one of the new dresses her sister, Amelia, had picked for her.

"You're fine," Maggie assured him. "I've been people watching."

"See anything good?" he asked.

"A few budding romances," Maggie said. "But I'm fairly certain a few of those people were married to someone else, so I tried to exude disapproval at them."

"I'm sure they felt chastised and will immediately rethink their behavior," he said.

"That's all any scold can ask for," she said. He opened the door for her and she edged her way inside. The room was crowded, so much that it was hard to navigate or even breathe. Ridge put his hand on her back and began trying to shepherd her toward the bar. When that failed, he clasped her hand and led the way. People moved aside for him, and Maggie felt grateful for his commanding presence as she did a quickstep behind him to keep up. At last they reached the bar. Her stomach rumbled with hunger, but there was no food, only exotic-sounding cocktails. What was a Moscow Mule? She had no idea, but several people seemed to be drinking them. Intimidated and hungry, she ordered a ginger ale.

"We make our own," the bartender said. He had a long, trendy-looking beard that came to a point in the center of his chest.

"Super," Maggie said. Until then, she hadn't known it was possible to make one's own ginger ale, but she supposed that explained the ten-dollar price tag.

Conversation swirled around them, loud and jarring. People jostled into her as they waited for their drinks, knocking Maggie into Ridge.

"Sorry," she said, pointing to the guy behind her who had bumped her without apology.

Ridge leaned close to speak in her ear. "Want me to kill him for you?"

"I don't want to react unreasonably. Let's wait and see if he does it a second time," she said.

Their drinks arrived and they shifted aside for the next people. They were quiet a moment as they sipped. Maggie began to wonder if the outing had been a mistake. Maybe their earlier camaraderie had been a blip. This wasn't her scene, but Ridge looked seamless here. Was it actually possible that he and she could be friends?

"You look like you fit in here," Ridge said. Or at least that was what Maggie thought he said. She had to lean in to hear him.

"Is that a bad thing?" she asked, refraining from telling him she had just been thinking the same about him.

He shook his head. "It's just that I have this image of you in my head from our last meeting, faded sweatshirt, reading glasses, warm cookies. And now you look so…sophisticated. I kind of miss the old Maggie."

Someone else jostled into her, knocking her into him. He put out a hand to steady her. "My sister picked the dress for me. I still prefer the sweats."

"This city is a rough place. I don't want it to change you," he admitted, sticking out a hand to block someone else from bumping her.

"Do you come here often?" she asked.

"I've been a few times," he said.

"Do you enjoy it?" she asked, practically yelling to be heard over the cicada's buzz of conversation.

He glanced around at the swarming mass of humanity. "Not especially."

"Do you want to go somewhere else?" she asked.

"Where did you have in mind?" he asked.

"I know a place," she said. This time she took his hand and led him out of the maze of people, breathing a sigh of relief when they reached the sidewalk.

He seemed to take the same breath. "Where do you want to go?"

"There's a diner three blocks over," she said.

He grimaced. "A diner? I'm not in the mood for a meal I'll still be digesting next week."

"It's not like that. It's farm to table."

"What does that even mean?" he asked.

"Do you trust me?" she asked.

He stared down at her, and she wondered if he was thinking the same thing she had been thinking. Were they wrong? Had the weird chemistry between them evaporated? "Yes," he said, though his tone lacked confidence.

"Come on." She held out her hand to him. "You're going to love this place, I promise."

"What if I don't?" he asked, eyeing her hand warily.

"Then you're a weirdo who doesn't know a good thing when he sees it," she said.

"I'm your boss. That's Mr. Weirdo to you," he said, but he clasped her hand and allowed her to lead him down the road and around the corner to the cute little all-night diner. Though it was crowded, the atmosphere was cozy rather than oppressive. Ridge found himself sighing in relief as they slid into a booth. Instinctively he took off his jacket and loosened his tie. The menu looked good and not like the greasy spoon he'd been dreading. He ordered salmon with some kind of wheatberry salad. Maggie surprised him by ordering grilled chicken with steamed asparagus.

"Are you on a diet?" he asked.

"No, but I've found it's easier to keep up on the running if I eat healthier," she said. "Although I still plan to order pie for dessert."

"But you already had cake today," he blurted without thinking. Of course it was none of his business if she ate two desserts in one day, but it was the unspoken rule he followed and sometimes he forgot others didn't do the same.

"You're not my dad," she retorted in the funny, non-filtered way she said things that made him laugh.

"You're right, I'm sorry," he said, smiling. "Eat whatever you like, no judgment here."

"When is the last time you were home?" she asked after the waitress brought their drinks.

"This morning before I left for work," he said, confused.

"I meant *home* home. Texas."

"Two and a half years," he said.

Her eyes bugged. "Why so long?"

"It's the job. There's not a lot of downtime. And, I don't know, it's not the same since my brother took over the ranch. It doesn't feel like my home anymore; it feels like his. Not that I'm not welcome there, but my parents moved to a condo, and it feels so…cold."

"What was it like to grow up on a ranch?" she asked, her chin perched in her hand as she awaited his answer.

He went into a long reminiscence about ranch life that lasted until their food arrived.

"That sounds like the best possible life for a little boy," she said as she began to cut her chicken.

"It was," he agreed.

"Does it ever make you sad your future children probably won't grow up the same?" she asked.

"It didn't, but now that you mention it, it kind of does," he said.

"Sorry," she said. "Here, taste this." She cut a bite of her chicken and plopped it on his plate. "You should know that my family is big into sharing food."

"Just not warm cookies," he said, reminding her of when she had smacked his fingers.

"For the record, I offered you a bite and you refused. You could be killed for that in some countries."

"Which countries?" he asked.

"You probably haven't heard of them," she said. "How's the salmon?"

"Would you like a bite?" he asked. When she nodded, he cut a piece and deposited it on her plate. His family was not big into sharing food. In fact, he couldn't remember ever sharing food with anyone before, not that he was complaining. Her chicken was delicious.

"That's really good," she said, eying his salmon with something like regret.

"Maggie, would you like to switch meals?" he offered.

"That's too weird," she said. "Isn't it?"

He rolled his eyes and switched their plates.

"Are you sure you don't mind?" she asked, taking a bite of the salmon before he could answer and change his mind.

"What is it with you and food?" he asked.

"It's how it is in my family. Food is love," she said. "Isn't your family the same?"

"Not really. Food was more a means to an end," he said. "You don't have to look at me that way."

"What way?" she asked.

"Like you feel sorry for me because my family didn't bond over baked goods. We had other things."

"What things?"

"The ranch, sports, anything that involved competition," he said.

"We literally could not be more opposite," she said.

"And yet here we are," he said and smiled because he was enjoying himself. The magic of Maggie hadn't worn off. He felt calmer and more at ease than he had in months, somehow more settled and less alone in her presence.

"What about holidays?" she asked.

"What about them?"

"Don't you see you family for those?" she asked.

"Occasionally," he said.

"What about when you don't?" she asked.

He shrugged.

"Alone?" she mouthed, as if it were some awful disease to spend Christmas alone. Maybe it was.

"I hate to be the bearer of bad news, but we don't exactly close when the holidays roll around. It's not like working at a bank. When something is going down, we stay until it's finished. You will work some holidays, and other times you'll work so close to the holidays that you won't be able to go home, either."

"Oh," she said, blinking. "What about girlfriends?"

He coughed, the abrupt change in topic having caught him by surprise. "What about them?" He took a sip of water to clear his throat.

"Don't you spend your holidays with them?" she asked.

"Sometimes, if I have one. Sometimes not. Depends on the year, I guess. Why? Are you worried about me or are you attempting to play matchmaker?" He left off the third option—that she was asking for herself. He didn't get that vibe from her, and he was more than a little relieved. He felt like a sniffer dog at the airport, except instead of checking for bombs, he was constantly searching for any signs of attraction on her part. So far he had found none, and so he continued to be comfortable around her, ridiculously so for the short amount of time they had known each other.

"It makes me sad, the thought of anyone spending the holidays alone, and I'm including myself in that. I've never spent a holiday away from my family."

"Tell you what, if it happens this year, we'll spend them together," he promised.

"What if you have a girlfriend by then?" she asked.

"I'll tell her I'm unavailable," he said.

"What if I have a boyfriend by then?" she added.

"You'll tell him you're unavailable," he said.

"What if we're really serious and it causes a big fight and we break up and it turns out you came between me and what was potentially the love of my life?" she said.

"Then he should send me a thank you because you're apparently exhausting and high maintenance. Also, I've probably saved him a fortune in cookie bills," he said.

"I told you I've cut back," she said, waving her fork and a bite of salmon at him for emphasis.

She was cute, adorably so, and not just physically. She was like his best friend's fun little sister—he shouldn't want to have her around all the time, but he did. "Are you enjoying my salmon?"

"I prefer chicken," she said, smiling when he rolled his eyes in exasperation. "What's a wheatberry?"

"No idea."

"You grew up on a ranch," she said.

"We didn't herd wheatberries," he said.

"I always assumed farm people know everything about agriculture," she said. "You're kind of letting me down here."

He pulled out his phone, Googled wheatberries, and gave her the description. "See? I knew you'd know," she said.

"I don't remember you being this much work before. I must have blocked out the parts of you that are exhausting," he said.

"Me, exhausting? I'm as low-maintenance as they come. I'm not into makeup or shoes or purses or fashion or decorating. I'm practically not even female," she said.

"You're definitely female," he assured her. "If you're not into any of those things, what are you into?"

"My dog, my family, my friends, travel, reading."

"That's a short list," he said.

"I'm a small person," she reminded him.

"You left one important thing off the list," he said.

"What's that?"

"Work." He pointed to himself.

"The job is still new. I haven't been doing it long enough to know if I love it," she said.

"What's not to love? The long hours, the stress, the relatively low pay?"

"When you put it like that, of course you're right. I love my job," she decided. They talked for several more hours, until, even after ordering pie and coffee, the waitress began giving them impatient looks. They left her a generous tip, and Ridge walked Maggie to the train station.

She prattled the entire way. Generally Ridge found it grating when people chattered incessantly, but in Maggie's case, he found it soothing. Maybe it was because he realized it was borne of the loneliness of being in a new city; she was saying all the things she had stored up for weeks of having no one to talk to. Somehow understanding her loneliness eased an echoing solitude inside him. Despite what he said to her about not being bothered he so rarely made it home to Texas, now that he thought of home, it opened an old ache inside him, one he thought he'd quashed long ago in military life. He had rarely been home since he was eighteen, and now he wondered why. What was so important that kept him from his roots? And then there was his future to consider. Did he really want to raise a child on the mean streets of DC? The flat, hot, vastness of home had helped make him the man he was today. Who would his children someday be?

A group of men on the street ahead pinged on his radar, the internal one that, since his early time in the navy, was always tuned to danger. The way they were eying him and Maggie, especially Maggie, told him they were up to no good. Without her notice, he eased her to the other side of the street, gently steering her with a hand to her shoulder. When they were on the other side of the street, she linked her arm through his. It was a companionable gesture, and it was nice. They were pals; she was safe and warm and pleasant and everything Ridge didn't know he'd been missing for a long, long time.

He deposited her at the train station with instructions to text him when she arrived safely home.

"What if I don't arrive safely home? What will you do?" she asked, the teasing glint in her eyes sparkling off the dim overheads at the train station.

"First I'll find you and fix what's broken. Then I'll avenge you," he said.

"And you expect me to believe you've never seen a superhero movie? Because that was literally a line from either Batman or Daredevil," she said.

"You're a grown woman. Why do you know superheroes so well?"

"I'm sandwiched between two brothers," she told him. "Superheroes and video games were the mainstay of my house until my baby sister came along, and then it was Barbie." She wrinkled her nose.

"Not a Barbie girl, were you?" he deduced.

"I was more into GI Joe, but I could never get my brothers interested. There's my train. Thanks for tonight, Cam. It was exactly what I needed." She patted his chest, smiling sweetly up at him.

He searched her features, once again checking for hints of misplaced attraction. When he found none, he was relieved. Wasn't he? "Text me," he reminded her.

"Yes, Mom," she said.

"Mom?" he echoed.

"I was going to say Daddy, but it sounded kind of kinky in my head, so I switched it up." With one last smile and wave, she boarded the train. Ridge stayed until the train pulled out of the station and then, reluctantly, walked to his car alone.

Chapter 6

A few days later, Maggie received a text from Ridge while they were at work. He was in a meeting, she knew, because she had watched him swish by her desk looking harried and important.

Dinner tonight?

Sure, but aren't you in a meeting?

Yes, but a bureaucratic windbag is speaking and if I give him my full attention, I might punch him and get fired. So, really, you're saving my job right now.

She smiled. How's pizza?

I don't know, I haven't talked to him today, he replied.

I meant for supper, dingus.

Food is your thing, and what's a dingus?

A super cool, handsome guy.

Nice, he replied.

See also: gullible, she texted.

I was about to say something nice to you but forget it.

Were you going to compliment my mad typing skills? The ones that handed in my last report an hour before it was due? she asked

Yes, I was going to say your mad typing skills are looking pretty cute today. I like the dress. He added a winking emoji that made her smile again.

Thanks. Another sister special. She keeps me clothed.

What does it mean that your sister and I have the same taste in clothes? he asked.

I'll have her buy you some dresses next time she's in town.

I prefer skirts, he said.

I feel like we should be having this convo in front of the company therapist

Gotta go. Giving a presentation in 3, 2, 1…

Quick question: could you get arrested for picturing a room full of generals in their underpants?

She didn't hear from him for about an hour, and then he texted again as he strode by her desk on the way back to his office.

Thanks for making me giggle like a little girl as I stood up to speak.

"Who do you think he could be texting?" Blue perched on the edge of Maggie's desk, his eyes following Ridge as he went into his office and closed the door.

"Who do *you* think he could be texting?" she echoed, shifting her phone into her pocket.

"I don't know. Who would Satan have on speed dial?" he mused.

"His mom?" Maggie guessed.

"No, he ate her soon after he was hatched, if the rumors are true," Blue said.

"He's really a nice guy," Maggie told him, and not for the first time.

He put his hand to her forehead. "Poor pumpkin. You're delirious with fever."

"Someday you're going to see it," Maggie assured him.

He gave her what appeared to be a pitying expression. "No, Maggie, someday you're going to see what we've all been talking about, and then you'll be sorry you ever tried to defend him."

"We'll see," she said.

"Yes, we will and, as your work husband, I want you to know I'm here to pick up the pieces when you eventually unravel," he said.

"Wait a minute, I thought Babs was your work wife," she said, squinting suspiciously up at him.

"I'm work polygamous," he informed her.

"I'm not. I'm a one work husband type of gal, and you're not it," she informed him.

He clutched his heart. "That hurts me."

She picked up a pencil and began poking him with the blunt end. "You have to go now. I have a report due."

"You're so diligent. No wonder you're teacher's pet," Blue said.

"I am not teacher's pet," she argued. "I'm merely conscientious."

"Mm, hmm. Tell me that next time you take Lucifer a piece of cake."

"That's called being a team player," she said.

"That's called borrowing trouble. The less contact you have with him the better." She opened her mouth to argue, but he put up his hands in surrender. "Friendly warning."

"Duly noted," she said, making a shooing motion for him to go away again as her phone beeped with another text. When Blue was safely gone, she picked it up and read.

Do you have food? I missed lunch, and I'm getting a headache.

Of course she had food. Her desk was loaded with snacks in case she got stuck at work and couldn't eat supper. She was not the type of person who could safely skip a meal.

I'll leave you something in the break room.

Can't you bring it in here? Head is pounding.

I'm being watched, she said, glancing around to make sure no one was observing her as she texted him.

I'll fix it. Load your pockets.

She loaded her pockets with the healthy snacks she knew he'd like. A minute later, he opened his door, stepped out, and strode purposefully to her desk. He gave it a knock, the signature thing he did when he was getting ready to summon someone to the inner sanctum for a berating session. "Maggie, my office." He turned and went back the way he came without another word or glance.

Maggie pushed away from her desk and followed him a few paces behind, wondering what it would be like if she actually were getting called to the carpet. It had happened to almost everyone but her. All eyes were on her now as she did what was known in the office as the walk of shame. Usually when people came out of Ridge's office after such a walk, they were either crying or on their way to the bathroom for a good cry.

Ridge opened the door for her and closed it behind her before speaking. "What do you have that's good? Hopefully a lot. I missed breakfast, too."

"No wonder you have a headache. You can't skip meals. Have you had water today? You're probably dehydrated," she said as she began to empty her pockets onto his desk. Nuts, granola bars, energy bars, candy, and trail mix tumbled out, along with an apple.

"This is spectacular. You're the best," Ridge said as he picked up the apple and took a bite.

"Of course you'd go for the fruit first, you weirdo. There's chocolate right here," she said, holding a candy bar in plain view for him.

"What kind of psychopath eats chocolate before the fruit?" he asked.

"You're hopeless," she informed him. "Oh, wait, I have one last thing." She turned her back on him. When she turned back around, she handed him a bottle of water.

"Where did that come from?" he asked, puzzled.

50

"Can't a girl have some secrets?" she asked. She took a step toward the door, but he tugged her back and kissed her forehead.

"Thank you, I really appreciate it. See you later. Text me the address of where we're meeting, I might be a few minutes late."

"All right. Don't skip meals again, and drink all your water," she scolded.

"Fine, Dad," he said.

"Dad?" she said.

"I was going to say Mommy, but it sounded kinky in my head, so I switched it up," he said.

She was smiling as she placed her hand on the door. With effort, she wiped it. If she came away from this meeting laughing, her work mates would hate her for sure. Instead she tried to look somber and subdued as she strode quietly back to her office.

Did you get reamed? Blue texted her, and even through the phone he sounded gleeful over the prospect.

No, just helping him with a problem. Everything is fine, she texted him.

He leaned around his desk so they made direct eye contact, wiped the end of his nose, and pointed at her.

Which was worse, being called a brown noser or teacher's pet? Was there a difference? She gave him an exaggerated shrug. He rolled his eyes and resumed working. She wished she could explain to everyone that they had woefully misjudged Ridge. He wasn't Satan; he was one of the kindest, funniest, silliest, and most thoughtful men she had ever met. For now, she would have to keep their friendship under wraps but, as she thought about it, she realized that wasn't such a bad thing. After all, a girl really did need to maintain some secrets.

Later, after work, they met at a restaurant of Maggie's choosing. Ridge wasn't into food as much as she was. She had an entire list of places she wanted to try. For tonight, she decided on a low-key pizza place, sensing he needed somewhere to unwind.

"It smells amazing," he greeted her as he slipped into the booth across from her.

"Thank you."

He smiled. "Are you taking credit for the restaurant's smell now?"

"It's not the restaurant, it's me. I'm trying a new cologne, *au de oregano*."

"You look normal, but then you open your mouth and the words disprove the theory," he said. He inhaled deeply and let it out slowly but it did nothing to ease the tense set of his shoulders.

"Give me your left hand," Maggie demanded.

He did so. "Are you going to propose?"

"No, I'm going to help you relax. Trust me." She began gently massaging his hand and he stared into space, entranced as the tension seemed to drain from his body.

"How are you doing this?" he asked as she switched hands and began massaging the right one.

"My college roommate was deeply into holistic health and massage. She went on to become a naturopath, and she taught me some lasting lessons about the healing power of touch, as well as the body's meridians."

"Meridians, you mean like where your toe is connected to your spleen and all that nonsense?" he said.

52

"Yes, and I believe it completely," she said.

"I didn't take you for a nut job. I mean, you are, but you also have access to mounds of scientific research," he said.

"It might surprise you to know the scientific community is beginning to come around to the nut job's way of thinking. Meanwhile you called the person who is massaging your hands a nut job."

"Sorry," he mumbled, closing his eyes and resting his head on the seat behind him. He might have fallen asleep if the waitress hadn't arrived to take their order. They quickly scanned the menu and decided on something.

"What is it with you, Maggie?" he asked when the waitress walked away. "I have never let a woman I wasn't dating massage me before, and yet here we are. For all intents and purposes, we barely know each other. And yet I feel more comfortable with you than most people I've known for years. What is that?"

"Do we have to give it a label, Ridge? Some people have natural chemistry. Sometimes it's romantic chemistry, and sometimes it's not. Ours is not, and so we're friends. Maybe we're friendship soul mates and we've found each other at last. This is so going to go in my movie."

"I liked it better before you tried to come up with a name for it," he said. "But fine, we're friendship soul mates." He squeezed the hand that was still holding his. "How are you holding up? You've had a huge transition."

"Great, actually. Everyone is so nice at the office," she said.

"Really?" he asked, surprised. "It seems like such a cold environment to me, or it did." Now that he thought about it, things had warmed up in the last few weeks. Ellen's birthday party was the first such celebration he could remember in the months since the team was assembled. And then it dawned on him: Maggie was the difference. Her warm, effusive nature was spreading to the others.

"What?" she asked.

"What what?" he said.

"You're smiling at me in a most peculiar manner," she said. She had stopped massaging his hand, but he didn't withdraw it. They were essentially holding hands now across the table, but neither seemed to realize.

"I'm glad I brought you on board, is all," he said. "Now, tell me something I don't know."

"It is physically impossible for you to lick your elbow," she said.

"I meant something about you I don't know," he said.

"It's physically impossible for me to lick my elbow, too," she said.

"Tell me the most fun thing you've done since you moved here," he said.

"I took my dog to Theodore Roosevelt Island," she said.

"That's it?"

"I'm a woman of simple tastes, and you're not allowed to make fun of my fun thing. What's your most fun thing?" she asked.

"My brother came to town and we went to a Capitals game," he said.

"And the Capitals are…"

"Hockey," he said.

"I've never been to a hockey game," she said.

"It's the best. Hey, let's go. There's a game tonight," he said.

"Tonight? I don't know if I could do that. I don't like riding the train home so late. That's when all the crazies come out."

"I'll take you home. You don't live that far from me, actually," he said. His thumb was gently smoothing over the back of her hand, and still neither of them realized.

"I'm not great with spontaneity," she said.

"You basically decided to give up your life and move here on a whim," he said.

"That's a good point. Okay, let's hockey. Aren't we a little overdressed?"

"It's DC. No one will bat an eye," he said.

In the end, he was right. There were other people overdressed for a hockey game, too, but Maggie wouldn't have cared because she had a blast.

"I love hockey," she declared.

"I know because that's the fourth time you said it," he told her as he drove her to her house after the game. They had picked up her car from the train station and dropped it at her house so she could check on her dog, and then she rode with him. "Plus you bought the shirt."

"Can I wear it to work?" she asked. He gave her a disparaging glance. "I'm going to take that as a maybe. This was so much fun, Cam. Thank you."

"You're welcome," he said. They reached her house and he walked her to the door.

"Do you want to come inside for coffee? I'm too wired to sleep anyway," she said.

"Sure," he agreed. He was curious to see inside, and his first glimpse did not disappoint. It was colorful and inviting, much like the woman herself. Not fancy, but still pleasant and homey. The dog was even more massive than he had expected, reaching halfway up Ridge's body when he came to greet him.

"How can you not be a dog person?" she asked.

"Who says I'm not a dog person?" he returned.

"Your face as you're attempting to sidestep my dog. He won't allow it, by the way. He demands to be greeted like a proper member of the family."

"It's not dogs I don't like. It's their messes. All the fur and slobber and whatnot. I always had dogs growing up, but they stayed outside."

"Ranch dogs are different," she said.

"That's where we agree," he replied. "Dogs should have a purpose, not be pampered playthings."

"Samson has a purpose. He's a guard dog."

"He's doing a stellar job," Ridge said as the dog practically fell over itself to lick him.

She put on a pot of coffee, and they sat on the couch. "Do you mind if I check the score of the game?" he asked.

"The game we just went to? Because I don't know if you were paying attention, but they won," she said.

"The other game," he said. Reaching for the remote, he turned to ESPN.

"Five minutes in my house, and you've commandeered the remote. Would you like to run real quick and put the toilet seat up to complete your domination of my space?" she asked.

"Sports now, talk later," he said.

She retrieved their coffee, set his on a coaster in front of him, and held hers to her nose.

"It's black," he noted.

"You take it black."

"I meant yours. You used to take it with cream and sugar," he said.

"That was before I got physically fit and lost twenty pounds," she said. "A fact you still haven't noted."

"I've noted," he said. He reached out a hand and patted her knee without removing his eyes from the television screen.

"If a naked woman walked through here, would you take your eyes off of sports to look at her?" she asked.

"Depends on the woman," he said. He reached for his coffee and drank while Maggie picked up her book and began reading.

"How can you read when the TV is on?" he asked.

"How can you have the TV on when there are books to read?" she countered.

He finally turned to face her. "You never watch TV?"

"Oh, I watch mounds of TV, but never sports," she said.

"Sports are fun. Remember hockey? They're all like that, you have to give them a chance."

"I'll concede sports are better in person if you'll concede watching sports stats on TV is boring for someone who doesn't follow sports," she said.

"Point conceded. I'm all caught up now anyway. What do you usually watch?"

"Things you'll hate," she said.

"Undoubtedly. So what's a good compromise?" he asked.

"Why do we have to compromise if it's my house?" she asked.

"Because I'm bigger and I have the remote," he said.

"Were you on the debate team? Because you're super good at it," she said.

"How about old sitcom reruns?" he asked.

"I could go for that," she said.

He found the channel that played reruns all night, and they settled back to watch. "I should go home," he said an hour later.

"At some point," she agreed, but neither of them made a move toward the door, and that was the last thing either of them remembered.

In the morning, he woke to the dog staring at him face to face as he lay on her couch. Maggie lay at the other end, still asleep. He glanced at the door, wondering if he could make his way out before she woke up. He felt…caught? Guilty? Something felt wrong about the situation. Though nothing had happened, he still felt like he shouldn't have stayed over. Gently, he moved one leg, and Maggie's eyes sprang open. She sat up and looked at him, confused.

"Were you here all night or did you break in to mug me?" she asked.

"I came for your gnome collection," he said, nodding to the group of gnomes on her mantel.

"You'll have to get by Samson first," she said as the dog continued to stare adoringly at him. She yawned and stretched. "Breakfast?"

His excuses to immediately flee died on his lips. "Are you offering to cook for me?"

"I always make breakfast on Saturday mornings for the random men who've stayed over," she informed him.

"Does that happen often?" he asked. To his knowledge, she hadn't dated since she'd been in DC.

"Literally all the time. I keep a selection of men's clothing, just in case, but they're all dirty now, so don't ask to see them."

He couldn't pass up a home cooked meal, something that so rarely happened in his world anymore. "Breakfast sounds good. What can I do to help?"

"Keep me company."

They eased into the kitchen. He sat at the table while she made bacon, eggs, and pancakes. They spent a long time eating and, though he had a lot to do, it was nearly noon by the time he reluctantly left her house.

Chapter 7

Maggie was exhausted. A new terror cell had sprung up seemingly overnight in New York with ties to London. The team had been working nonstop the last few days to try and get ahead of it. Ridge had flown to New York while Maggie and Blue fed him information from DC. Blue was an extraordinarily talented hacker. It had been fun to watch a master at work. Maggie had compiled everything he gathered into an easily accessible database, one that could cross reference with social media and all the chatter they received from intercepted phone lines. Thanks to their hard work, arrests had been made in both cities. Now, after a whirlwind trip back home to DC, Ridge was flying to London to debrief and compare notes with their intelligence committee.

"You look cute," Ridge said.

"If you like girls in glasses, yoga pants, and hair that screams, 'I haven't slept in days'," Maggie said. Traffic was tight, and she couldn't take her eyes off the road to look at him.

"I do," he assured her. He didn't normally. He was a man who liked women to put as much effort into their appearance as he did. But with Maggie things were different. Seeing her dressed down was a reminder of when they first met. Usually at the office she looked so sophisticated and put together, like any typical DC urbanite. But when she got comfy, she became his Maggie, the silly one who made him laugh and got excited over warm cookies. "Thanks for doing this."

"No problem," she said. She honestly didn't mind driving him to the airport at three AM, but who knew there would be so much traffic so early in the morning? Or was it late at night? New York was supposed to be the city that didn't sleep, but they had nothing on DC.

"Are you and Blue an item?" Ridge asked and Maggie nearly swerved into an embankment.

"No. Why would you even ask that?" She fought hard to keep her eyes on the road, but she wanted to look at him, to read what was in his face. By his tone, she couldn't imagine what was going on in his head.

"You're together a lot."

"We're friends," Maggie said.

"There seems to be something more there, a certain chemistry," Ridge said.

"I'm not his type," Maggie said. "He likes girls with interesting tattoos and colored hair. I'm way too plain Jane ordinary for him."

"It sounds like what you're saying is that if he were interested in you, you'd go out with him," Ridge said.

"What? No, how are you getting that from what I said? Neither of us is interested in the other. We're friends, the end. What is this about?"

"You spend a lot of time together," he said.

"So do we," she pointed out.

"And look at us now." He reached across the console to squeeze her knee.

"Blue and I are friends, just friends," Maggie reiterated.

"Good, because office romances are not allowed, not on my watch," he said.

"You're in luck because there aren't any. Well, except with the food cart guy who brings warm muffins on

Wednesdays. I think he and I might have something special," she mused.

"If you have to pay a guy to bring you warm muffins, you're doing it wrong," he said.

"Dating advice from Cameron Ridge. I should be writing this down, this stuff is gold," she said. "What else can you tell me?"

"Actions speak louder than words, always. Don't listen to what a man says. We'll say anything. Pay attention to his actions. They'll tell you his intent every time." His hand still rested on her knee. He gave it a light squeeze.

"I actually should write that down. It's good advice."

"All my advice is good," he protested.

"Like when we were in the park last week and you told me that hornet's nest was empty, so I touched it and a bunch of angry hornets came out and Samson and I had to run away screaming?" she reminded him.

"You got a good workout that day," he said. "No complaining."

They arrived at the airport. She tried to leave him at the passenger drop off, but Ridge was having none of it.

"You're not going to walk me in? I'm flying overseas. I may never come home again. Someone needs to see me off," he said. "This is bad deployment etiquette."

"Liar, liar pants on fire. You want me to be a pack mule and help carry one of your twelve thousand bags," she said.

"That's not true—I want you to carry two of my bags," he said, grinning.

"Fine, but you know what this makes us?" she said.

"Too cheap to pay a valet?" he guessed as they unloaded his bags from her car.

"This seals the deal between us. We're official airport buddies now. Do you understand the implications, and are you ready to accept them?" she asked.

"What are the implications, besides me getting to see you with your glasses on and hair a mess while you mutter darkly at interstate traffic?" he asked.

"This is an official next step in our friendship. It means we have no one else who likes us enough to take us places in the middle of the night. We're officially friendless losers, minus each other," she said. "Though, to be fair, my dog would totally drive me to the airport, if he knew how to work the pedals in the car. So really, you're a loser. I'm doing all right."

"You're considering teaching your dog to drive so you can use the carpool lane. I wouldn't say you're doing well," he said.

"Can we talk about the fact that you're a former navy guy, and yet you over pack like a thirteen-year-old girl?" she complained, shifting his bags around to relieve the pressure from her shoulders.

"Let me guess: if you were going to London, you'd only bring one bag," he said.

"No, I would stuff a couple of pairs of underwear in my backpack and call it a day," she said. She loved to travel, and she always traveled lightly.

"You're awfully cranky for someone who hasn't slept in days and is driving around DC at three in the morning," he noted.

"I'm not cranky; I'm insanely jealous," she informed him.

"Why?" he asked. "Because I'm taking the redeye? I've got news for you, it's not as glamorous as I'm making it out to be." They reached the last security gate before they had to separate and stopped, facing each other.

She set his bags down and clutched his lapels. "You're going to London, Cam. *London.* Do you even understand how exciting that is? You have to go to Piccadilly Circus. And that big market with all the food, and London Bridge, and the Palace. Please take a picture of the changing of the guard for me, pretty please. And have formal tea. Ask London intelligence if there really is a Double 07 and if he's single. And try to figure out what clotted cream is and why everyone eats it when it sounds like a biological dysfunction."

"Maggie, you understand that I'm going there on business, right? I'm jetting over for a few days to have endless meetings and flying right back. It's not going to be fun."

"But you won't be having fun in *London*," she said.

"This is a productive conversation. I'm glad you're hearing me." He rested his hands on hers, which were still attached to his lapels. "Are you going to miss me while I'm gone? Driving me to the airport doesn't count if you're not going to miss me."

"Obviously. There's a birthday party this week. Who is going to rudely refuse my cake and offers of social interaction?" she said. "Try to get out for a little fun. At least have tea."

"I had no idea you liked London so much. I should have taken you with me," he said.

"Was that an option?" she exclaimed, aghast.

"You were the primary contributor to the report that spurred this entire visit. I think I could easily have swung it," he said.

She made a pained sound, something between a gag and a whimper.

"I thought I was saving you," he said, his tone apologetic. "It's going to be completely exhausting."

"*Completely exhausting in London, Cameron.*"

"Next time," he promised.

"I would love that, *love*. Do you think maybe we could arrange to cover a terrorist cell with ties to Paris next time?" she asked. "I could really go for a croissant."

"I'll see what I can do," he said. He brushed some wild hairs off her face. At work her topknot was straight and neat, the quintessential librarian hairdo. After, it was loose and messy, often springing free in a mad dash to escape. There was a metaphor for the woman herself in there somewhere, but he hadn't yet found it. "Take good care of the office while I'm away."

"Sure thing, Boss," she agreed.

"Thanks again for the ride," he said.

"Anytime, airport buddy."

"You're going to remember to pick me up, right?" he asked.

"I will be here at three in the morning, four days hence," she said.

"Don't say 'hence' in everyday conversation. The other spies will know you're a librarian and tease you," he urged.

"Remember, if you get confused by the language barrier, say, 'Ello, guvna, care for a cuppa?'" Maggie said.

"I have been to London a half dozen times and never once heard anyone talk that way. You seem to be under the delusion everyone there is an extra from *Mary Poppins*," he said.

She stood on her toes to hug him and whispered in his ear. "At least eat a scone while you're there. For me."

"For you, I will eat a scone," he agreed. He returned her hug, picking her up off the ground so her toes skimmed the carpet a few seconds before he set her down again. With a final wave, he shouldered all of his bags and headed through the gate.

Maggie turned toward the exit, feeling a bit lost and empty. It was only a few days, but she had come to depend on him an enormous amount. Though it had never happened, Ridge would be the person Maggie would call if she got a flat tire or ran out of gas or had any other sort of cataclysmic emergency. She had even amended her personnel records to make him her hospital contact, in case she landed somewhere unconscious. The fact that he was temporarily unavailable to her made her feel insecure. She supposed she could call Blue if she needed something, but he lived in Downtown DC, far away from her suburban house. And, while she and Blue were friends, they didn't share the same comfort level she and Ridge did.

She was doubtless overthinking things because she was tired. The chances she would have a flat tire or other emergency in the next few days were slim. Ridge would return soon, and all would be right with the world again. In the meantime, she could join the automobile club, if she felt it was necessary.

Trying hard to stay awake and alert, she found her car, drove home, and fell into much-needed sleep.

On the airplane, Ridge looked out the window and contemplated taking a nap. He would be jetlagged no matter what he did; flying east was a lose-lose situation, and there would be no time to recoup. Once he landed, he would be in nonstop meetings until he returned back home. He tried to picture Maggie by his side through the exhaustion and smiled. She would be frazzled, but she would be fun. One secret he had learned about Maggie—the more tired she felt, the slap-happier she became. When sleepy, she was the very definition of punch drunk.

"You two were cute." The middle-aged woman beside him spoke with a deep southern twang.

"Excuse me?" he said, turning to her with a questioning glance.

"You and your girlfriend. Or maybe your wife? Are you newlyweds?" she asked. "The blond, at the gate. I was watching. It brought back good memories of me and my husband."

"Oh, thank you, but that wasn't my wife. And we're not dating. She's a coworker."

Her brows rose. "Coworker? I worked at the same company for thirty years, and if I'd ever had a coworker like that, I would have worked another thirty." Smiling, she closed her eyes and put on her headphones.

Ridge turned his attention back out the window with a shake of his head. What would give anyone the idea that he and Maggie were dating? They were like night and day, just friends, nothing more. It was probably a generational thing. Older people were always trying to pair off the younger generation.

Thinking of Maggie renewed his feelings of guilt. He should have brought her along. It would be nice for his team to get out of the office, to get some recognition, and Maggie was by far the only one he would want to accompany him on such a long and tedious journey. If she were here now, she wouldn't be contemplating a nap. She would have her nose pressed to the window—after finagling him out of the window seat, of course. Her excitement level for the upcoming blitz of boring meetings would be at a ten. If she were here, the meetings likely wouldn't be boring. She would scribble asides in the margins of his notes, as she did back home, inappropriate little comments that tempted him to laugh at the worst possible moment while she sat straight-faced and serious, giving no outward indication of the naughtiness within. Maggie made everything warm, alive, vibrant, and plain old fun.

He was relieved to hear there was nothing between her and Blue. He assumed she would have told him if there was, but sometimes people didn't realize what was going on until another person pointed it out. That was why he had asked, to make sure. The way Blue looked at her sometimes made Ridge wonder, but at least now he knew Maggie wasn't interested in Blue. Since Maggie arrived, his team had started to click. An office romance would mar the perfect symbiosis they were beginning to establish. He was glad he wouldn't have to deal with that sort of thing.

He rested his head on the seat and closed his eyes, warm thoughts of Maggie lulling him to sleep.

Chapter 8

The Friday following his return from London, Ridge wasn't at work.

"Let's get a piñata!" Ellen suggested, so gleeful she could hardly contain herself. Maggie couldn't deny the party atmosphere was fun, but she was worried. Cameron Ridge was not the kind of man to take a sick day, unless it was dire. She tried to call him, but there was no answer. After arguing with herself a few times, she finally cashed in some personal time and left a couple of hours early. After the long train ride home, she checked on her dog, packed up a few things, swung by the store and, at last, landed on her boss's doorstep.

After knocking three times, she was tempted to give up when he finally stumbled to the door, shirtless and disheveled.

"I brought soup," Maggie said when he continued to stare at her without saying a word.

In answer, he groaned and turned back inside, toward what was presumably his bedroom. She followed him and sat by the bed after he crawled in and pulled the covers up. It was a tangled, sweaty mess and it smelled like staleness and fever, though the rest of the house was immaculate.

"Sit up and let me doctor you," she commanded.

"I can't, I'm dying. Maybe I'm already dead," he said. He sounded stuffy and as miserable as he looked.

"Cam, I brought an entire bag of goodies to make you feel better," she said, in the soothing voice of a mother cooing to a toddler. "But I need your cooperation. Sit up, please." She tapped him.

He scowled but grudgingly obliged. She cracked open a can of soda, inserted a straw, and handed it over. He opened his mouth to protest, and she used the opportunity to shove the straw between his lips. He took a tentative sip and then guzzled half the can. If her guess was correct, he'd had no food or liquids all day. "I brought soup. Shall I feed you?"

It was a sign of his weakness and misery that he nodded. She sat on her knees in the bed beside him and spoon-fed him some of the broth. When he reached his limit of that, she gave him a cracker, followed by a piece of peppermint candy and a dose of elderberry syrup.

When he was properly hydrated and fed, she filled her hot water bottle and tucked it under his cheek, straightening his sheets and blankets and pulling them up around him. Next she plugged in the essential oil diffuser she'd brought and tapped in a few drops of eucalyptus. When that was finished, she applied an oil blend to his chest.

"Is there a voodoo doll in your bag, too?" he asked before a coughing fit took him.

"Talk to me in an hour when you feel like a new creation," she said. She retrieved a cool washcloth for his head, gave him a bit more of the soda, and went to prepare a cup of tea.

She force-fed him half of the tea, and then he was ready for sleep. Maggie retreated to the living room and walked around, looking at his bookshelves. The house was shockingly well decorated for a former navy man and current bachelor. It had a woman's touch, and she wondered who had done it for him. Or maybe his tastes ran more feminine than she gave him credit for. Somehow she doubted it. The house felt too formal and less like Ridge actually lived there.

Maybe he'd had a serious girlfriend and they broke up. Or maybe he had hired a decorator. She had no idea. Instead of continuing to speculate, she made herself a cup of tea, washed up the few dishes in his sink, and sat down on his couch to read the book she'd brought.

A couple of hours later he stumbled out of his bedroom, looking still sick and sleepy but more than halfway human now. He lay down and rested his head in her lap. "Will you please put some more oils on my chest?"

"Are you sorry you made fun of my home remedies?" she asked.

He nodded contritely.

She rubbed more oils on his chest, fed him another spoonful of elderberry syrup, made him another cup of tea, stood by while he drank all of it, and then refilled the hot water bottle.

When all of that was done, he sighed in contentment as he settled his head back into her lap. "Thank you, Maggie. I can halfway breathe again, and the unceasing pounding in my head has finally ceased, and even my sore throat feels a tiny bit better. I don't ever remember being this sick before."

"Want me to make you some eggs and toast?" she asked. "That's what my mom always made for me when I was sick."

"Yes, please," he said meekly.

She went into the kitchen and made him scrambled eggs, buttered toast, and juice. "Where did you get these things? I don't have any food," he said when she returned with his food on a platter.

"I brought them from home, just in case," she replied.

"Aw," he said. "Thanks."

"No problem. I kind of figured you were on your own here with no one to help out. Having no one to take care of you when you're sick is the absolute worst. Also, we're now officially sickness buddies, in case you were keeping track," she said. He nodded his agreement as he shoveled more eggs into his mouth. "Who decorated your apartment?"

"How do you know someone decorated it for me?" he asked.

She tapped her temple. "Intuition."

"My sister-in-law," he said.

"You only have the one?" she said.

He nodded, reached for his phone, and scrolled until he found the picture he wanted. He tapped the screen. "My sister-in-law, Isabel."

Maggie pulled the phone closer and immediately wanted to push it away again. The woman was stunning and exactly the type of woman she had imagined Ridge with. "Was she a beauty contestant?"

"Winner," he said. "Miss America, ten years ago."

She blinked at him. "Your sister-in-law was Miss America?"

He nodded.

"Let me see your brother."

He scrolled again and handed her the phone. She didn't think it was possible, but somehow Ridge was the ugly one in the family. "What does your brother do?" she asked.

"He used to play pro football. Now he runs the family ranch," Ridge said.

"A regular J.R. Ewing," she replied.

He laughed and touched his fingers to his throat. "Sore," he croaked.

She gave him a piece of peppermint candy. He lay back down with his head in her lap and turned on the television, tuning to a game. Maggie stared into space, thinking. Even though there was nothing romantic between her and Cam, the pictures of his siblings still left her feeling more than a little insecure. What kind of family was he from? And, with such an exclusive lineage, could she trust the validity of his friendship with her?

"Do they have kids?" she blurted after a while.

He shook his head. "Isabel doesn't want," he said.

"Why not?" she asked.

"Career, figure, selfishness. Love her, but probably not mom material." He winced and pressed his fingers to his throat again.

"How does your brother feel about that?" she asked.

"Not good," he whispered. He picked up her hand and ran it over his head like Samson using his paw to beg for her attention. "You're supposed to be nursing me."

"You're a big baby," she accused, but she began smoothing her hand over his head and neck, pausing to massage the swollen glands in his neck occasionally. He was getting sleepy again. He twisted so he could see her.

"Thank you for coming to take care of me when I was dying."

"You're welcome," she said.

"You're really good at it. You'll be a good mom," he said, slight emphasis on the "you'll," as if he were still thinking of his sister-in-law and making comparisons.

"Are you hinting that you want me to have your baby or that you want me to leave? The haze of sickness makes it hard for me to tell," she asked.

He frowned, rolled toward her, and pressed his face to her stomach.

"I'm going to take that as a no on both counts," she said. She grabbed the remote and turned to the home and garden channel, seizing the opportunity while he wasn't paying attention. The remote had become a silent battle between them. Usually he won, but Maggie hadn't given in completely. Ridge clutched her hand and again urged her to pet his head.

She did so, sifting her fingers gently through his hair and down the back of his neck. His arms cinched around her middle.

"Never leave," he said, his words muffled against the softness of her belly. Only one of them had abs of steel, and it wasn't her.

"I think you'll feel differently once the virus moves on," she told him.

He shook his head and winced at the pain the motion caused him. "We could be roommates," he surprised them both by saying. He pulled back to look at her. "It would save on money and time. We could commute together."

She petted his head a few times before answering. "Why, Agent Ridge, I do believe you're delirious."

"I think I'm serious," he said, squinting.

"I have a ninety pound dog that sheds and drools," she told him. He grimaced. "And I like my space, and you like your space. And then there are the women."

"You have women?" he asked, confused.

"*You* have women, the women you will eventually have over, the ones who look like your sister-in-law. What would they say about your girl roommate and her giant, slobbery pooch?"

"You don't have to decide right now," he said, nestling his face against her stomach again.

She chuckled. "Poor baby, you're going to regret this entire conversation when you're back in your healthy mind again."

Ridge didn't argue, but he wasn't entirely sure. All he knew was that this morning he had woken up sicker than he could ever remember and utterly alone. And now Maggie was there, and she had taken care of him. He felt leaps and bounds better after eating and drinking and being petted and coddled. Why would he not want that in his life all the time?

Her words reminded him of Isabel, his sister-in-law. When he was a kid, he had been intensely jealous of his brother's beautiful bride. But as the years waned, he began to see the cracks in their relationship. Isabel was…cold. There was no other word for it. She was passionless, unless keeping up her appearance counted as a passion. She worked out, she ate healthy, she kept up on the latest fashions and supplements, but that was the entirety of her existence. She was good with people and worked well in her capacity as the wife of a ranching mogul. But that was the extent of her. Ridge wanted more. He wanted the beauty, sure, but the brains and heart to go with it. Some women had it all, and he would hold out until he found it. Meantime there was Maggie with her gentle brand of kindness, good cheer, and so much warmth it was like being near a woodstove all the time. Only, with her, she warmed him from the inside out.

And now he realized something else about her. She smelled good, really good. So good that he opened his mouth and bit her, without really questioning why. She yelped and pushed his face away from her stomach.

"What are you doing?" she demanded.

"I'm a sleep biter. Sorry," he said.

"Is that actually a thing?" she said.

"Apparently so," he said. "I'm sorry." He smoothed his palm over the spot he'd bitten. Why had he done that? He had no idea. All of a sudden, he had *wanted*. Not her, of course because it wasn't like that between them. But something. He pressed his face to her again, vowing to be good, and to seal the vow he placed a gentle kiss on the spot he had bitten, so soft she didn't feel it. But the kiss was a mistake because he wanted more, more of her body, more of everything. He imagined himself…no, he would not imagine himself because this was Maggie and it wasn't like that between them. They were friends, pals, amigos. He was, as she had said, delusional with illness. That was why he had bitten her, and that was why he was now having sultry, tempting thoughts about her. It would probably help if he moved away from her body and the enticing scent of her. Instead he cinched her slightly closer and pressed his face slightly closer to her belly with a groan of frustration at himself and his weakness. Why did he have to be a man? Why couldn't he enjoy the purity of their friendship with no intrusive hormonal urges?

"Are you feeling bad, bud?" Maggie asked, her tone oozing sympathy.

He nodded, not daring himself to speak.

"What can I do to help?" she asked.

"Absolutely nothing," he said. "Just don't move."

Misconstruing his words for continued misery, she resumed sifting her fingers through his hair. Meanwhile Ridge was white knuckling his way through a wave of desire.

This is Maggie, she's only a friend, I will not mess this up, this moment will pass, I don't really mean it, do not hit on your coworker, do not bite her again, why does she smell so good?

At last when he could take it no more, he rolled off the couch away from her and stood. "I'm going to go to bed, goodnight."

"Want me to rub some more oils on your chest?" she asked, smiling innocently as she held the bottle aloft.

He took a step back and nearly fell backwards over the coffee table. "Geez, no. I mean I think maybe I'm having a bit of a reaction or something." For emphasis, he itched his chest.

"Are you okay?" she asked.

"I'm good. And you have been so great, you are so great…" he broke off, staring at her, his fists clenched at his sides. Maggie stood.

"You don't look so good. Do you want me to help you to bed?"

"Maggie, you have to go," he blurted desperately.

She reeled back and her face closed up.

"That came out wrong, please, I'm sorry. I didn't mean it like that. I love having you here, truly. But I kind of feel like I might get sick." That part wasn't an exaggeration. The unwelcome swirl of desire was making him feel dizzy and nauseated. "And it would be really embarrassing to me if you were here for that."

She smiled. "All right. I'm going to leave you the elderberry syrup, the soup, some soda and crackers, and my hot water bottle, but you have to promise to use them and take good care of yourself. Stay hydrated, it will make a world of difference."

"I promise," he said. He was willing to promise anything to get her out of arm's reach.

"Call if you need anything," she said.

"I'm sure I'll be fine. This will all blow over by tomorrow."

She chuckled. "That would be a miraculously short run for a virus but, sure, let's think positively."

He wasn't talking about the virus; he was talking about the temporary insanity that had taken over his brain, caused by weakness that was doubtless caused by the illness. Of course he wanted her; his normal defenses were down. He would want any female right now. She opened the door and stepped through.

"Wait," he called.

She turned toward him and paused, her pretty, pleasant face alight with a smile. What was he doing? He was supposed to be getting rid of her, not hailing her back. All he knew was that it felt like all the light and life in his house would be leaving with her. Tentatively, he took a step forward and pressed a kiss to her cheek. "Thanks."

She touched her palm to his cheek. "You're welcome, sickness buddy. Get some rest."

Not likely tonight, he thought, but he didn't say as much. He nodded and leaned on the door for support while she walked to her car and started it up. He remained standing in the open door, long after she had driven away. It occurred to him that it was becoming a repetitive theme for them, him watching her drive away with something like yearning in his heart.

At last he closed the door and wandered inside. He lay down on the couch, but couldn't get comfortable without Maggie's soft body as a buffer. Now that she was outside the realm of temptation, he wondered why he had sent her away. Now what was he to do with no one to take care of him, no one to feed him or bring him drinks and water bottles and pet his head?

The home and garden channel was on. He hated the channel, but he left it on because it brought him an echo of comfort, a reminder of Maggie.

Chapter 9

Over the next few months, Ridge and Maggie's outings became a weekly standard. Sometimes Ridge chose the venue—usually a baseball game, in his ever-increasing desire to teach Maggie to enjoy sports. And sometimes Maggie chose the activity—usually something outdoors where they could bring the dog. One morning in the park, they ran into each other as they were jogging and decided to do that together, too. But at work, they maintained their distance. No one knew they were friends or had any contact outside of the job. Sometimes Maggie went out with Babs and Blue. They were also becoming good friends, but it was never the same as with Ridge, with whom she seemed to share some sort of supernatural affinity. He didn't notice when she tumbled out of bed and threw on jogging pants any more than he seemed to notice when she spent a long time on her hair and makeup. To him, she was simply Maggie, his friend. And he was becoming her rock in the city, her person, her home away from home.

Neither could articulate why they chose to keep their friendship a secret. If pressed, Ridge might have said it was because he didn't want to appear to have chosen favorites, though Maggie was by far his favorite. He didn't want her to be a source of resentment among her coworkers. Maggie would have said something similar, though people were already talking about the fact that she had never left his office crying, only smiling. Her insistence that he was, in fact, a nice guy didn't hold any water for people who believed he was the boogeyman. In their defense, he did nothing to dispel the notion. He seemed to store all his kindness for Maggie and lash out at the remainder of their crew. Maggie was disturbed by the dichotomy and had yet to find a tactful way to bring it up. She felt torn. No one was able to see the man she adored in all his silly sweetness. On the other hand, she didn't have to share him with anyone else. She suspected he went out on dates, but he never talked about it. And he for certain wasn't in a serious relationship, given all the time he spent with her and at work.

Her efforts to get him to leave his office and join their celebrations never let up, and he never relented. It had almost become a game, her trying to coax him out and him flatly refusing.

When it was Blue's birthday, Maggie made a bright pink cake. "To keep life unpredictable," she told him. When Ridge made no move to join the festivities, she dutifully cut him a slice to carry to his office.

"Why do you keep trying? You're like the Energizer Bunny," Babs said. "He's never coming out."

"Let's pray," Ellen said, shuddering as she glanced at Ridge's closed door.

"Someday he'll come out," Maggie replied, as she always did.

"Girl, you've got it bad," LuAnn said.

"I solemnly swear I do not have a crush on our boss. I simply think he should be a part of things, and it gets sad and lonely in his office," Maggie replied, but everyone had shared a collective eye roll, so convinced were they of Maggie's unrequited feelings for him. The misconception annoyed her, and she marched to Ridge's office with purpose.

"Come in, Maggie," he called when she knocked on the door.

"How did you know it was me?" she asked when she opened the door and stepped inside. It was the kind of heavy door that closed automatically. It did so, and she leaned on it.

"I heard the off key rendition of the birthday song echoing down the hallway," he said.

"Why didn't you come join us, Yeti?" she said.

"I'm busy. Leave the cake and go, woman," he said, tapping the spot on his desk where she always set the cake.

"No," she replied, and that got his attention.

"If you're not bringing me cake, why are you here holding cake?"

"You've become too complacent in your role as birthday cake consumer. If you want this cake, and I know you do, you're going to have to work for it."

He sat back and laced his fingers together. "What did you have in mind? Some kind of gladiator duel to the death over frosting?"

"No, I simply want you to walk over here, take the cake and say, 'Thank you, Maggie,' like a normal person with good manners."

He shook his head and tapped the spot on his desk.

She shook her head and reached for the door. Sighing, he stood, walked around the desk, and strode purposefully forward until he was so close to her she had to press herself into the door to avoid him. He took the cake from her and noticed a spot of frosting on her thumb. He brought her hand to his mouth, pulled her thumb between his lips, and licked the icing away.

"Thank you for the cake, Maggie. The frosting is delicious."

"Was that so hard?" Maggie asked, her voice husky and breathless.

"No, I rather enjoyed it. Now get back to work, minion."

"Give me a minute, my knees seemed to have failed me."

"Play with fire, enjoy the burn," he said. He walked back to his desk, finishing the cake in two bites.

"You're ridiculous," she said when she could rightfully speak again. "And it's unfair you can turn on whatever that is and do it to me and I have no recourse with which to retaliate."

"Players gonna play, baby," he said, returning his attention to his work.

"Ridiculous," Maggie muttered before letting herself out. When she was safely gone, Ridge stopped pretending to type whatever gibberish he'd been typing and let out a long, shaky breath.

Two weeks later, the scene repeated itself, though this time Maggie fully intended to drop the cake and go. She had learned her lesson about what Ridge could do when provoked. She cut him a slice and knocked on his door.

"What," he barked.

She opened the door and poked her head in. "I have cake."

"I don't want cake," he said. "And did I say you could come in?"

"I'm not going to make you work for it. I'll leave it and you can eat it when and if you get hungry." She took a step inside.

He stood and yelled. "I said I don't want cake, Maggie, are you deaf? Why do we have to have these idiotic celebrations every five minutes? Can no one function here like a normal, workday office? Get out!" Then he picked up a glass and threw it at the door where it shattered into a million pieces, narrowly missing her head.

Her face drained of color, she backed out of the room and made the long walk of shame back to her desk. People in the office were sympathetic, yet slightly gleeful. At long last, Maggie had witnessed the beast. She got it now, what people had been saying about him; that had been terrifying. No one had ever spoken to her that way. The fact that it had been Ridge was doubly disappointing and confusing.

He didn't emerge from his office the rest of the day, and Maggie was glad. She had no idea how she would face him again, today or any day. How could their friendship continue after such a display of unwarranted rage?

She went home silent and sullen and spent a long time being consoled by Samson, who was always happy to see her and never angry. Part of her was still numb from the shock of the encounter. In all the many, many, *many* hours she had spent with Ridge, she had never once seen him lose his temper, and especially not with her.

When there was a knock on her door, she almost didn't answer. Who else would it be but him? With trepidation, she opened the door and saw him standing on the other side, a large bag of Chinese food in his hand.

"I don't even know what to say, Maggie. I'm so incredibly sorry. My behavior was inexcusable, and I deeply regret it. Can we pretty please be friends again?"

She regarded him solemnly for a moment and then, to her horror, burst into tears. He dropped the food and pulled her into his embrace, holding her tightly. "I'm so, so sorry," he murmured, kissing her head and stroking her hair with his fingers. Eventually her tears came to an end, and she invited him inside.

"I brought makeup Chinese takeout," he said, holding the bag aloft. He headed toward the table, but she tugged him back.

"Where are you going?"

"To the table," he said, confused.

"What is this, the Ritz? Who eats Chinese takeout at the table? You sit on the floor like an impoverished college student," she said. She sat in front of the coffee table and patted the spot beside her, urging him to do the same. He kicked off his shoes, sat beside her, and began taking out containers.

"Did you get crab Rangoon?" she asked.

"Are you serious? Would I have been allowed inside without it?" he asked.

"Doubtful," she said, smiling a little. He picked up her hand and kissed it and they started to eat. Some things they both liked, and they passed the containers back and forth, each maintaining his or her own chopsticks. They ate in comfortable silence, broken only by Maggie's tremulous sniffles. Each sniffle was a stab in Ridge's heart, piling the guilt a little deeper.

"Whose birthday was it?" he asked at last.

"My dad's," she said. He frowned in confusion. "It's my dad's 60th birthday, and my family is having a surprise party for him today. I'm the only one not there, and I was feeling a little sad. So everyone got together and brought in a cake to celebrate so I wouldn't feel left out."

He bent his head over until it touched the coffee table. "I'm such a jerk."

She rested her hand on his arm. "That's what's so confusing to me. I know you're not. What happened?"

He took a breath and sat up. "It's a combination of things, some lingering flickers of PTSD and the operative who was killed."

"I read about it," Maggie said. It had been in the daily briefing. She had been sad, but it hadn't affected her as much as him.

"I knew him. We came up through the navy together, were both SEALS, went to Quantico together, and have worked in the field together too many times to count. Four years ago I was in his wedding. Three years ago, I was at his first baby's christening. And now he's gone."

She set down her chopsticks. "Cam," she whispered. "You lost a friend, a good friend."

He nodded.

"Why didn't you tell me?"

"I wasn't ready to talk about it," he said, staring at his chopsticks as he twirled them mindlessly between his fingers.

She sat on her knees and hugged him, pulling him against her chest like a mother comforting a child. At first he resisted, and then he gave in, pressing his face to her and crying a little. He hadn't cried in ages, since he couldn't remember when. But this was Maggie, his safe place.

"I'm so, so sorry," she whispered when he had himself back under control. "Would you like to tell me about him?"

He didn't think he would want to, but as he opened his mouth to say no, stories began to pour out of him, about their shenanigans in the navy, their harrowing adventures on duty, some of the dicey situations they'd faced in the field together, and his memories of the man himself, aside from the job. The pain and pressure inside him flowed out, along with the words until, eventually, he felt drained of everything.

Maggie listened quietly, sympathetically. Her phone buzzed, probably her family at her father's party back home.

But she ignored it and kept her focus on him, alternately smiling and pressing her hand to her mouth in anxiety, depending on the story. Eventually, when he was out of words and feelings and food, they sat on the couch and turned on the TV.

"What do you want to watch?" she asked.

"You choose," he said, a sign of his exhaustion. Usually he controlled the remote, even at her house. She turned to mindless reruns, something they both enjoyed, and sat back beside him. He put his arm around her. She slung her arm over his waist and rested her head on his chest.

"I should go home," he said.

"I feel like I've heard that somewhere before," she said.

"I mean it this time," he said, but he made no move to leave. He was tired, drained, exhausted, and immensely comforted all at once. This afternoon he thought he had ruined things between them forever, and that hurt more than he could have imagined. And now they were closer than ever, because of Maggie and her warm-hearted willingness to forgive his odious display. He gave her a squeeze and kissed the top of her head. When she didn't respond, he knew she was already out. He should cover her with a blanket and make his escape before he, too, gave in to sleep. But he didn't. Instead he turned off the television, put a blanket over them both, and closed his eyes.

Chapter 10

In the morning, he had regrets. Usually in the rare event one of them stayed over at the other's house, they either took separate ends of the couch or one took the couch while whichever homeowner it was slept in his or her own bed. This morning they woke up twined together, her fully in his arms like a lover's embrace. Ridge broke out in a cold sweat because, as he reviewed their relationship, he began to believe Maggie was in love with him and he had somehow missed it. How could she not be with all the time they'd spent together? Worse, he began to wonder if she believed he was in love with her. Did she view their friendship differently than he did? He began to feel the same choking sense of panic he always did when it came time to define his relationship with a woman. Had he been naïve in his behavior toward Maggie, fully believing she was immune to him? She was a woman, and women were different than men. After so much time, attention, talking, and laughter, how could any woman help falling in love with him?

He was pondering how to make a quick escape when Maggie woke up, her face a mere two inches from his. "Well, this is new," she said. She extricated herself from him and sat up. "Do you want breakfast?"

"Um," he said, searching for a handy way to say no without hurting her feelings.

"I kind of need to talk to you about something, so if you can stay, that would be great," she said.

"All right," he said, a sinking feeling of dread in the pit of his stomach.

Smiling, she patted his cheek. "I need to see to Sam, and then I'll get started."

"'Kay," he said, forcing a smile. *No, no, no, no, no.* Yesterday he thought he had ruined their friendship, and now Maggie was about to ruin it for certain. How did one handle hearing a love confession from a best friend? "I want to keep you in the friend zone," lacked finesse as an answer.

He used her shower as she cooked, mostly as a way to avoid her. Her toiletries smelled just like her. Normally that would have made him smile. Today it made him sad. Would things change forever after this? He hoped not. He loved Maggie as he had loved few people in his life. She was too important to lose. Maybe that was what he would tell her.

"Thanks for letting me use your shower," he said as he emerged into the kitchen.

"Just so long as you didn't use my underwear, we're golden," she said, and he smiled. Her back was to him as she finished flipping omelets, and her hips wiggled slightly as she jostled the pan. He smiled wider, enjoying the view, as well as the fact that she was a good cook. Occasionally, when neither felt like going out, they stayed in and she cooked supper. He had never told her those were the nights he liked the best because it reminded him of home. Everything about Maggie felt like home.

She plated the food and poured the juice and coffee. He sat by feeling inept compared to her usefulness. Though, if he were being honest, he liked it when she took care of him. She waited to speak until he had a bite of food in his mouth.

"Cam, I need to tell you something, and it's a little awkward. So I'm going to preface it by saying that I hope it won't change anything between us," she said.

"If you're afraid it will change things, then maybe you shouldn't say anything," he said.

"I've struggled with it for a while, believe me. I vowed not to bring it up, but last night something changed, and now it feels like the elephant in the room."

"Maggie," he began, desperate to stop her confession of love, but he was too late.

"Cam, no one likes you," she blurted.

He blinked at her, trying to make sense of her words. "What?"

"That came out more blunt than I meant because I'm nervous, but the essence is true. No one at work likes you. They think you're an ogre."

He waved her words away, smiling with unfathomable relief. "No one likes their boss."

She put her hand on his. "Cam, they call you Satan. There are rumors you're some kind of reptile because you're there before everyone, leave after everyone, and no one has ever seen you eat or drink or use the bathroom."

"I'm sincerely glad no one has ever seen me use the bathroom," he said.

"This is serious. It's affecting morale. People are looking for other jobs."

He scowled. "Which people?"

"I'm not going to tell you so you can ream or fire them," she said, exasperated.

"Then why are you telling me?"

"Because you're great, and I want everyone to know it," she yelled, tossing her hands up in exasperation. "You're the best boss I've ever had, but I'm the only one in the office who thinks that. Everyone else says the opposite."

"Maggie, honey, I don't need to be liked," he said, squeezing her hand.

"But you need to be effective, and I am telling you as a friend and an employee that you're not right now. People are so terrified to make a mistake that it's stifling performance and productivity."

He withdrew his hand, blinking.

"I don't like telling you these things, they hurt me. They're awkward and uncomfortable to say. But I'm doing it because I know to the essence of my core that you are capable of being an amazing leader. But your volatile, angry displays are holding you back."

"I don't agree with you," Ridge said, beginning to get well and truly angry. Maggie stood and put her hands on his shoulders in a desperate attempt to preempt his anger and get her point across.

"You are one of my closest friends in the world, so please believe me that I'm saying what I'm about to say with all the love in my heart: you're a jerk sometimes. It hurts me to see people dislike you so, and it hurts me to see you abuse my other friends at work."

"You have other friends?" he asked, sliding her onto his lap.

"Yes, I've been friend cheating on you," she said, and he smiled a little.

"The thing is, I was raised to believe there should be a distinction between bosses and employees," he said.

"I wholeheartedly agree with you," she said.

"You know you're saying that unironically while my hand is literally on your thigh," he said.

"We're non-binary, but for everyone else, yes. I'm not saying you have to have a game of catch with them. Poke your head out from your hidey-hole once in a while and mingle. Come to a birthday celebration, give a pat on the back for a job well done, stop making people sob in the bathroom. They're leaving puddles on the floor, and it's a hazard. And maybe, just maybe, come out with us some evening like a regular human instead of a disciplined machine."

He rested his forehead on hers. "I will consider it."

"That's all I'm asking," she said. "By the way, your hand is still very much on my thigh."

"Is it? Fascinating," he said, giving her thigh a squeeze.

"You're a different kind of boss."

"This is how I mingle," he said.

"Blue is in for a big surprise come Monday," she said. He laughed and her phone buzzed. "I have to take this, sorry." She slid off his lap and answered her phone. All of her family was gathered around her sister's phone.

"Hey, Maggie," they called.

"Happy birthday, Dad," she said. "I'm so sorry I couldn't be there."

"We missed you," her older brother, Johnny said, pushing his way into the camera's view.

"I missed you, too. I miss you always," Maggie said.

"I love you," Johnny said.

"I love you, too," Maggie said, blowing him kisses. She had three siblings. Her oldest, Johnny, had Down Syndrome.

"Where were you last night? We tried to call," her mother asked.

"I had a thing," she replied. "Sorry."

"Did you have to work?" her dad asked.

"No, but my boss is here. Want to say hi?" she asked. Behind her, Ridge was shaking his head furiously.

"Sure," her family agreed. Maggie turned the phone toward him. "This is Ridge."

"Hi," her family called, except her little sister, Amelia who practically trampled everyone in her haste to get closer to the phone.

"Holy crap," Amelia called.

"Amelia, language," their mother said.

"Is he for real?" Amelia asked.

"Don't encourage him," Maggie said. Ridge smiled and Amelia actually gasped.

"You have pretty teeth," Johnny called.

"Thank you," Ridge said.

"Is he single?" Amelia blurted.

"Gross, Mom, why does she say stuff like that?" their middle brother, Darren, said.

"Amelia, control yourself," her mother said.

"Mom, look at him," Amelia said, pointing.

"He's single, but he has issues," Maggie said.

"I don't have issues," Ridge argued.

"More issues than *People* magazine," Maggie added in a loudly whispered aside.

"You are in for such a beating when you hang up that phone," Ridge whispered, and her family laughed.

"We'll not keep you honey, we wanted to check in and tell you we miss you," her mom said.

"I miss you, too. I'll call again soon."

"Sounds good. Goodbye, and goodbye, Ridge. Nice to meet you."

"Nice to meet you," Ridge echoed waving.

"I love you," Johnny said.

"I love you," Maggie replied.

"I love you, too," Amelia added. "And I was talking to Ridge."

"Mom," Darren complained, "Make her stop."

"Amelia, act like a lady," her mother said before she pushed the button to disconnect. Maggie sat staring at the blank phone for a minute in silence.

"Are you going to make it?" Ridge asked.

She nodded.

"Good." He put her in a headlock. "How could you tell your family I have issues?"

"Because you have issues," she said, struggling free of his grasp.

"I do not have issues," he said.

"Tell me the truth. When I told you I needed to talk to you this morning and you got that panicked look, as if you were searching for a way to gnaw off your own foot to make an escape, were you afraid I was about to confess my passionate love for you?"

"I hate when you read me like that," he said.

She poked him. He batted her hand away.

"Fine, but only because I don't want to lose the good thing we've got going here," he said.

She leaned forward and wrapped her arms around his neck, letting her lips brush his. "But, Cam, what if the good thing we've got going could be even better?"

He froze. "I…"

She let him go and pulled back with a smile. "Kidding."

"I cannot believe you did that," he said when his tongue finally dislodged from the roof of his mouth.

"Play with fire, enjoy the burn," she said. She licked her finger and touched it to his shoulder, making the "tss" sound of a fire being doused.

"You're ridiculous," he said.

"Players gonna play, baby. You want another omelet?"

"Yes." He handed her his plate. She stood and prepared another omelet while he sat back and enjoyed the hip wiggle she had no idea she was doing. All in all, it was a perfect Saturday morning.

Chapter 11

After that, things were slightly different at work. It started with the next birthday party. Maggie did not take a piece of cake to Cam and try to lure him out. Instead he emerged from his office like a groundhog in February, tentatively, as if uncertain of his welcome. And with good reason. As soon as he entered the break room, conversation came to a standstill, except for Maggie who picked up where everyone left off.

"Hey, you made it, and you're in time for cake. It's LuAnn's birthday," she said, knowing he would have no idea who they were celebrating. "She loves chocolate, so it's a triple fudge cake today."

"Girl, I don't love chocolate. I want to marry chocolate and have its baby," LuAnn said.

Maggie cut Ridge a piece of cake and handed it over. "Happy birthday, LuAnn," he said, smiling the megawatt smile that made everyone, including men, come to a complete standstill and ponder whether or not his teeth were real. They were, Maggie knew, making his freakishly brilliant smile even more extraordinary.

"Thanks, Mr. Ridge." The usually outspoken LuAnn sounded tentative.

"It's just Ridge," Ridge said, but kindly. Conversation tried and failed to resume again, and he knew he had reached his max with the group. "I should get back. Thanks for the cake, Mags. Have a good day, y'all." With another smile—toothless this time—he turned and went back to his office. Everyone waited until he was safely tucked away to speak.

"What was that about?" Ellen hissed in a whisper.

"Do you think he found religion?" Babs asked.

"I think he found something else, huh, *Mags*," Blue said and everyone turned to look at Maggie.

"Yeah, why did he call you that?" LuAnn asked.

"A lot of people call me that," Maggie said.

"None of us do," Blue said.

"That's because I hate you all," Maggie said. "Don't be conspiracy theorists. I told you he's a nice guy, and he seems to be trying to convey that. Take it for what it is."

"And what was the 'y'all' about?" Ellen continued undaunted. "Is he trying to be folksy?"

"He's southern," Maggie said, and they all turned to look at her again.

"You're joking," Babs said.

"I thought southerners were supposed to be nice," LuAnn said.

"He *is* nice," Maggie told them. "In fact, I was kind of thinking of inviting him to join us at Barney's next week."

That suggestion was met with dead silence. "Because you have a vendetta against us or you simply want to kill all fun?" Blue asked.

"Give him a chance, pretty please. Wouldn't it be nice to work in a place where you like your boss and everyone gets along?" Maggie said.

"Yes, but Heaven keeps rejecting my applications," Blue said.

"Try, please. If it doesn't work, he never has to come with us again. Please." She clasped her hands and put them under her chin.

"Saying no to you is like kicking a bunny," Babs said.

"I've kicked plenty of bunnies," Ellen said. "I'm still a no."

Blue sighed. "Sorry, Ellen, you're outvoted. Let's have Satan try to join us for our super fun and relaxing after work outing next week. Hurray."

"That's the spirit," Maggie said, and then spent another hour later that week trying to convince Ridge to show up.

"I will only go if we go together," he said.

"You realize that's going to notch up the awkwardness and speculation," she said.

"Final offer," he said.

"You are a stubborn old goat," she said.

"And you're fine, young nag," he replied, pinching her waist.

"This must be how Reagan felt when he was trying to negotiate an end to the Berlin wall," Maggie said.

"Would that make me east or west Germany?" he asked.

"What do you think, comrade?" she replied.

When the night in question arrived, she wasn't sure who was more nervous, her or Ridge or her coworkers. "Why am I doing this? You already told me they hate me," Ridge said.

"Because they don't know you," Maggie insisted. "This will give them a chance to see you outside of work."

"Seeing your boss outside of work is like running into your teacher at the mall," he said. "Horrendous."

"It's going to be fine," Maggie said, reassuring them both.

"Maggie, do you want to walk in like this?" he asked, noting their joined hands.

"Good point," she said, shaking free of his clasp. "How does that keep happening?"

"Because you can't keep your hands off me," he said.

"Like chicken pox," she said and then pointed a finger at him. "Don't touch me tonight. They'll notice, and they'll think it's weird."

"Which of us is the queen of affectionate gestures? You're the one who's touchy-feely. I keep my hands to myself like a normal, emotionally repressed man."

She shook her head. "You touch me first every single time, all the time. I'm beginning to wonder if it's some kind of OCD obsession for you to have your hands on my person."

"And then you wake up and realize you're the one who touches me," he said.

"Compulsive liar says what?" Maggie muttered.

"I don't know, you tell me, Touchy McFeelington." He poked her arm.

"You just did it, right there," she said, pointing to the place he had poked her.

"Video or it didn't happen," he said.

"I swear sometimes it's like being with my little brother," she said.

He frowned, not liking the comparison. It was bad luck that the frown landed as they reached the table of coworkers. "Hey, guys," Maggie said with forced calmness and good cheer.

The table looked up collectively and froze in uncertainty. "Hey," Blue said at last. "Welcome."

"Thanks," Maggie said. She sat. Ridge sat beside her. He was being quiet, which she knew meant he was assessing the mood while also scanning the room for danger and making note of the exits. But to the waiting crowd of coworkers it looked a whole lot like grumpy disapproval. "What were you guys talking about?"

"Eagles."

"Did someone see an eagle?" Maggie asked, excited.

Blue put his hand on hers and gave it a pat. "Babycakes, not eagles, *the* Eagles, as in Philadelphia."

"Who likes the Eagles?" Ridge said, tuning in at the mention of football. He leaned forward and rested his hands on the table beside Maggie's forcing Blue to withdraw his hand or risk touching fingers with his boss.

"The guy from Philadelphia," Blue said. "Don't tell me you like the Redskins."

"Pfft," Ridge said. "I like the only team in America, the Cowboys."

"And you're willing to admit that?" Blue said.

"I haven't hit a man in a while, but I'm not opposed to it, Blue," Ridge said, and everyone "ooohed."

"And I haven't hacked anyone's credit report in a while, but I'm not opposed to it, Ridge," Blue said.

"And I haven't had anything to eat since lunch, and I'm starving," Maggie said.

"Where's the waitress?" Ridge asked, looking around.

"You order at the bar," Babs said.

"Did you guys already order?" Maggie asked.

"We're starving, too," Blue said, nodding.

Maggie started to stand, but Ridge put a hand to her shoulder. "I'll get it." She watched him walk away. When she turned back around, everyone was staring at her.

"What?" she asked.

"We get it now," Blue said.

"Get what?" she asked.

"You guys are a *thang*," LuAnn said.

"We are not a thang. We're not even a thing. We're pals."

"You came together," Babs said.

"We live five minutes from each other," Maggie said.

"See, that's another thing. None of us has any idea where he lives, or that he's from the south, or if he sleeps or blinks or makes blood sacrifices in his office, or anything else about him. But you seem to be a fount of information," Blue said.

"I'm a research librarian. I research," Maggie said.

"Before, I would have bought that because we all assumed you had a one-sided crush going on. But it's not one-sided, is it?" Blue insisted.

"There's no side because there's no crush. We're friends, that's all."

"No, no, no," Babs said. She pointed between herself and Blue. "We're friends. You and Ridge are a whole other level."

"Guys, come on. Have you seen him?" Maggie said.

"Have you seen you?" LuAnn said.

"Don't tell me we're going to have to give you a self-esteem intervention," Blue said. "That's so sad."

"I don't have low self-esteem, I simply see reality. He dates supermodel types. Besides, it doesn't matter anyway because he and I are friends, and that's all. I solemnly swear." She held up her right hand.

"Are you saying the pledge?" Ridge asked as he returned with drinks. He set hers in front of her. "I got you regular Coke because they use grenadine to make their cherry, and I know you don't like that."

Across from them, Blue snickered into his hand while Babs faked a cough. "What's up?" Ridge asked, looking at them askance.

"They think we're a couple," Maggie blurted.

"I can't believe you tattled to Dad," Blue hissed.

"Friends," Ridge said, pointing between himself and Maggie. "Don't you guys have friends of the opposite sex?"

"We're friends," Blue said, pointing between himself, Babs, and LuAnn. "But watch this, hey, guys, what do I want to drink tonight?"

"No earthly idea," Babs said.

"Couldn't tell you if you paid me," LuAnn agreed.

"Hmm," Blue said. Maggie winced, waiting for Ridge to blow up, but he surprised everyone by laughing.

"We're *good* friends," he said.

"How come none of us knew that?" Blue asked.

"Because you're woefully unobservant and self-absorbed?" Ridge guessed.

"He's got us there," Blue agreed, taking a sip of his drink. "How long have you been *good* friends?"

"Hmm," Ridge said, eyeing Maggie. "Forever, maybe."

"Did you know each other before?" Babs asked.

"Before what? The earth began?" Ridge asked.

"Before we all started working together," LuAnn clarified.

"Some," Maggie said. There was no need to tell them she had only met Ridge when he recruited her, and that they had formed an almost immediate connection. They might find it weird. *She* found it weird.

"So, you're like friends outside of work," Blue said.

"Why is this so shocking to everyone?" Ridge said. He hugged Maggie, pressing his cheek to hers. "Best friends, yes. Do stuff outside of work, yes. Romance, no. Love her to pieces, yes. In love with her, no." He kissed her cheek and let her go.

Babs poked Blue. "Why don't you do cute stuff like that with me?"

"Because if I tried to touch you like that you would rip my cheek off with your bare teeth," Blue said.

"Do you have a girlfriend?" LuAnn asked tentatively. It was clear they were testing the limits, trying to figure out how casual and comfortable they could be with Ridge.

Ridge paused before answering, as if wondering the same thing. "No," he said at last.

"And we know Maggie's not dating anyone," Blue said.

"What's that supposed to mean? I could be dating someone," she said.

"Are you?" he asked.

"No, but I could."

"Have you gone on one date since you've been here?" Babs asked.

"I…shut up," Maggie said. "Dating is hard. Where am I going to meet someone? On the train? The only eligible man on my commute picks his nose and eats it."

"Can you get his number for me?" Babs asked.

The food arrived and conversation paused while everyone began to eat. Maggie picked the olives off her pizza and gave them to Ridge while he gave her his breadstick and dipping sauce. When they looked up, everyone was watching them.

"What now?" Maggie snapped.

"Nothing, it's cute," Babs said.

"My parents do that same thing. Of course they've been married for forty years, but whatever," Blue said.

"One more observation about our relationship, and you're all fired," Ridge said. Everyone laughed and resumed eating, but the look Blue gave Maggie told her the ridicule was far from over.

The remainder of the night was upbeat and fun. Eventually everyone left until only Ridge and Maggie remained. They had purposely waited so they wouldn't be observed walking to his car together.

"How do you feel? It went well, don't you think? I think this evening humanized you, in their view," Maggie said.

"Maybe," he agreed.

"You maintained your bossness while letting the stench of the little people touch you," she said.

"Some people stunk more than others. What was their obsession with us? How many times did we tell them we're not a thing?" he asked. His arm was around her chair, his fingers skimming her back.

"I know, right?" She was turned toward him, resting both hands on his thigh. "It was so annoying. I told you we should have come separately."

"Who cares? It's over now and I'm sure eventually they'll let it go. Your place or mine?"

"Mine, I need to be with the dog," she said.

"You love your dog more than me," he pouted.

"In his defense, I knew him first," she said. She squeezed his leg. "Let's go, I'm exhausted."

Chapter 12

They assumed their usual spots on Maggie's sofa, with the dog taking up two thirds of available space.

"We're becoming couch potatoes," he said.

"We run five or six days a week," she said. "Well, you run. I jog lamely behind."

"You do fine," he said, giving her a squeeze. His arm was around her shoulders, and her head was on his chest, tucked under his arm like a baby chick.

"We watch too much TV," he reiterated.

"It's midnight. What would you like to do instead, learn to hula hoop?" she asked. "There's probably a YouTube video for that, and I actually have a hula hoop. Don't ask why."

"I don't know," he said. "It feels wrong somehow."

She sat up, eyes wide. "You know what I figured out?"

"What?" he asked, missing her warmth. Her house was chillier than his.

"Today is September 13th. We met a year ago today."

"Hey, you're right."

"Happy friendiversary," she said.

"That's not a thing," he said.

"It's a thing because I made it a thing. Don't ruin it," she said.

"You're right. Happy friendiversary." They hugged and when they pulled apart, they were facing each other, both hands clasped and resting between them. "What should we do to celebrate?"

"Let's eat cookies," she suggested.

"The answer to everything is not cookies," he said.

"How do you know unless you've tried to make it the answer to everything?" she said.

"Let's review the year. Tell me your highlights," he said. He brushed the stray hairs off her face, the ones that were trying to escape again. In the last year, he had never once seen her hair down, and he found that odd. After the many, many hours they had logged together, both at work and during their downtime, shouldn't he have seen her hair loose at least once?

"I moved to a city I thought I would hate and ended up loving. I started a job I didn't know if I could do."

"And you're rocking it. Consider this your performance review," he said.

"Thank you. And I lost twenty pounds, something I never thought possible, given my aforementioned love of cookies," she said.

"That's right, you did," he said, surveying her waist. His hand moved there and rested on her hip. "I've almost forgotten what you looked like before, but I'm happy to know you've retained your curves."

"I don't think you're allowed to comment on my curves from the friend zone. Stay in your lane. Also, your hands are on my body," she said.

"My hands almost always seem to be on your body," he commented. He had long given up on trying to puzzle together exactly what their friendship was. It defied definition, but he liked it.

"I think I'm beginning to understand why people think we're a thing," she said.

"It's all in their heads," he said. "They don't understand the complexities of male/female friendships."

"Neither do I, come to think of it," she said.

"Don't you want to know my highlights from the year?" he asked.

"For sure," she said.

"I met this woman."

"Do I know her?" she asked.

"Shh. She's smart and sweet and fun and funny and weird and an awesome cook."

"You could have left out weird."

"No, I really couldn't. It's an integral part of her," he said.

"Is she hot?" Maggie teased.

Ridge nodded. "At first you think she's cute, pretty, maybe even beautiful. But then you get to know her better, and she's so, so hot." His thumb began tracing a slow circle on her hipbone. God bless yoga pants and their skin-hugging clinginess. "Maggie, it's been a year. I need to test something." He let go her body and reached for her hair, pulling it out of its ubiquitous topknot. She shooed his hands aside when he got her ponytail holder hopelessly tangled. At last she pulled it free and fluffed the blond cascade gently over her shoulders.

"Yowza," he breathed. "Keep wearing the bun thing to work, okay?"

"Why's that?' she asked.

"Otherwise I might genuinely drool and spend my day writing, 'Mr. Cameron Eldridge' on my desk."

"You'd take my name?" she said.

"What do you think?" he asked.

"I think you're the kind of man who likes to put his stamp on a woman," she said.

"You know me so well," he said. His fingers couldn't resist sifting her hair a few times. He started at her scalp and let the silky strands flow through his fingers. Maggie closed her eyes, sighing a little.

"That feels nice," she whispered.

"Yes, it does," Ridge agreed. His hands slid from the crown of her hair to the nape of her neck, still skimming gently along her scalp. She went limp and leaned in to him slightly, her eyes still closed. The look of pleasure on her pretty face was so intense, he couldn't look away. One of his hands eased forward, framing her face in his palm. His thumb slid along her jawline and skimmed lightly over her bottom lip.

Maggie's eyes opened. They stared at each other, but neither said a word. The silence grew and stretched between them, along with the tension. "Let me check something," he said. He took her hand and placed it over his heart and stretched out his palm and pressed it to her heart. "Our heartbeats are synched, and they're thumping out of control. What do you think that means?"

"That we're happy to be friends?" she guessed.

The silence returned. The tension was unbearable. They were both struggling to breathe, as if they'd run a marathon, when in fact they'd barely moved. At last he spoke, his voice ragged. "Maggie, I…I think maybe we should…" His phone buzzed and they both jumped, breaking apart and adding a few inches between them. Samson huffed in displeasure when Maggie bumped him. Ridge pulled out his phone and checked it, glad for a reprieve.

"I have to go to work," he announced.

"Now?" she blurted.

"Now," he said.

"Should I come with you?" she asked.

"No, but I'll buzz you if I need you, so better get some rest and keep your phone handy." He stood. She started to stand, but he pushed her back down and quickly removed his hand. "Don't walk me to the door tonight. I can't right now with you. I just can't."

"All right," Maggie said, trying hard not to be hurt by his apparent rejection.

He reached the door, turned, and blew her a kiss. "Happy friendiversary, love."

She pretended to catch the kiss, and he smiled. When he was gone, she opened her hand and stared at her empty palm, wondering over the strange turn the night had taken.

Chapter 13

Ridge texted Maggie at 5 AM on Saturday telling her to come to the office but first swing by and bring him a new suit and some food.

"Anything else, your majesty?" she muttered to herself. She hadn't slept well, and the imperious text made her feel even crankier. She wondered if he was being terse because of their confusing encounter the night before, but her arrival at work dispelled that notion. The boss was there, the big boss, her boss, Ridge's boss, everybody's boss.

"What's happening?" Maggie asked as she stood in Ridge's office with him and fed him bites of a granola bar while he changed out of one suit and into a fresh one.

"We got some intel on a new cell that's threatening mass casualties in the US. It's cropped up in the last few hours, and it's high priority because they're already in the country."

"What?" Maggie hissed. "How did it get this far?"

"I don't know," he said. "They slipped under the radar. Everyone missed them, and now everyone is on them. This is bad, Maggie. This is very, very bad." He slipped the final leg into his pants and stood upright to zip them.

"Wait, you have granola on your face," she said, standing on her toes to brush it off. He stood patiently by while she wiped his lips.

"You look especially amazing today," he said. "I notice you wore your hair down."

"My neck was cold," she replied.

"Temptress," he accused. "Let's go."

"You want me to come with you?" she squeaked. She had never been in a meeting with the highest of the higher ups before, and this would be a meeting with all of them.

"I want my own translator, and I want you to get a read on the situation. You don't have to talk, just use that famous intuition of yours."

"Okay," she said, taking a steadying breath. It was a bad day to wear her hair down. The bun made her feel more grownup and professional. "Hold on." She wound her hair into a chignon at the base of her neck and secured it with a rubber band from his desk. "Does that look okay?"

"There's this one hair," he said, touching one long strand that had escaped the knot. "But I kind of like it, it's a hint of sexy, sort of our little secret." His fingers were still holding the strand of hair, but his eyes fell to her lips.

"Now is so not the time," she said.

"I know," he said. He let her hair go and took a deep breath. "Here we go." They headed out of his office and up three floors to the secure conference room. It was soundproof, checked for bugs daily and unable to be penetrated with any outside infrared technology. Even the windows had been specially installed to not only be bulletproof but lacking in vibrations that would have given way to high-tech outside listening devices.

"You've got this," Maggie said, squeezing Ridge's hand before they stepped off the elevator.

"Thanks," he said, returning the squeeze. It was his first time in the big leagues, too. Previously he had been a field agent, doing the daunting work of gathering intel. It was a whole new learning curve on the other side of the desk. They entered the conference room and sat down. Their boss's boss, Admiral Hagan, gave the rundown of the situation, making it sound even direr than Ridge had. Based on his language, that of a first-year sailor and not an esteemed admiral, he was irate and maybe a little bit panicked. Though, having never met him before, Maggie supposed it was possible he always talked that way.

The next higher up, marine General Briggs, was no less angry or articulate. Basically it was feared that someone in the intelligence line had messed up. Fingers were ready to point, but no one could figure out where. Who had dropped the ball and how?

"We have three Saudi nationals in the country, ready to carry out the next 9-11. We have no idea who they are, how they got here, or exactly what they're planning. This is unacceptable, people." He yelled so forcefully that some of his spittle landed on the table in front of Maggie. She refused to look at it, let alone wipe it away. With the current mood of the room, they might toss her out the window for blinking.

"How did this happen?" The next to scream at them was Ridge and Maggie's direct boss, a Colonel Caruthers, an old army man. Previously Maggie had seen him as being grandfatherly. Not after today. Right now he looked like a bulldog in search of a jugular to rip.

Ridge spoke up. Maggie thought it was brave of him. She was too petrified to so much as turn her head to watch him talk. "What do we actually know? Can we go over it again?"

The Colonel huffed but pushed a button. People popped onto the screen, along with some audio that had been laid overtop of the photos. There were two older men talking. Maggie closed her eyes for a second to hone in on their voices. One said the plans were nearly finished while the other said there could be up to ten thousand casualties. And then the tape stopped.

"That's it," the Colonel said. Maggie opened her eyes and froze as all air was sucked from the room. She legitimately couldn't breathe and thought she might pass out. Ridge somehow noticed. His glance turned into a stare of alarm. He leaned closer and whispered.

"Maggie, are you okay?"

She pointed to the man now on the screen, his superimposed face seeming to dominate the room. "That man."

"You know him?" Ridge asked, leaning in. "Have you come across his picture before?"

She shook her head and turned to face him. Everything felt surreal, and the room seemed to be tipping. "He's my fiancé."

Everyone was ordered out of the room. The only ones who remained were Maggie, Ridge, and the three top brass.

"How could you have hired a woman with a terrorist for a boyfriend?" The General screamed in Ridge's face.

"I'm not the one who did her background," Ridge replied.

"It never came up?" The General yelled.

Maggie couldn't take it anymore. "Please, stop yelling at Ridge. It's not his fault."

"Then whose fault is it? Yours?" The General screamed. "Did you purposely mislead the government of the United States, Missy? Because that's a felony."

"Maggie would never," Ridge began, but Maggie shook her head at him and took a breath.

"He's dead," she said.

"He's apparently very much alive," the Admiral said quietly.

"I thought he was dead. I went to his funeral. I have the program, if you'd like me to show you. It was so long ago, my first year out of college. It never occurred to me to mention it," she said. "To anyone," she added, with an apologetic glance at Ridge.

"You work for an anti-terrorism unit, and it never occurred to you to tell the US government that your ex-boyfriend was a Saudi national?"

"He's not Saudi," she insisted.

"What's his name?" the General barked.

"Sam, although that's his preferred nickname."

"Where's he from?" the Colonel yelled.

"He's from…I can't…if you could give me a minute to…"

"We don't have a minute," the General shouted.

"Leave her be and let her get a breath," the Admiral said. "You can see the girl's had a shock, and she's not a marine. Stop berating her. Take a breath, Maggie. Pull yourself together and tell us what you know."

Maggie nodded and took a shaky breath. "Thank you, sir. His name is Din Chatti, but he's gone by Sam since he was a boy. His mother is a US citizen with Saudi ancestry. His father was Saudi, but the family moved to Jordan when Sam was born. He has dual citizenship, and he attended college with me. We met freshman year, became serious right away, and dated all four years. We were engaged our senior year and planned to marry immediately after. He died in a car accident two months before our wedding. Or at least I thought he did."

"You visited Jordan with him," Ridge said.

Maggie nodded. "I spent a semester abroad, studying the language and living with his parents, and I visited several times with him over the four years we were together."

"Was there ever any talk of anything you would consider suspicious?" Ridge asked. With him asking the questions in his gentle, probing, and familiar way, it was easier to think.

"He had uncles, Saudi uncles, who were estranged. They were talked about in whispers, so I assumed it was something nefarious."

"What were their names?" the General barked.

"I don't know. I don't think I ever heard their names."

"Anything else," Ridge prompted.

"His father also died right before Sam did. The uncles in question were his brothers."

"Anything else?" the Admiral asked.

"Not that I can think of, sir, but I'll try my hardest to come up with more."

The Admiral nodded at her and turned to face the other two, disregarding Ridge from their circle. "Are you gentlemen thinking what I'm thinking?"

"Yes, sir," the Colonel and General agreed.

"With all due respect, sirs, what are you thinking?" Ridge asked.

"Bait, Lieutenant," the General said.

Ridge dashed to his feet. "Absolutely not."

"Pardon me, Lieutenant?" the Admiral said.

"Sir, she is a librarian," Ridge said.

"Has she not had the same training as everyone else in this building?" the Admiral asked.

"Yes sir, but…"

"There are no buts, Lieutenant," the Admiral said.

"Look at her," Ridge said, pointing. "It would be like sending a lamb to slaughter. She's a civilian in every sense of the word."

"She looks okay to me," the General said.

"I've seen worse," the Colonel agreed.

The Admiral remained focused on Ridge. "You're coming within a hairsbreadth of insubordination, Lieutenant."

"All due respect, sir, but I'm a civilian now, too," Ridge said.

"And an employee under my command. Sit down, son."

Years of military training kicked in and Ridge sat.

"She's doing it," the Admiral said.

Ridge opened his mouth to speak again, but Maggie preempted him. "I'll do it," she said, and all the men turned to look at her in surprise as if, during their power play, they had forgotten she was there and able to speak for herself.

"Maggie," Ridge started, but she held up a hand.

"What's the alternative, Cameron? That ten thousand people die because I'm better with research than combat? I can't live with that, and I know you can't, either. What's the plan, sirs?"

"There's a party where we strongly suspect some kind of handoff or meeting will take place. You'll go to the party with a handler and try to make contact with this Sam person."

Maggie nodded.

Ridge stood again. The other three men regarded him warily. "I'm going with her."

"We have field agents for that," the Colonel said.

"I brought her into this company, and I'm not going to hand her off to some cowboy out to make a name for himself. I'm a qualified field agent, more than qualified, if I say so myself, and I will be her handler," he said.

"I see no problem with that," the Colonel said. He turned to the other men. "Gentlemen?"

"It's a go, we'll get it set up. In the meantime, debrief your agent, Lieutenant. Thoroughly."

"Yes, sir," Ridge said, and he and Maggie were dismissed.

Chapter 14

The walk back to Ridge's office was long and silent. He held the door for her, ushered her inside, and closed and locked it behind her. He closed the blinds and turned to face her.

Maggie sat in the chair in front of his desk, miserable and silent. Ridge paced back and forth behind her. "Maggie, how many hours have we spent together?"

"Ridge…"

"How many hours?" he asked.

"I don't know. About a million," she said.

"We've run together every morning, we've gone out every weekend, and often during the week. We've slept at each other's houses; you nursed me back to health when I was sick. I've held you when you cried; you've held me when I cried. During all that time, we've had conversation after conversation after conversation about intensely deep and personal topics."

"I get it, Ridge," she said. "I neglected to tell you I dated a terrorist, and you were embarrassed in front of the brass. I'm incredibly sorry, but I also spent the last hour getting reamed by some of the highest-ranking members of the intelligence community, and I really don't want to hear it from you."

"A terrorist? You think that's what this is about?" he said.

"Isn't it?" she asked, confused.

"I don't care if he was a terrorist, I don't care if he was the leader of the free world. You had a fiancé, and you never said a word, not once. You had a wedding planned, you had a life planned, and you never even mentioned it. Would it have been so hard to say, 'Hey, Ridge, guess what? I was all set to marry another man. Surprise!'"

"I don't recall hearing about any of the women in your life," she said.

"If I'd ever had a fiancée, you'd be the first to know," he said.

"What about the other women you've dated since I've been here?" she asked, standing to face him.

"What other women, Maggie?" He spread his arms wide and looked around the room as if expecting phantom females to drop from the ceiling. "There's been no one since you. Do you think I'm Hugh Heffner with some sort of supernatural testosterone level, the kind of guy who can juggle multiple ladies? Because, spoiler alert, you are more than enough for me. You exhaust me," he yelled, jabbing his finger in her chest, his own chest heaving. "That was not supposed to make you smile," he added, in a significantly calmer tone.

"But it did," she said. "Cam, the reason I didn't tell you about Sam was because it hurt too much. He was my first kiss, first date, first love; he was my everything. And when he died, he took a piece of me with him. It was two months before a wedding we had been planning for a year. Everything was booked, the invitations were sent. I had to write everyone and explain why there wouldn't be a wedding and send back their gifts, and I couldn't stop crying to write the words. I thought I would never stop crying. It's been six years, and it still hurts. Do you understand what it's like to believe you will never love again, that you'll never get close to anyone again? Do you know what it's like to realize the last man who touched you drove off a cliff?" she asked.

"I believe I have the distinction of being the last man who touched you," he said. He eased closer and slid his arms around her. She returned his embrace and rested her forehead on his chest.

"Seeing him again was...you have no idea," she muttered.

"I can guess," he said. He tipped her face up. "Maggie, don't take the assignment. Go back to Washington or go back home. Please. Do something else, anything else," he said.

"You want me to go?" she asked.

"Who said I'm not going with you?" he replied. "You can become a librarian again and support me until I figure out what to do next."

"Cam," she said.

He touched his finger to her lips. "Listen to me. You don't know what you're getting into. The Saudis...remember what they did to that journalist? And all he did was have the audacity to disagree with the prince. They will kill you, and they will do it in such a manner that will make you beg for death first. Please don't do this."

"If I don't do this, then what's it all been about? So others can sacrifice but not me?"

"That's heroic in theory, but you haven't seen the reality. I have," he said.

"It's going to be okay," she said.

"How can you possibly say that?" he asked.

"Because you'll be there," she said.

He touched his forehead to hers and closed his eyes. "I can't lose you."

"Then don't."

His hand ran down the length of her spine and back up again, she tugged him impossibly closer. A knock sounded on the door, startling them apart. Maggie sank into the chair as Ridge answered the door.

"Did you debrief her?" the Colonel asked.

118

"Thoroughly, sir," Ridge said.

"Good. Report on my desk in an hour. We're working on the logistics of the assignment, it should come together soon."

"Yes, sir," Ridge said. They shared a nod, and the Colonel departed. "Can you write a report for me?" he whispered to Maggie.

"Should I put in some grammatical errors and typos to make it look legit?" she asked.

"Probably," he said. He perched on the edge of his desk, facing her. "I just realized something. Your dog's name is Samson, and you call him Sam."

"My parents bought him for me, after. They thought it might bring some sunshine into my life again. They were right," she said.

"Now I feel like a jerk for disparaging the shedding and drooling," he said.

"As well you should. He's an awesome dog," she said. They shared a smile.

"It's going to be a crazy blitz around here until this thing is over. I probably won't see you much until then."

"All right," she said, not sure if she was receiving the brushoff.

"What I'm trying to say is that I'm here, if you need me. Even if you can't tell. I'm always here."

"Back at ya, sailor," she said. "Always."

They shared another smile that lingered much longer than necessary. "I should go write your report," Maggie said at last, snapping to attention.

"Back to work, minion," he said, tapping his foot to her backside when she turned to go.

She whirled. "That's harassment, sir."

"What are you going to do about it?" he asked, grinning.

She moved very close, until they were almost touching but not quite. "What did you have in mind?"

"You're in a dry forest playing with matches right now," he warned.

She mimicked striking a match and opening her hand to release it, but he caught her wrist.

"Who knows you better than I do?" he asked.

"No one," she said.

"That's right, so I know when you're teasing and when you're not. If you're in the mood to be serious, come back and I'll help you with those matches. In the meantime, go write my report, worker bee." He released her wrist.

"I'm going to write an amazing report, and I'll sign it with your new handle, 'Big Talk, No Action,'" she threatened.

"You think you're safe because we're at work, huh?" he asked.

"I think I'm safe because you're all hat, no cattle," she said. She had learned the phrase from him and rightly assumed it would drive him crazy if she used it on him.

He picked her up, bringing her face in line with his and pressing her close. "Uh-oh, now you've gone too far."

Maggie tried not to let on how nervous she was. He had that look, the same one he'd used when he licked the frosting off her finger. He could drive all the common sense from her brain, if he chose to. "Cam…" she began.

"What's that, chicken feathers? Is someone having second thoughts?"

She frowned, not liking the challenge she heard in his mocking tone. "No. I was going to tell you to bring your A game." She wrapped her arms around his neck, closing what little distance remained between them.

"Baby, I don't have anything besides an A game," he said.

Maggie rolled her eyes. "You know, I was thinking this moment needed some cockiness. It's so universally appealing." She squirmed, and he released her, setting her gently on her feet a few inches away.

"Just so we're clear—you broke first," he said, poking her bicep.

"Just so we're clear—you're twelve," she said, batting his fingers away.

"Am I getting a report today or nah?" he asked.

"You men and your reports. It's all you ever think about," she accused.

"That's because your reports are so incredibly sexy. I can't get enough," he said.

"I'm going to put a little something extra in this one, just for you," she said, tossing him a wink as she let herself out of his office.

Ridge walked her to the door, making a shooing motion with his hand. When the door was closed and she was safely on the other side, he pressed his forehead to the cool, solid wood, trying to draw a deep, steadying breath for the first time in what felt like years.

Chapter 15

The next week was a blitz of meetings, so many, many meetings that Maggie lost track. They all went by different names: briefing, de-briefing, rundown, conference, session, consultation, prep time. But in Maggie's mind, they were all a mind-numbing parade of bureaucracy. She only saw Ridge once during the week, when he accompanied her to her polygraph. In addition to all the meetings, she had to be thoroughly investigated to make sure she hadn't lied about Sam. She told the same story so many times it began to feel rote, despite the fact that it had been the greatest tragedy of her life. She was exhausted, but she knew Ridge was more so. He wasn't even going home anymore. Instead he began sleeping in his office, asking Maggie to bring him fresh clothes from his house each day.

Despite everyone's exhaustion, the team began to feel cohesive. Ridge didn't lose his temper with them once, even when everything seemed to be falling apart. It took a massive, group effort to pull off the type of operation they were about to undertake, and everyone was giving it their all. The fact that Ridge and Maggie were physically going to be heading the operation made everything feel more personal and real than usual. Previously all their work had gone toward compiling reports for important people in DC, sometimes the president himself. Now all their work was going toward keeping two members of their own team alive, and everyone was feeling the pressure.

In addition to the blitz of meetings, Maggie was also being prepped for the upcoming event. Apparently the government didn't trust her fashion sense because they brought in a consultant to dress her, including hair, makeup, and jewelry on loan from Harry Winston.

"The point is for you to stand out and garner attention. In a room full of billionaires, that won't be easy," the consultant, Marla, said.

"Are you going to take me shopping?" Maggie asked. She had no idea how that would fit into her already crammed schedule.

"This isn't an off-the-rack type event. You'll be wearing a designer original. He'll be here in…here he is now," Marla said as a man even Maggie, with her limited fashion sense, recognized. A few years ago he had won a reality design television show and become famous for, among other things, his flamboyant personality.

Maggie wondered if it had all been an act for the show because now he seemed low-key and professional, if rather abrupt. "She's still dressed," he said, addressing Marla.

"Strip," Marla commanded her. "He only has an hour."

"No one told me there would be nudity," Maggie said. It had been a long time since laundry day, and she was down to her white cotton granny panties.

Instead of answering, Marla and the designer reached out and began to undress her themselves, quickly and efficiently. In seconds, she stood in the aforementioned granny panties and her most tattered bra.

"I haven't had much time for laundry lately," she explained, trying and failing to cover herself with her hands as the designer took her measurements and Marla wrote them down.

"Can you really make a dress in a week?" she tried, though she wasn't sure if they could actually hear her. Maybe she was invisible now. In her current state of disrepair and nudity, she hoped so. At that, the designer tossed her a glance.

"Honey, I can make a dress for a tank blindfolded while a goat does the cha-cha. But it so happens that I brought some things I already had. We'll find what works best for you and have it altered. You recently lost weight?"

"Yes," Maggie peeped.

He clucked his tongue in disapproval. "Buy some new underwear and a bra. These don't fit. You're a 34-C now, by the way. Get something with underwire."

"I'm not really accustomed to strange men talking about my bra," she said.

"Don't think of me as a man; thing of me as a doctor for your underwear. And, honey, your underwear are dying. Get help immediately."

Maggie nodded, feeling more than a little mortified. They let her put her clothes on and go back to work. Apparently whatever he was making for her would be ready on the night in question. In the meantime, she went back to her desk, took a five-minute break, and ordered a handful of new bras and underpants.

"Why are you looking at underwear on company time?" Ridge, who happened to be striding by her desk on his way from yet another meeting, paused and leaned over.

"Because the man said I need new ones," she said.

"Do I want to know what you're talking about?" he asked.

She shook her head

"Good." He leaned closer and whispered in her ear. "Get the blue ones, you look good in blue."

"You can't tell me which underwear to buy," she said.

"I'm not telling; I'm requesting," he said. He tapped her desk and continued on his way. Once he was safely in his office, Maggie returned to her computer and bought the blue ones.

The night before the event, Maggie called her family. "Steve, it's Maggie," her mom yelled away from the phone. "I think he's outside. Here talk to your brother."

"Hi, Maggie," her brother, Johnny, took the phone.

"Hi," Maggie said.

"When are you coming home? I miss you."

"I miss you, too. I love you."

"I love you, too. Hey, did I tell you what happened at work?" Her brother worked at a fast food restaurant, and he viewed every day as a grand, new adventure. Maggie loved how much he loved it, and she was always happy to hear stories, but tonight she felt the desperate need to talk to her parents, just in case. She listened to Johnny's story and tried to show the proper amount of enthusiasm.

"Hey, Johnny, is Mom still there?"

"No, I think she ran to the store."

"What about Dad?"

"I don't know where he is. Outside, maybe. Hey, I love you."

She felt tears prick the backs of her eyes. "I love you, too, so, so much. Will you do me a favor?"

"Yes," he said. There was never a qualifier with Johnny, he was always ready to help.

"Will you tell Mom and Dad and Darren and Amelia that I love them so much and give them kisses for me?"

"Yes," he said. "Hey, put Samson on."

She dutifully put her dog on the phone and let Johnny talk to him for a while, and then it was time to go. "Don't forget to tell everyone I love them, okay?"

"Okay. Come home soon, Maggie. I miss you."

"I'll try, and I miss you, too, and I love you."

"I love you, and I love Samson. Tell him for me."

"I'll tell him, if you'll tell everyone there, promise?"

"Promise," he said. He blew her a few kisses, and she ended the call. She hadn't felt so alone or bereft since Sam died, and she dashed at a few tears.

"Maggie? I let myself in, I hope that's okay."

It was Ridge. They had exchanged keys a while ago, but he had never used hers. She jumped up, ran at him, and flung her arms around him, knocking him back a step.

"I guess it's okay," he said.

"How did you get away?" she asked.

"I just did," he said. "Are you doing okay?"

She nodded, but she was also clinging to him like a koala. He sat on her couch, and still she didn't budge.

"You sure you're doing okay?" he asked.

She nodded again. She didn't want to talk, didn't want to cry, she simply wanted to hold him and be held. "How did you know how much I needed you?"

"Intuition," he said, and she laughed a little.

"I hate it when you read me that way," she said.

"Really?"

"No." She pressed her face to his neck and inhaled, drawing strength from the solid warmth of him.

"Do you want to talk about it?" he asked.

"No."

"Do you want to eat the junk food I brought you?"

That gave her pause. "Maybe later," she said.

"You just want me to hold you?" he guessed.

She nodded. "And I want to hold you back."

"Best plan ever," he said. He secured the blanket around her, kissed the top of her head, and reached for the remote.

"We're having a moment, and you're going to watch ESPN," she said, incredulous.

"We have a lot of moments, and I still want to know the score of the game," he said.

"Hey, Cam, if things go wrong, I want you to know that…"

He interrupted her. "No. We're not going to talk like that. Everything will be fine."

"But if it's not…"

He grasped her biceps and set her away from him. "Stop it, and I'm serious. I have never lost anyone on a mission, and you're not going to screw up my perfect record. Got it?"

She nodded.

"Good." He tucked her back against him and let her go. She pressed her face to his neck again, grumpy and frustrated with his can-do attitude. How dare he be cheerful and optimistic when she was ready to wallow in pessimism and negativity? She did the only thing she could think to do in the situation.

"Ouch, did you bite me?" he asked. He sat back so he could see her face.

"I'm a sleep biter," she said.

He set aside the remote. "You know what's going to happen now."

She stood and began backing away from him. "Cam, don't do it."

"Don't blame me, you asked for it," he said, standing to his full and impressive height. She turned and sprinted away from him, heading for the safety of the bathroom. He easily caught her in three strides, returned her to the couch, and tossed her onto her back.

"Please, please don't," she pled.

"I'm sorry, but I have no choice," he said, and then he tackled and tickled her until tears streamed down her face and she begged for mercy.

"Say you're sorry," he demanded, pinning her arms over her head.

"I'm sorry," she wheezed.

"Say you'll never bite me again," he said.

"Never," she said, trying to shake the tears out of her eyes and stop giggling.

"Tell me you love me the most," he said.

"I love you," she said, and it was as if all the levity was sucked from the room. He was still on top of her, her arms trapped over her head. His face was an inch away.

"The most," he prompted.

"The most," she whispered. They locked eyes. His face descended toward hers. At the last moment, she turned her head to look at the floor. "What junk food did you bring?"

He let his head fall onto her shoulder with a sigh, whether it was relief or regret, she didn't know. "Cookie dough and those gummy bears you like."

"Nothing for you?" she asked.

"I thought we could share," he said. He rolled to the side, releasing her from his grasp, though his arm rested on her waist.

"What in our history has taught you to think that?" she asked.

"You're right, I don't know what I was thinking," he said. They shared a smile and the tension was back, pulling and stretching between them.

"I'll preheat the oven," she said. She spun away from him and off the couch. Ridge turned onto his back and stared at the ceiling. How long could they reasonably push away what was brewing between them? Eventually it would have to be dealt with, one way or another, and then what? Past history told him the friendship he had with Maggie was far better than any romantic entanglement he'd had with anyone else. Romance messed everything up, and so did attraction. He didn't want to go there, didn't want to mar the purity and perfection of their friendship, and he sensed she didn't, either. How long could they hold out before one of them snapped?

It won't be me, he vowed. He had passed rigorous SEAL training. If he could do that, he could do anything. He was disciplined, more disciplined than Maggie. It was up to him to be strong for both of them until this stressful time was over. Then, he was sure, everything would go back to normal with her. All they had to do was survive the impending crisis that made them want to cling to each other, and they would be able to breathe again without the threat of death pushing them together.

I can do this, he told himself. *I can totally do this.* He rolled off the couch to see if she needed help in the kitchen and saw her opening a package. Unaware of his presence, she opened the piece of mail and held a pair of lacy, blue underwear aloft. Wordlessly he turned, went into her bathroom, and locked the door, not trusting himself to leave again until the cookies were ready and the coffee had been poured.

Chapter 16

When the big night finally arrived, Maggie felt strangely calm. In fact, she was almost having fun. It felt a little like prom. Marla whisked her away and dressed her in the designer gown, and she finally got why people had designer gowns made instead of buying off the rack. It was a cliché, but the dress fit her like a glove, so much that she had to be sewn into it. It was strapless, another first for Maggie. Previously she had never had the type of body that would allow her to wear something she considered revealing, but she didn't look bad. In fact, since the dress had literally been made for her, it showed off the best parts of her while obscuring the worst. Her slightly poochy tummy, for instance, was well hidden under the voluminous folds at the bottom of the dress. It was some kind of metallic gray fabric that caught the light, as well as the gray highlights in her blue eyes and, without a doubt, she had never looked better.

"How much would it cost if I bought this dress?" Maggie asked as she turned to admire the stranger in the full-length mirror.

"Somewhere between seven and ten thousand," Marla said distractedly while she finished sewing the back of Maggie's dress.

"Dollars?" Maggie exclaimed.

"We don't deal in pesos," Marla said in the dry, deadpan way Maggie was growing used to. Marla had seen a lot, if her unaffected style of delivery was any indication.

"Do I get to keep it?" Maggie asked and, for the first time since she'd known her, Marla laughed and laughed.

They argued over her hair. "The style of the dress demands it be worn up," Marla said.

"He likes it down," Maggie insisted. Finally they compromised on a side-swept updo that left most of her hair cascading down the side of her neck.

"You really have fabulous hair," Marla said. "Too bad you have no idea what to do with it."

"Thank you?" Maggie tried, not sure if it had been a compliment.

Her makeup was another argument. Marla did it for her, and Maggie wasn't pleased. "It's too much."

"It's an evening ball; it's supposed to be dramatic. You don't wear enough anyway," Marla reproached.

"He's from an extremely conservative family, and he knows me. He's going to be suspicious if I show up with my nose contoured like a Kardashian," Maggie said. "Can you take it down a notch?"

"Fine," Marla huffed. "I'll take off the contouring and some of the blush, but I'm leaving your eyes."

"Good, I'll need them to see," Maggie replied, earning another rueful smile from Marla.

"Jewelry time," Marla said, sounding excited.

"I'm not really into jewelry," Maggie told her.

"What a shocking surprise," Marla said, deadpan again. "Are you sure you're a woman?"

"I've never been able to use the bathroom standing up, despite repeated failed attempts, so yes," Maggie said. But when Marla opened the briefcase of loaned jewelry, Maggie thought she might finally have found her missing female DNA. "Ho-ly cow."

"I know, right?" Marla said and the two women came together in a moment of mutual fawning appreciation over the stunning diamond and sapphire necklace. Maggie reached out a hand, Marla smacked it away, and the moment was over. "You're not allowed to touch it until you sign all the papers."

"I have to sign papers?"

"You have to sign your life away. If anything happens to this, the government will hold you personally responsible and probably put you in some kind of work camp until you're able to pay it off, which will be never."

"Are you a motivational speaker in your downtime?" Maggie asked.

"No, I'm the keeper of the keys for this necklace, and if anything happens to it, I will hunt you down like a dog in the street," Marla said. She handed Maggie a stack of papers to sign and then, when they were all in order, gently removed the necklace and placed it on Maggie's neck.

"Wow," Marla said as she fastened the necklace and stepped back. "Is it bad that I'm jealous of you right now?"

"Well, there's a chance I could die, so that should tamp down the envy some," Maggie said.

"You'd think so, but no," Marla said. She reached out and lovingly touched the necklace, practically drooling over the sight of such large gemstones.

"Do you need a moment alone with the necklace?" Maggie asked.

"Just don't get blood on it," Marla said, and Maggie didn't know her well enough to know if she was joking.

After Marla, the sound tech came in to fit her with a tiny and obscure microphone. "They couldn't have sent a woman?" Maggie complained as the guy worked furiously to tape the tiny device inside her bra.

"I always get the hard jobs," the guy said, grinning at Maggie in a way that made her want to punch him more than a little. Sensing her wrath, he wiped his smile and became all business. "Remember this is an extremely sensitive instrument.

You don't have to tilt your head down or speak into it in any obvious manner. It will not only pick up your conversation, it will pick up what's happening in the room around you."

"What if I have to use the bathroom? How do I turn it off?" she asked.

"There is no off," he said. "So I will hear everything you say and do. Everything."

"I do not get paid enough for this," Maggie said.

"Neither do I," he agreed.

"Neither do I," Ridge agreed as he entered the room. He tapped his ear. "Mic's live."

"Oh, you get to be in on the eavesdropping, too? Goody," she said.

"About forty people get to be in on the eavesdropping," he reminded her, and Maggie went silent. In theory, she knew how many people were watching and listening to them. But now it was reality, and she felt suddenly shy. The sound tech finished taping her and left. "Where exactly were his hands?"

"Everywhere," Maggie said.

"How do I get his job?" Ridge asked.

"According to his level of enjoyment, I think you need to be a sex offender," she said.

"I'm halfway there," Ridge said. He withdrew a notebook and pen from his inside breast pocket and scrawled her a note.

You look spectacular.

"And you look…" She scanned his outfit and tilted her head. The suit was nice, but it was topped by a bolo tie with silver tassels and a giant silver belt buckle. On his feet were leather cowboy boots. "Well, you look like a male Annie

Oakley. Does Marla hate you? Where did she find that hideous getup?"

He took her face in his hands and touched his forehead to hers. "These are my real clothes."

She burst out laughing. "I am so going to make fun of you later."

"Something to look forward to. Ready?"

She nodded. He released her face and they walked to the car in silence, an ostentatious luxury vehicle with vanity plates. "It's kind of unfair that I get to be a princess and you have to be Yosemite Sam," she noted.

"Oh, the people in the trailer are loving you right now," he said, and she was once again reminded they weren't actually alone.

"I keep forgetting," she said.

"I don't," he said, his eyes scanning her with more than a little appreciation. They had staged near the event, so it was only a short drive to the party, but still long enough for Maggie's nerves to begin to jangle.

"Can we listen to the radio?" she asked.

"Only if you want everyone to run screaming from the trailer. Too much reverb," he said. "We could sing."

"I could try, but it would probably have the same effect on the people in the trailer," she said. "You sing." She poked him and, to her surprise, he opened his mouth and sang "Friends in Low Places," the entire song with all the words. And he was good.

"I went through a big Garth Brooks phase in high school," he told her.

Maggie sat back astonished. "You think you know a person, and then it turns out he's a genuine rootin' tootin' cowpoke."

"I *am* from Texas," he reminded her.

"I'm not sure the people of Texas want you broadcasting that tonight. You look like the county fair ate too much and spit you out," she said.

"You're going to be the audio they play at the company Christmas party for sure," he said, tapping his ear. Maggie winced. She had forgotten again. When she was with him, it was too easy to be herself.

The party was being held on a massive gated compound. They arrived at the gate and were greeted by two security guards, Saudi.

"Identification," one said to Ridge in a heavily accented and commanding tone. The other bade Maggie roll down her window and stuck his head in, inspecting the vehicle and her body. She tried not to fidget while the men looked everything over and spoke to each other in their native tongue. After a brief, laughing exchange, they tossed Ridge's license back to him and waved them through.

"What did they say?" he asked.

"Eh, are you sure you want to know?" she asked.

"Yes."

"They said you look like an American cartoon character and, let's see, how can I clean it up, they wondered exactly what was holding my dress up and took bets on how easily it would come off."

"Hmm," he said. His expression told her he wanted to say more, but he was reining it in for the sake of all the listening ears. He parked in the spot being designated by yet another guard and then came around to open her door and help her out of the car. He kept her hand on the walk to the house and paused under a streetlamp. He reached into his jacket again, withdrew the little notebook, and penned another missive.

So much I would say, if no one was listening.

Maggie smiled, kissed her fingertip, and pressed it to his lips. Knowing it would make her laugh, he stuck out his tongue and licked her finger. As anticipated, she laughed and wiped her finger on his sleeve. "Weirdo."

He took her hand again. "Ready?"

"As I'll ever be," she replied, trying not to sound as breathless and petrified as she felt.

He gave her hand a squeeze, and they stepped up to the door.

Chapter 17

The party was unlike anything Maggie had ever seen. The food table alone was a Bacchanalian feast to rival the best Vegas buffet. All around her was the kind of hedonistic display she had only witnessed on television. To her right, two men snorted a line of what she guessed to be cocaine off a table, while all around the room sashayed beautiful women whose very essence told anyone who was looking they were for hire.

"What is this?" she whispered. She had expected a classy, catered event. Instead it was a pagan dystopia.

"They like to party," Ridge whispered.

Maggie had no idea how to behave in such an environment. She had never felt more innocent or small town before. She had never seen drugs, not even marijuana, and now the most illicit drugs were on full parade.

"What do I do?" she whispered, panicked.

"Not that," he said, nodding toward the two men who began snorting yet another line of coke. "Be yourself, that's why you're here."

"And who will you be?" she asked.

"As obnoxious as possible," he said. "Hey y'all." He hailed a group of men standing in a circle, took Maggie's hand, and dragged her over. "Ridge Colton," he said, letting go of Maggie to thrust his hand in their faces, forcing them to shake. "You may have heard of my family, they just discovered the big Houser well on our property. Woo, it was a gusher."

He blathered on and on about his family's immense wealth and the newly acquired well while the men listened with barely disguised disdain. Maggie tuned him out and scanned the room, as she was supposed to. There was no sign of Sam or his uncles, but there were plenty enough people to provide cover for anything or anyone. With so much illicit activity taking place in plain view, she could only imagine what was happening behind closed doors. She needed to leave Ridge and mingle, but she was terrified to do so.

You're not a guest, you're an agent. Act like it. She touched her fingers lightly to Ridge's arm. "I'm going to get some food."

"Sure, darlin'," he said, not bothering to look at her as he waved her away. Maggie made her way to the immense and overloaded food tables, took a plate, and began to put anything on her tray she thought she might be able to stomach. She was both starving and nauseated after having been too nervous to eat all day.

"Hello." The man across from her at the buffet spoke. He was American and looked nice enough, but who could tell under such conditions?

"Hello," she said.

"Are you with someone?" he asked.

"The cowboy," she said, pointing to Ridge. "Are you here on business?"

"I guess," he said, chuckling uncomfortably. "My boss is here for a meeting and dragged me along. Not my scene."

"Mine, either," she said. "I was doing the guy a favor by being his date, but I had no idea it would be like this."

"Little tip: don't drink anything," the man said.

Maggie nodded and set down the glass of punch she had picked up. "Thank you. So, what kind of business brings one here? Because, as far as I can tell, you either have to be a hooker or a drug mule to be invited."

"Well, I'm not a hooker," he said, smiling enigmatically, and Maggie suppressed a little shudder. She had entered a world where even wholesome-looking men like him couldn't be trusted.

"We have that in common," she said. She took a bite of fruit and froze. "Is the food safe?"

"Food's safe," he said. "They only drug the drinks, for some reason." He shrugged.

"Who's hosting this party?" she asked

"A couple of Saudis. You don't want to meet them."

She smiled innocently. "Why not?"

He looked around and leaned in to whisper. "Because they're not good guys."

"Drugs?" she whispered.

He shook his head. "Worse."

"What could be worse than drugs?" she blurted, a genuine question she wouldn't have asked if she'd been thinking about it.

He chuckled. "You're fresh off the farm, aren't you?"

"More like the cherry orchard, but yes," she said, picking up another piece of fruit.

"What do you do?" he asked.

"Promise you won't laugh?" she said.

He nodded.

"I'm a librarian."

He laughed. "Sorry, I'm sorry. It's just so…" he waved a hand at her. "If my librarian looked like you, I would for sure be a dedicated reader."

She gave a self-deprecating glance at her outfit. "My date arranged it for me. He's really into appearances. If I had my druthers, I would be in my fleece pajamas watching Netflix right now."

He laughed again. "You might be the strangest thing at this party."

"I'm going to take that as a compliment," she said.

"You should," he agreed.

She scanned the room. Still no sign of Sam. "Everyone here seems so old. Are we the youngest people here?"

"There's your date," he said. Maggie's spirits fell until he continued. "And there's this other guy, but he's kind of elusive. He's supposed to be meeting with my boss, but I only caught a glimpse."

Maggie tensed. "Is he one of the hosts?"

"There's some connection there, but I haven't figured it out. These aren't the sort of people you want to question." He eased closer to her, and Maggie's senses went on alert. Something about him said he couldn't be trusted, despite his outwardly wholesome manner. "There are a lot of private rooms here."

"It's a huge mansion," she said, holding herself stiffly away from him.

"Do you want to see one?" his fingers trailed down her arm.

Maggie froze. What was she supposed to do? Going with the guy would give her a chance to check things out and look for Sam. On the other hand, she didn't think a tour was what he had in mind. At last she decided to take Ridge's advice and be herself. She turned to him with a smile. "If you're genuinely offering to let me see the place, then I'd be delighted. If you think I'm for hire, or even for free, then you're sadly mistaken and I'll break every one of those fingers you put on my arm."

He withdrew his hand. "I see. Okay, but I'm still bored, so if you want to walk around, I'm game."

"Sounds good," she said.

"Do you need to tell your date you're going? Will he come looking for you?"

Was he checking to see if Ridge was keeping a protective eye on her? "He might, if I'm gone long enough, but I don't want to disturb him when he's trying to make a billion dollar deal on his new oil well. He was fairly explicit about not getting in his way tonight."

"How could you ever be in anyone's way?" the man asked with a smile that was beginning to look a little smarmy.

Maggie pulled her sequined clutch close and gave it a little pat, feeling the reassuring outline of her gun. When she had first been issued a weapon, she had thought it was a waste because she would never need it. Now she had never been more thankful for the thing, and for the ability to use it. "It's a mystery for the ages. Let's go."

She trailed behind him as he meandered out of the massive hall and down a dim, narrow passage. Behind some of the closed doors she heard sounds that told her more than business deals were taking place, and her nausea increased. This was definitely not her scene, and she hoped never to repeat it.

"Whose place is this?" she asked.

"The Saudis bought it. They wanted privacy to conduct their, ah, business."

"Wow," she said, not needing to feign awe. The place was spectacular, a giant wood and stone monstrosity that looked like it could house ten families.

"I know, it's incredible. And this is only part of it. There's a whole hidden portion."

Her ears pricked. "Like secret passages and stuff?"

He nodded. "Old, underground bomb shelters or whatnot. I think this was some sort of gangster hideout during prohibition."

"That's fascinating," Maggie said sincerely. "I don't suppose we could see that part."

He paused and turned to face her. "You want to see something more private?"

"I'm a history buff," she said, feeling concerned and a little confused. Was she sending him mixed signals? Did he think she meant something other than what she said? "Truly, that kind of thing fascinates me."

They were at the end of the long, dark hallway. "I could show you some things," he said. His arm stretched out in front of her, his palm resting on the wall, blocking her path, should she choose to go forward.

"My only interest here is the history of this house," she said.

"It's an interesting house. It might take some time to explain things thoroughly." His free hand rested on her bare shoulder.

Maggie tensed. "I told you not to touch me."

"Your words say that, but everything else says something different," he said.

"Listen to my words. Get your hand off me and let me go."

He smiled, and it was fully creepy and threatening now. "Or what? You'll scream? Do you think anyone will hear you or care if they did?" He backed her against the wall, which she now realized was a door. "Let's step inside, we'll talk more about history."

She wasn't frightened. Not only had she had enough self-defense to get herself out of the situation, but there was an entire team of trained agents listening in, plus Ridge who would likely be along any minute. But she didn't want to have to blow their cover for this chump, so she brought her knee up hard and disabled him. He doubled over, retching, but recovered quicker than she thought he might. Before she could step around him and make an escape, his hand shot out and pinned her to the door by her throat.

"Not a good idea," he choked. He stood upright again, and the look on his face had been transformed into something terrifying. Maggie began to feel a flicker of worry. He could do a lot of damage in the short time it took anyone to get to her.

"Don't," she said.

He opened his mouth, but she never got to hear what he had to say because someone spoke from behind him.

"Release her."

The man dropped his hand and spun immediately, and now it was his turn to be terrified. "We were just playing around," he said.

"It didn't look like playing to me," the man said. He nodded his head down the hallway, and the man who had been tormenting her scurried away like the cockroach he was. Maggie was left alone with her rescuer and, for the first time in six years, came face to face with her dead fiancé.

Chapter 18

"Sam?" Maggie said, and she didn't have to force the shaky wobble into her words. Her knees gave out and she slumped hard against the door.

"Hello, Maggie," Sam said, much calmer than she felt. Then, as if suddenly remembering where they were, darted furious glances up and down the hall before shoving her into the room behind her. He flicked on the lights and grasped her biceps. "What are you doing here?"

"How?" she asked. "How are you here?"

"What are you doing here?" he asked, giving her a little shake.

"The guy, I came with the guy."

"Who is he?"

"I don't know, some friend of a friend from work. He needed a date, and I thought it would be fun to go to a fancy party. Apparently not." She stared up into his face. "How are you here? You're dead."

"Apparently not," he said, his lips twisting into a wry smile. "Maggie, don't cry, please don't cry. I can't stand it."

She hadn't realized she was crying until he said so. All she knew was that the pain of seeing him again hurt worse than she could have imagined. She thought she was fully over him, but seeing him again, up close and in person…It was an agonizing mixture of love, longing, grief, and anguish. He brushed his fingers on her face and then kissed her cheeks.

"I'm not sure I want you to touch me," she said, but she clung to him nonetheless. The smell of him, so familiar, knifed through her senses, making her feel almost delirious with confusion. She had cut him out of her memory, told her brain over and over that he was gone and needed to be forgotten. And yet he was *here*.

"How can this be?" he asked.

"How can you be the one who is confused?" she countered.

"I followed your steps to Washington and the college job, but then you disappeared."

"I needed a change. I thought it would be fun to live in the city," she said.

"You hate the city."

"A lot has changed in six years," she told him, remembering her fury all over again. She would have pulled away, but he had her sandwiched between himself and the wall. "Why, Sam, why did you do it? You could have told me you didn't want to get married."

He gave a humorless little chuckle. "You think this is about our wedding?"

"Isn't it?" she asked.

"Maggie, if I'd had my way, you would be with our second child as we speak."

"I never agreed to that many kids," she said.

"I would have won that argument, and you know it," he said. "Look at you. *Look at you.* You look even more beautiful than when we met, and until this moment I never knew that was possible. You know I still remember the first time I saw you, strolling through campus, reading a book, and smiling. I had never seen anyone do all three things at once. And do you remember what I said to you?"

"You said you were about to change my life forever, and I suppose that turned out to be true."

He continued, undaunted. "Do you remember your response?"

"I laughed and said stranger danger seemed suddenly all too real."

He laughed and she smiled. He had the best laugh. "Then when I finally, finally convinced you to go out with me, you wore your hair down on our first date, and I begged you to wear it down from then on."

"I haven't been able to wear it down since you died. Or since I thought you died. Sam, what happened? Why? It's been six years and twenty minutes, and I still don't have an answer."

"I can't give you an answer," he said.

"You owe me an explanation," she said.

"Do you not understand that I'm trying to protect you? That everything I've done has been to protect you?"

"No, I don't because you won't tell me. You used to tell me everything. We had no secrets, or so I thought."

"We had one very big secret," he said. He put his hands over his face and drew a deep breath.

She peeled his hands away and looked in his eyes. "Please, I need to know. Please, Sam. I need an explanation. You can't understand what it's like, thinking you were dead. Do you care what that did to me? Do you have any idea how I grieved for you? I threw myself on your coffin and begged them to put me in the ground with you. My dad and my little brother had to peel me off and carry me away, kicking and screaming and clawing to get back to you."

He covered his ears. "Stop it, stop."

"I was catatonic for three weeks. They had to put me in the hospital and give me fluids through an IV because I couldn't eat or sleep or even function. I'm not sure I was alive during that time after your funeral because it's all a black blur."

He put his hands back over his face. "Maggie, don't."

She peeled them away again and held his wrists. "Do you think I was the only one who grieved for you? Do you

146

think my mother and father and brothers and sister didn't also weep for you? Do you understand what your disappearance did to Johnny? He cried every single night for a solid year, and I seemed to be the only one who could hear him, so it was up to me to comfort him, and I couldn't stop crying, either.

"I haven't been able to get close to a man, for fear he'll disappear like you did. You have made me untouchable. I died when you went away, and now you have the audacity to stand here and say you can't tell me what it was about? How dare you?" Her chest was heaving. She had completely forgotten all the people listening to their conversation, forgotten Ridge, forgotten her assignment, forgotten everything but her pain and the aching need for answers.

The silence hung heavily between them as Sam refused to speak. Eventually the energy drained from her. She sagged against the wall and let go his wrists. He touched his fingers gently to her chin and tipped her face toward his. "I can't tell you what happened, but I can tell you that I loved you then, I love you now, and I begin to believe I will always love you. Why would I hurt you without reason?"

"I don't know. You tell me," she said, her tone more bitter than she intended.

In answer, he pressed his lips to hers, gently, tenderly. Maggie didn't mean to respond, but it had been so long, and she was under such a confusing pall of emotion. She slid her arms around him and deepened the kiss, and it took on a life of its own as six years of emptiness and longing came pouring out of her.

"You are not to be in this part of the hallway," a man outside the door said. Sam stepped away from Maggie as if he had been electrocuted.

"It's them," he whispered, his dark face going pale.

"Who?" she whispered, though she already knew.

He shook his head and put his finger to his lips.

"Have you seen my date?" Ridge twanged. "Little blond gal, gray dress?"

The uncles were coming, and Ridge had intercepted them. And she would be caught with Sam. How could they all possibly get away unscathed?

"I'm so sorry," Sam whispered.

"For what?" Maggie started to say when the door was ripped open and the three men from the hallway tumbled inside. She barely had time to register what was going on before Sam's open palm cracked across her cheek, striking her so hard she reeled into the wall behind her. He hurled an epithet at her in Arabic, something so horrible and ugly Maggie would never utter it, not in a million years. Then he turned his back to her and spoke to Ridge.

"There's your trash, I'm done with her." Head up, he walked out of the room, followed by his uncles, who didn't utter a word.

Maggie thought she might black out, the pain and shock were so intense. She had taken a few hits during her training at Quantico, but never like that, not a purposeful assault to her face. She could already feel her cheek swelling and a goose egg beginning to form on the back of her head. Were her molars loose? They felt so, at least a little.

"We're done," Ridge said, rushing forward to offer her his arm for support. She thought at first he was talking to her, and then she remembered their eager crowd of listeners.

"We didn't get the…" she began, but he cut her off.

"I said we're done," he snapped, his tone brooking no rebuttal. She nodded, dazed, and allowed him to lead her back through the mazelike house and outside to the car. Miraculously, no one seemed to notice them. Possibly because some type of belly dance performance was taking place in the main party hall and everyone was absorbed.

He tucked her in the car and knelt beside her. "Are you going to pass out?"

She shook her head.

"Are you going to throw up?"

"Possibly," she said. He opened the glove compartment to search for something but came up empty.

"At least it's not my car," he said. He closed her door and came around to his side. "I'm taking her home."

"Are you talking to the car?" she asked, still very much dazed.

He tapped his ear. "She's had enough. I'll do the report and de-brief myself. I'm taking her home." He was using the tone again, the one that said you'd be a fool to argue. She dearly hoped he wasn't talking to the Colonel, but realized he probably was. He plucked the earpiece out and tossed it into the console.

"We can go to the office. I can do the debrief," she said weakly.

"How many fingers am I holding up?" he asked.

"Three?" she guessed.

"Both hands are on the wheel. Home for you," he said.

"Are you going to get fired?" she whispered, covering her bodice to block the microphone in her bra.

He shook his head and winked at her, and she realized they could hear her, regardless of how she tried to stop it. For all she knew, the car could be wired and probably was. She closed her eyes and tried to stave off the encroaching nausea by breathing purposefully through her nose.

A minute later they stopped at the sound trailer, the one being used as a staging area by their team, the one where Maggie had gotten ready only a few hours ago. Marla met her at the car, removed the necklace from Maggie's neck, stuck a pen in her hand, and had her sign a release paper.

"You did good, Maggie," Marla surprised her by saying. Maggie was about to argue with her, to protest and point out how badly she had failed, when Marla continued. "No blood on it," she said, inspecting the necklace with something like reverence before snapping the lid shut and closing the car door.

Maggie tipped her head back against the seat and closed her eyes. *Home.* The safety and shelter of her house and dog were all she wanted right now. It came as a surprise when they stopped sooner than she would have imagined, but when she opened her eyes, she saw they were in the drive-thru lane of a fast food restaurant.

"You haven't eaten all day," he explained. "And neither have I. You'll feel better with something in your stomach."

She didn't argue, but she doubted it. When the aroma of food filled the car, however, she realized she was famished and polished off her meal and soda immediately, all while handing him his food so he could eat, too.

"Better?" Ridge asked after she had eaten.

"Yes, thank you," she said.

"What are bosses for?" he asked. His tone was casual, but his expression was anything but. His left hand white-knuckled the steering wheel while his right reached for her hand and twined their fingers together. "You okay?" he mouthed when they came to a stoplight.

She shrugged, not knowing how to answer. Which hurt more—her face, her heart, or the fact that she had failed her mission?

At last they reached her house. Ridge used his key to let them in and then checked Samson's food and water while Maggie remained standing in the entryway like a stranger. He clasped her hand and led her to her bedroom, Samson trotting happily behind them. Once there, he turned her around and tried to unzip her but, as she had been sewn into the dress, there was no zipper. He pulled a knife out of his pocket and cut the seam. The dress fell to the floor like the empty shell it was. Maggie stood in her underwear and bra. She should be embarrassed about that, but she was too numb. Ridge searched in her top drawer until he found a pair of pajamas. She dutifully and wordlessly lifted her arms while he slipped the shirt over her head and then held the legs for her while she stepped into them like a child.

When she was dressed, he led her to the bed, tucked her in and perched beside her. She reached into his inside pocket, pulled out the little notepad, and wrote him a note.

I'm sorry.

He scowled, perplexed. "Why?" he mouthed.

I failed, she wrote.

He shook his head. She nodded. He pulled her upright so he could whisper directly in her ear. "You did perfectly. You made contact, you got information."

"Not *the* information," she said.

He chuckled. "It would be great if intelligence worked that way, if you had gone in and found out exactly what they were planning and brought back evidence. But that rarely to never happens. It comes in bits and pieces. You got a foot in the door, you gave us a start. The plan went as it was supposed to, and I can't think of a way it could have gone better. We know mounds more now than we did before tonight."

"Like what?" she asked, lying back again. It was safe to talk about work out loud.

"Like the fact that the uncles own the house. That gives us a paper trail. Like the fact that there are hidden rooms that didn't show up on our blueprints. Like the fact that...Sam," he had to force the name out, "is terrified of his uncles."

"What does that tell us?" she asked.

"That he might not be working with them willingly."

"It never made sense that he was," she said.

"We'll see," Ridge said, sounding surly once more. He caressed her head, smoothing the fallen hairs away. He took the notebook and wrote.

You're beautiful.

I'm purple, she wrote, and pointed to her cheek.

"It's a good color for you," he said. "I have to go do the de-brief and write my report."

He took the notebook and wrote, I'll be back after.

She nodded.

He pulled out his notebook and scribbled again, his mouth sliding into a wicked grin as he wrote.

Do you want to peel off the mic, or do you want me to do it?

She reached into her shirt, peeled off the mic, and placed it in his palm.

"I don't have to tell you how disappointed I am you chose to do that yourself." He took her hand and kissed the inside of her wrist. "You were brilliant, as good or better than any fulltime field agent. You kept your cool and stayed on task."

She had done neither of those things, but she didn't argue. Maybe it had sounded like she was doing her job when she was pleading with Sam for answers. She hoped so.

"Thanks for having my back, boss," she said.

"Always," he mouthed.

"Hey, can I ask you one more thing before you go?" she said.

He stood and paused by her bed. "What's that?"

"Do you have chaps and spurs, and what are the chances that I could get you to yodel?"

He took the notebook and scribbled furiously.

When you're all healed up, you will pay dearly for that remark.

She took the notebook and replied, Big talk, no action.

He kissed his finger and touched it to her lips, laughing when she licked him. "Weirdo," he said, wiping his finger on her pajama shirt. He paused to scratch Samson behind the ears. The dog had grown on him to the point where he didn't so much mind the slobber and shedding. Maybe when this was over he would broach the subject of being roommates again.

He reached the door and turned once more to look at Maggie. She was curled into the fetal position, eyes closed. He could see the purple rise of her cheek from across the room and had to force himself to turn and walk away.

Chapter 19

Ridge walked to the car, got in, started it, and sat for what felt like a long time. Leaving Maggie felt wrong, but he had a job and he had his orders. At last he reversed the car out of her driveway and pulled onto the road, fighting a wave of his own nausea that had nothing to do with an empty stomach. The night had been a train wreck.

What he said to Maggie had been true, and he had meant it. She had done an excellent job, even better than he expected. She was so sweet, innocent, and unaffected. He had no idea how she would react to the debauched atmosphere of the party. But after her initial shock, she had adjusted like a pro, taken herself to the food table, and begun asking probing questions, garnering them a treasure trove of information about the house and its inhabitants.

When she disappeared with the man, Ridge wanted to go after her. But what could he do when she had already established that he was a casual date intent on making business deals? It was the right way to play it, but he had hated it. Seeing her go with a man whose intentions had been clear from the start had felt like sending his favorite calf to the slaughterhouse, only much, much worse. When the man put his hands on her, Ridge gave up any pretense of trying to maintain his cover and began sprinting away, down the long hallway. But Sam got there first. And that was when things really went downhill.

It was one thing to hear her being manhandled by a creep and another entirely to hear her relive the worst heartbreak of her life. Her grief and pain had been raw, the wound re-opened by an assignment that forced her to relive it in the worst possible way. He had felt sick and guilty and ashamed that they were using her so, and for what? On the speculation that something big was about to go down? What if they were wrong? They had been wrong before. What if they had put Maggie through the wringer for nothing? How would he live with himself if that were the case?

And then there had been the confessions of love and all the kissing. It was obvious to anyone with ears that Sam was still in love with Maggie. The question, at least in his mind, was whether Maggie felt the same.

Finally, as an apex of the emotional trainwreck they had all been riding, he'd had to watch Maggie get hit, smacked so hard he had wondered if she might have a concussion. And there hadn't been one single thing he could do about it. Not only would he have blown their covers, but he understood why the man did it, and that made him feel even more angry and helpless. If their situations were reversed, he supposed he would have tried to do the same, but could he have done so? Could he have belted his precious Maggie in the face? Maybe, to save her life, as Sam had doubtless done. The uncles had been coming for her. If he hadn't showed up and Sam hadn't put on his little display, they might have tried to take her still. Armageddon could have broken out in the hallway with his guns and their guns and his team and their guards all shooting it out for supremacy. But Maggie, his poor, sweet, lovely Maggie, had been the scapegoat that saved everyone. Now she was a bruised flower, sick, exhausted, emotionally spent, swollen and in pain. And he had left her there when he should have remained, holding her and putting the broken pieces back together.

He didn't know he was going to turn around until he did a squealing U-turn in the middle of the road. And then he was speeding back to Maggie, far faster than he had gone away. How could he have left her like that? For what? He had his laptop, he would do the debrief from her house. Why hadn't he thought of that in the first place?

He tried to call her, to tell her he was on his way back and see if there was anything she wanted. There was no answer. He was tempted to stop at the store and pick up a snack, but a pervading sense of doom and urgency drove him onward. Something felt off, something felt wrong. He'd had the feeling before, when missions went wrong, and he had always been correct in his premonitions of disaster. Why had he left her? Why?

As soon as he screeched to a halt in front of her house, he saw the door standing open and called in his team. He had no idea what lay before him, but it was sure to be something bad. He wouldn't think the worst yet. Maybe they had simply tried to scare her, to warn her away.

There was no waiting for backup in the field, not when Maggie's life may hang in the balance. He withdrew his gun from its holster and crept up to her house. The lights were off and there was no greeting woof from Samson. Ridge rounded the corner of the door, gun in hand. He paused, letting his senses adjust to the darkness and silence. His gut told him the house was empty, but his brain told him to make sure. They might have left someone inside to tie up loose ends; they might have booby trapped it to explode. He had seen both, and was prepared for anything.

He swept the house, quickly and efficiently. There were no trip wires and there were no humans. What had happened? He flicked on the lights, and that was when he saw the blood.

Chapter 20

They gagged her, bound her, blindfolded her, and stuffed her in the trunk. *I'm going to die,* was Maggie's first thought, followed quickly by, *No I'm not.* She wasn't a helpless victim; she was a highly trained federal agent. She had skills and knowledge they didn't know she possessed, and it was time to use them to her advantage.

She tried to keep track of the turns they made along the road, but it was too disorienting. Panic clawed at her throat, but she resolutely pushed it away. If she gave in to fear, she would be lost. Her only hope was to use her brain to tap into the things she had learned in the academy.

The car came to a stop, the trunk was opened, and Maggie was hauled out. They ripped the blindfold off her, and she took a quick look around to make note of her surroundings, inhaling in surprise when she easily recognized the compound she'd just left. In fact, the party was still going on and growing louder.

She considered making a run for it, but quickly discarded the idea. The two guards who had taken her far outweighed her, and they were armed. She was half their size, bound, and disoriented. The odds weren't in her favor.

They led her around the back of the house and through a basement garage. Inside the garage was a keypad. The bigger of the two men pressed in a code and another door opened. The fact that they had removed the blindfold and let her see the code didn't bode well for her, but Maggie tried instead to focus on how best to make an escape, should the opportunity present itself. The hidden portion of the basement was a maze, but she forced herself to memorize turns and count steps in order to get herself back out again.

At last they stopped in front of a room and opened the door. The room looked very much like a windowless cell and, she noted, locked from the outside. The guards had been talking to each other the whole way, and the tone of their conversation made Maggie intensely uncomfortable. They dithered outside the cell, debating how much they could do to her before their bosses arrived. At last when she could take it no longer, she turned to face them and spoke in their language.

"If you touch me, they'll kill you. They want me whole."

She wasn't certain if they believed her or if they were merely surprised to hear a blond American speak perfect Arabic. Either way, they gave her a hard shove inside and closed the door, remaining firmly on the opposite side. Maggie took a deep breath and tried to quell the quaking in her hands. She toured the room, and it didn't take long. There was a single bed, more like a cot than an actual frame and mattress, and that was it. There were no windows to try and climb out, no pictures to break and use as a weapon, no chair to shove under the door. The bed was metal and had no weak spots to break apart. The mattress was a useless piece of fluff. She supposed she could tear the mattress apart and try to use the material as a garrote, but it would require brute strength to gain the advantage over even one of the huge guards, let alone two.

The guards worried her as much or more than the men who had ordered her detained. Her captors at least had a purpose. To the guards she was merely a tempting distraction. How much longer would her threat hold them off? And what if they asked their bosses if they could have her and they said yes? If, as she suspected, she had been brought forth as a punishment to Sam, then what better punishment would there be than letting the men have their way with her before they killed her? She had read enough daily briefings to know how things operated. Rape was a weapon wielded by the most brutal of men. If even half of what they suspected of Sam's uncles was true, then allowing her to be brutalized would be merely a drop in the bucket of their crimes.

She alternated pacing and jumping to keep the blood flowing to her legs and brain. She had to stay sharp, had to stay focused, had to stay free of fear.

That plan evaporated when one of the uncles entered and stood staring at Maggie, silent and foreboding.

"Sit down," he commanded at last, in Arabic.

She wondered if now was the time to make her stand. Could she reasonably overpower the uncle? And, if not, would it benefit her at all to disobey him?

"I know you can understand me. Stop pretending and sit."

She sat, but slowly. There was no gain in being combative, just as there was no benefit in being a scared rabbit. Maybe there was a middle ground to be found—compliance without obsequiousness.

"Why were you at the party tonight?" he asked, still not bothering to switch to English.

"I was invited by the man I was with. He needed a date," she replied, also in his language. At one time she was so fluent in Arabic she didn't have to think. Now speaking it made her realize how rusty she had become. It was one thing to read it and another entirely to have a conversation.

He stared at her, his eyes cold and calculating. "I know my nephew's former connection to you. What did he say to you?"

"Nothing," Maggie said, touching her bruised cheek. "I was understandably upset about his disappearance from my life. I wanted him to tell me why he left. He refused. He was angry and distant, and then he smacked me." She looked up, letting her eyes blaze into his with what she hoped passed for honesty. No matter what Sam had done, his life might be in her hands right now. She had to make sure she did her best for him.

"You have always been a weakness for him."

"Why do you care?" Maggie demanded. "Because I'm not Saudi? Because I'm an American? Neither of those things mattered to Sam, or his parents."

"His parents were weak," the uncle said. "And they are not in charge of our family's legacy."

She frowned.

"I see you do not understand me, and that proves your unfitness to be near us."

"Kidnapping me from my home seems extreme. Sam and I already broke up when he disappeared six years ago," she said.

The uncle stared at her again, his dark eyes boring into her. "I know who you are, and I know who you work for. The only question now is how to get the most value from your presence." Abruptly, he turned and left the room.

Maggie remained on the cot, shivering now. She was still wearing her pajamas, the ones Ridge had lovingly placed on her after he cut her out of her dress. The room was cold, but that had nothing to do with her shaking. *They knew.* If there was any doubt in her mind before about her fate, it was gone now. They would kill her, slowly and painfully after they tried to extract as much information as possible.

She was going to die. Despite all of her training and newly acquired knowledge, she was at their mercy. They outnumbered her, were larger, and armed. She had never felt so helpless, alone, or frustrated. Why had she let herself get taken in the first place? True, she had been sleeping peacefully when they burst in on her, but, in retrospect, she should have done *something* besides scream and kick and flail, all of which had been fruitless after they so easily bound and gagged her.

Her family came to mind, one by one, first her parents and then her siblings. Her death would be the hardest on Johnny whose emotions were pure and deep and close to the surface. Her parents would grieve, naturally, but they had three other children. Out of everyone in her life, the loss would doubtless hit Ridge the hardest. He would take it personally, probably blaming himself for leaving her alone, but how could he have known? Neither of them could have guessed the uncles would track her down and take her. It was a bold move that smacked of desperation, practically an act of war. They had taken an American agent captive, in America. And not even at an embassy; they had ripped her from her home and taken her to their compound.

Strangely, that thought heartened her. She *was* an American agent, and that had to mean something. Surely they wouldn't leave her stranded. Ridge would never, even if the agency insisted on it. He would come for her, she was sure. Whether he would make it in time was another question. And doubtless they would be ready for him, with an arsenal of weapons and who knew what else at their disposal. The situation could very easily turn into a siege. They might all be killed.

Head in hands, she rocked back and forth, trying to maintain a shred of reason against the crushing press of fear. The thing she needed most right now was to keep her head and be ready, something easier said than done. She was exhausted, frightened, helpless, and confused. That was doubtless how they wanted her, and she refused to submit to their desires, if only out of stubbornness.

The door opened again. She sat up and pressed her back to the wall, trying hard to look defiant, though she knew she probably resembled a wounded bunny more than a brave warrior.

"Maggie," Sam breathed. He sank to the cot beside her. She shrank away from him and his mouth opened in wounded surprise. "You think I'm going to hurt you?"

She pointed to her cheek.

His head dropped to his hands. "Why can't you understand that I must hurt you to protect you? Do you think I enjoyed that?"

"I don't know what to think anymore," she said.

Tentatively, he took her hand. She didn't pull away. "I'm sorry, so very sorry about everything. I did the worst thing I could think of to keep you safe six years ago, and now I did the worst thing I could think of tonight to try and keep you safe again, and I failed. Who would have believed a twist of fate brought you to this party?" He frowned, dismayed. Either he had no idea she was an agent, or he was a better actor than she gave him credit for.

She let out a shaky breath. He eased closer and slipped his arm around her. She rested her head on his shoulder. Despite the dire situation, they sat in comfortable, easy silence. It might have been six years ago with no interruption in their relationship, if not for the fact that she was a bruised hostage and he was a possible terrorist and captor.

"I missed you," he said. "Setting aside the attraction between us, you were my best friend, the closest thing to me on earth. I have never met anyone else like you, before or since. You were and still remain the best person I've ever known."

"It's hard to not feel like those words are hollow sentiment," she said.

He shook his head. "I'm going to get you out of this."

"How? They'll kill you."

"Yes, they will," he declared. "I don't care. I haven't cared for a long time. You have no idea the misery of my existence. You said you've been alone and unable to love, but at least you've been alive. I've been a shadow, an echo of my former self. Gone is the innocent boy you knew. In his place is some kind of monster."

"Sam, what have you done?" she asked.

"You wouldn't, couldn't possibly understand."

"Try me," she said.

"They killed my mother."

She gasped. "Sam, no." Sam's mother had been beautiful, soft, and lovely. She had accepted Maggie like a daughter, not caring about their differing nationalities or religions. She and Sam had been close, extraordinarily so.

"This was after they threatened you, after I had to fake my death so they'd leave you alone. You were a weakness, a softness, and so was my mother. They wanted to remove temptation, to make me as hard as they are. They succeeded."

"Why? What did they want you to do?" she asked.

"Mostly I've been their business liaison, but their business is brutal. I've seen things, done things…" he trailed off. "Lately, it's…" he paused again. "I find that I can't speak the words to you. You are too pure, and you wouldn't believe me if I told you."

Maggie took a breath, hating to disillusion him further than he already was. "Sam, someone is coming for me."

He blinked at her in confusion. "No one is coming, Maggie. I'm your only means of escape, but I swear I'll get you out."

"Someone is coming for me," she repeated. "If you mean what you say, if you truly want me to be safe, you'll help him."

"Who is it?" he asked.

"The man I was with tonight."

His brow wrinkled in confusion. "The loud cowboy?"

She nodded, trying to convey the truth with her eyes without having to say the words. She was not authorized to blow Ridge's cover, or hers, based on the suspicion that they might already know.

"Maggie?" he said. "What is going on?"

"I can't tell you the details. Suffice it to say things aren't always as they seem in both our worlds. But the man who is coming is good, and he's coming to get me out."

He blinked at her, shocked. "Who are you?"

"I'm the same person I've always been with a slightly different job," she said.

"You…you're not. Are you?"

"I can neither confirm nor deny anything," she said, smiling slightly.

"Look at you," he said, shaking his head, but he was smiling. "When I pictured you as the mother of my children, you were never holding a gun."

"And when I pictured you as the father of my children, you never faked your own death to get out of diaper duty," she said, and he laughed.

"Only you could make me laugh at a time like this," he said, giving her shoulders a squeeze. "All right, I'm going to go keep an eye out for your coworker and try to devise a plan. He is only your coworker, yes? Please tell me you're not married to another man."

"I'm not married," she assured him.

"Are you…is there someone in your life?" he asked.

164

"Tell you what, let's get out of this alive, and then we can compare dating histories," she said.

"You were always good at playing hard to get," he said.

"Thanks, but right now I'm playing 'trying hard to stay alive,'" she informed him.

"You will stay alive, I swear it," he said. He stood, and she could see that he was simmering with rage.

"Sam, don't be reckless. Don't do anything unnecessarily crazy," she said.

He gave a humorless chuckle. "Oh, Maggie. I have no idea what's crazy anymore. My frame of reference is gone." He pulled her up to stand in front of him. "For various reasons, this could be the last time we ever see each other. So I want you to know what I said earlier is true. You were my first love. I loved you deeply, and I continue to believe I love you still. When this is over, and if it ends favorably, I want to have a conversation about us, about the possibility of a future."

She opened her mouth to respond, but he kissed her instead, a deep, intense kiss of longing. Maggie responded because there was still a part of her that longed for him in return, and it might be the last pleasant thing that happened to them before they both died. Now was not the time to say no to kisses.

He let her go and took a step back, as if to remove himself from the temptation of reaching for her again. He pulled a memory stick on a lanyard from beneath his shirt and gave it to her. "Don't lose this. It's what they're willing to kill for. There are six guards in total, including the two standing outside this door, and they're all armed with automatic weapons plus a leg holster. I'll do what I can, but a lot is going to rest on your friend." He kissed her forehead. "Good luck."

"You, too."

"I'm going to need it," he said and, not allowing himself to look back, let himself out of the room.

Her anxiety now in full bloom, Maggie secured the lanyard around her own neck and resumed pacing, wondering how long it would be until the action began.

Chapter 21

Cameron Ridge had never been more grateful for his years of training, first as a SEAL and then as an agent. Being in the field was his comfort zone, far more than pushing papers behind a desk, as he had been doing for the past few months since taking command of his new team. When he was on a mission, as he had been for most of the last decade, he didn't have to worry about people's *feelings* and whether or not his employees liked him. Budget constrictions didn't bother him. He never had to worry if the copier was on the fritz or if someone didn't get the time off they requested and would now quit and leave him short handed. In the field only one thing mattered: failure or success. But unlike every other mission he had ever done, the stakes had never included the life of someone he knew, someone he personally cared about. That was why he was thankful for the training that allowed him to compartmentalize his emotions and focus on the job at hand. For now, he wasn't rescuing Maggie; he was simply carrying out a mission, and failure was not an option.

It was likely, but it wasn't an option.

"You know what this means," the Colonel had said when he showed up at Maggie's house soon after Ridge cleared it. The fact that he arrived in person was a testament to the seriousness of the situation. One of their own had been taken by terrorists on their own soil, and no one took that lightly. It didn't help matters that Maggie was well liked by all who knew her and had eyes as gentle and kind as a newborn foal.

"I know what it means," Ridge had replied, and from there he was on his own. He had gone outside their agency to assemble a team he trusted, a mix of current and former SEAL guys who could do an op, do it well, and keep it covert. There was no protocol for what he was about to do, no written rules, and no budget to pay any of the players. They were there because they lived by a certain code—a brother in trouble is in need of help, the end. None of them even knew Maggie, but they knew Ridge and, by extension, knew he wouldn't be asking for their help for anything less than the direst emergency. And, truth be told, they were the crazy adventurous sort for whom breaking into a well-guarded Saudi compound sounded like a fun way to spend a Friday night.

The only fly in the ointment, as far as Ridge was concerned, was the complete lack of preparation. He liked to have a plan, and he liked to run it at least once before they carried it through. Planning made or broke a mission. But he had enough experience to know a plan wasn't always possible. Sometimes in an emergency, one had to roll with the punches. Maggie in the hands of a couple of madmen qualified as the highest sort of emergency.

So he threw together a team, told them what he knew of the house and its occupants, and that was that. Lethal force had been authorized for anyone who got in their way. Within two hours after finding Maggie's house empty, Ridge was back at the party site with his assembled team, all of them dressed, armed, and ready to go.

First they had to cut the concertina wire surrounding the compound. There were no dogs, and for that Ridge was thankful. He hated it when they had to dispose of animals, hapless victims who had no choice in what their owners were up to. The lights were off outside, and that was strange. They had been on when he and Maggie left the party, which was still in full swing, despite being the middle of the night. Maybe the party was continual, a constant source of cover. They split into three teams of two and flanked the back entrance, but there were no guards outside.

Ridge and his team looked at each other. No lights, no guards, and no dogs. Was it a trap? They proceeded to the door to disable the security system, but it wasn't on. In fact, the door was ajar.

The forward team opened it and swept the hall before signaling the next team inside. The third team would wait outside and guard the door.

They turned the corner and saw two guards posted outside a door. They were down before they had time to raise their weapons, easily and silently. The forward team waited outside while Ridge and his partner opened the door. Maggie stood in the center of the room, her arms crossed over her chest as if she had been waiting patiently the entire two hours, as if she was certain he would come for her.

"Cam?" she whispered, tilting her head at him. He was in full gear and not easily recognized. He nodded and motioned her forward, his eyes scanning her for obvious blood or bruises.

"Are you hurt?" he whispered.

She shook her head. He wanted to sag in relief, but he couldn't because, somehow, they had to get back out again. He sandwiched Maggie between himself and Ethan, his partner, and they turned to go.

They made it almost back to the door when a man stepped out of a room, intercepting their path. The forward team raised their weapons, but before anyone could act, Maggie rushed forward and threw herself in front of the man.

"No," she hissed, shaking her head.

"Maggie!" Ridge exclaimed, albeit in a whisper. All Sam had to do was reach out an arm and secure it around her neck, thereby using her as a handy shield.

"He's on our side. He helped," Maggie insisted. Sam remained motionless, staring at them with unreadable eyes. Everyone looked to Ridge for direction. Slowly, he reached out a hand and pulled Maggie back to his side.

"Hands up," Ridge said, and Sam complied. "Face the wall." Sam turned and put his hands on the wall, but his head swiveled to watch Maggie and the team as they finished their exit.

Maggie turned to look at Sam, pressing her fingers to her lips before offering him a wave goodbye. She may never see him again, but she couldn't think about it now. She couldn't think about anything, not until they were safely away from the compound.

Outside, things became dicey. Their presence had been discovered, and the four remaining guards were back.

"Take her and go," Ethan said, shoving Maggie toward Ridge and turning toward the guards. They went forward to engage and provide cover while Maggie and Ridge made their escape. The guards were coming from the area of the hole they'd made in the concertina wire. There was no choice but to go around the building, back up front, and leave by way of the party.

Ridge had a firm clasp on Maggie's hand, and she flat out ran, despite the fact she was barefoot, in her pajamas, and it was freezing outside. But they made it, and there were no guards left to give chase. He shoved her into a car and peeled off.

"Where are we..." she began but he shook his head, his finger to his lips. She had no idea what that meant, but her brain was too tired to do anything but obey. Instead of talking, she sat back and stared at him in the dim moonlight. He looked a little like a bug, black helmet, black glasses she assumed were equipped with some type of night vision, black clothes, vest, weapons, ammo. He was foreign and intimidating, but when he rested his hand on her leg and gave it a gentle squeeze, he was all at once familiar.

After a long drive to the middle of nowhere, he pulled off the road, got out of the car, and motioned for Maggie to do the same. To her shock, he then turned her around, pressed her against the car, and began to do a combination of a frisk and full-body scan.

"What is going on?" she managed to whisper.

"Searching for bugs," he whispered in her ear, using the opportunity to push aside her hair and scan her neck and there, below her left ear, was an invisible little dot. How he saw it, she had no idea. How it had had been placed there without her notice was an even bigger mystery. Carefully, he peeled it off, tossed it inside the car, and closed the door. When that was done, he turned her to face him and wrapped her in a hug, the full weight of his body smashing her against the car.

"Are we able to talk now?" she whispered.

He nodded. His face against her neck felt odd with so much plastic protection between them. He must have realized the same thing because he ripped off his helmet and goggles and tossed them aside.

She found that, now she could talk, there was too much to say. The words bottlenecked inside her, so she contented herself with holding him and being held in return. There was no air between them, as if they both felt desperate to reassure themselves of the other's safety using only the power of touch. They were plastered together, their faces pressed to each other's necks.

"Maggie," Ridge breathed, loading the one word with all the mixed up emotion he felt—guilt, terror, relief.

"It's okay," she assured him. Her fingers smoothed over the back of his neck, trying to ease the spot where he stored the most tension.

"I…" Ridge began, but the sound of an approaching motor broke them apart. Maggie tensed, but Ridge seemed to relax. A similarly dressed operative stopped a motorcycle two feet away and slipped off, coming to rest beside Ridge. He peeled off his helmet and goggles, surveying Maggie with a charmingly lopsided smile. "You must be Maggie."

Maggie nodded, dazed. She had no idea who he was or what was going on.

"I'm Ethan. Look how adorable you are, in your jammies and everything." He picked her up in a quick, tight hug before setting her down.

"I'm sorry, who are you?" Maggie said.

"I'm Ethan," he repeated before turning his attention to Ridge.

"How many casualties?" Ridge asked.

"Three but I don't think any fatalities. In and out, the guys are probably already out celebrating and disappointed it was so easy," Ethan said.

"I owe you," Ridge said.

"If only there was some way to repay me," Ethan said, bestowing another smile on Maggie.

"Not a chance," Ridge said. "Here." He handed Ethan the keys to the car, and Ethan gave him the keys to the motorcycle.

"Um," Maggie began, but Ridge interrupted.

"I'll explain in a minute, Mags, I have to give Ethan some instructions," he said, not really looking at her. He and Ethan were doing the guy thing where they dismissed the

172

female presence, a punishment for not having enough testosterone to be part of the club.

"But I have this, and I think it should go to the Colonel," Maggie said, holding aloft the flash drive Sam had given her. Now she had the men's full attention.

"Is that what I think it is?" Ridge asked.

"According to Sam, yes," Maggie said. She couldn't be certain, but she suspected it was everything they needed to know about whatever Sam's uncles were planning.

Ridge palmed it and stared at it in silence.

"That should go to the Colonel, and he'll want to hear about it from you," Ethan said. His tone held a teasing note Maggie didn't understand. "You go do your report. I'll see to Maggie."

"If you need to go, then go," Maggie said, though the last thing she wanted at the moment was to be left alone with another strange man, even if he was apparently someone Ridge trusted completely.

Some kind of internal battle raged through Ridge's features before he eventually pressed the flash drive into Ethan's palm. "I don't have to tell you how many lives might depend on this making it to the Colonel. Tonight."

"Such a worrier, LT," Ethan said, rolling his eyes. "Now, you kids have fun." He knocked his fist against Ridge's bicep before turning his attention back to Maggie. "Maggie, a true pleasure to meet you. Something tells me I'll be seeing more of you in the future."

She stood on her toes to hug him. "Thank you so much for coming to get me, whomever you are."

"She said 'whom'" Ethan said, giving her a tight squeeze before letting her go.

"I told you she's a librarian," Ridge said, sounding amused.

"I thought that was her handle," Ethan replied.

"She doesn't have a handle. She's not in the field," Ridge said.

"She is now," Ethan said, his arms swinging wide to encompass the fields around them. "How about QT?"

"How about you get out of here and leave her to me?" Ridge suggested.

Ethan put up his hands and took a step back. "Just a suggestion, LT." He winked at Maggie, slid behind the wheel of the car, and drove away.

"Why did he take the car?" Maggie asked.

"Car's bugged."

"But it's bugged by the agency, right?"

"Yes, and that's the problem." Ridge turned to face her. "The agency can't be trusted anymore. There's a mole."

Chapter 22

They drove for what felt like hours, until the sun began to steal over the horizon. Maggie wanted one thing: sleep. But she had never ridden a motorcycle before. Fear off falling off kept her from giving in to her exhaustion. Occasionally when they stopped at a sign or light, Ridge patted her hand reassuringly, the one that was clasped around his middle. In return, she gave him a squeeze. If not for the terror of the last few hours, it might have been a pleasant ride.

Ridge drove through a fast food place for breakfast, which Maggie would have found funny, if she had any energy leftover for humor.

"How are we supposed to eat it?" she asked, holding the bag aloft.

"Hold it. We'll be there in a bit," he replied before speeding back onto the road.

A half hour of twisty, turning driving later, he pulled off the road onto a hidden drive Maggie wouldn't have otherwise noticed. The driveway was nearly two miles long and almost as twisty as the road, winding sharply back and forth between dense forest. At last he stopped in front of a small, dark cabin.

"Here," he said, hopping off. He lifted Maggie down, a necessity since her legs were now permanently conformed to fit the motorcycle. It took a few hobbling steps before she remembered how to walk again. Ridge was quiet as he led her up the steps and opened the door.

"What is this place?" she asked when it became clear he wasn't going to volunteer the information.

"Safehouse," he said, as if words were an economy.

"If there's a mole, won't he know we're here?"

"There are a lot of safehouses. Only the Colonel knows which one we're at," he said.

Maggie stepped inside and gazed around. The cabin felt like an abandoned vacation rental, as if it had been used occasionally but left to deteriorate in the interim. It was closed up, mildewed, and dusty. Ridge set their food on the small table and held Maggie's chair for her. She tried to catch his glance, but his eyes wouldn't meet hers.

He set out their food. "Cam," she began, but he shook his head.

"Eat first."

She dutifully ate. Everything tasted like sawdust, but it filled her empty belly. Chewing and swallowing became her focus as she imagined the food going down her gullet like a pâté goose. Toward the end of the meal, her eyes began to leak and tears ran unchecked down her cheeks. Unable to continue for one more bite, she pushed away her last few bites of food.

"Cam," she began, her voice tremulous. "Samson?"

At last he met her eyes, and she knew. "He was still alive when I got there. An emergency vet came to your house. He did everything he could, but…He didn't suffer, Maggie, I swear. I sat with him and petted his head while the vet gave him a shot, and he thumped his tail, closed his eyes, and went to sleep. I'm sorry, I'm so sorry."

"I knew they shot him, and I knew it was bad. But he was so big and so healthy, I hoped…The way he looked at me, and I had to be carried right over him, as if I were abandoning him."

"He knew you weren't abandoning him; he knew you were in trouble," he countered.

She nodded. "He tried to attack them. You would have been so proud. He earned his guard dog stripes, in the end."

176

She put her hands over her face and sobbed. He scooped her up, carried her to the couch, sat down, and held her in his lap. She cried until she was exhausted and there were no more tears while Ridge petted her head and kissed her temple, trying in vain to soothe her. Her heart was broken, and it broke his in turn. He wished he could fix it, to make a way for Samson to still be alive. Barring that, he wanted to destroy the men who had hurt her so badly.

Eventually, when she was quiet, he spoke.

"You should go to bed. The bedroom is through that door." He indicated the doorway with a nod of his head. "I'm going to go outside and turn on the gas so we can get some heat and hot water. Maybe after you wake up, the water will be hot enough for a shower." His hand smoothed gently over her hair a few more times.

She nodded, sniffling. "Thanks, Cam. I know we have more to talk about, and you need to do the debrief, but…"

"Maggie, don't worry about it. Sleep, we'll talk later," he said. She slid off his lap and practically stumbled to the bathroom before heading to the bedroom. Ridge went outside, hid the motorcycle, covered its tracks, lit the gas, and did a perimeter check before going back inside.

Maggie appeared in the doorway. "Cam, there's only one bedroom in this place."

"You take it, I'll crash on the couch," he said.

"The couch is disgusting," she said. "I can see the stains from here. Come to bed. It wouldn't be the first time we've shared a sleeping space." She turned and went back into the room without waiting for an answer. Ridge glanced at the couch. It *was* disgusting and tiny and hard. The bed, he knew from prior experience, was almost as uncomfortable as the couch, but Maggie was there, and that was its own inducement. He wanted to be near her, in case she needed him. Or in case he needed her. His mind was still in work mode; he hadn't yet processed his emotions from the last couple of days.

He shucked off his shoes and headed in her direction. By the time he arrived, she was already asleep. He peeled down to his boxers and a t-shirt and climbed in the bed, turning toward Maggie who, even in her sleep, snuggled against him in search of warmth. He was too happy to provide it, slipping his arm over her waist and pulling her close as his face performed a cracking yawn.

Despite his exhaustion, sleep was elusive. He had almost lost her because he chose work over her. Was that what becoming a bureaucrat had done to him? Had he turned into such a boss-pleasing sycophant that he could so easily put filing a report over staying to make sure Maggie was okay when he clearly knew she wasn't? The weight of guilt pressed down on him, making it hard to breathe.

Maggie rolled toward him and curled into a ball, her clutched fists touching his chest. He stared at her so long and so hard she eventually woke, blinking sleepily up at him. "What's wrong with you?" she asked.

He shook his head.

"It's not your fault, Cam. None of it." She reached a hand up and ran it soothingly over his temple.

"Then why does it feel like it is?" he asked. "I shouldn't have left you."

"I'm a grownup and, despite what you might believe, you are not responsible for my safety or wellbeing. You did what you needed to do; you did your duty. There was no way either of us could have foreseen what happened." She let her palm rest on his cheek. He turned his head into it and kissed it, taking comfort from her words.

"I'm not sure I'm cut out for office life," he admitted. "Being in the field is so much easier, it feels more natural."

"You're thirty two years old. At some point age or statistics are going to catch up with you. If you want to build a future, the kind where you're a husband and a father, then you need to start somewhere."

"It's not what I thought it was going to be, and I don't know if I'm good at it," he confessed. He wouldn't have been able to say the words to anyone else, but this was Maggie; he could tell her anything, even his deepest fears and insecurities.

"I think you're good at it. I think you're spectacular at it," she said.

"I thought you said I wasn't," he reminded her. "Because everyone hates me, remember?"

"No. I said you had the potential to be amazing, and you're growing into that potential. Every job comes with a learning curve, and you're learning. When I see you enter a room, people sit up and take notice. You're a natural leader, someone who walks into a meeting and makes everyone pay attention. You have that kind of commanding presence that makes people want to listen to what you have to say, and what you have to say is pretty great. Do you know you're the only person in meetings who doesn't make me want to gouge out my eyes with a pen to try and stay awake? You are good at what you do, amazing, really. And I get that maybe it's not as exciting or rewarding as being in the field or being a SEAL, but the survival rate is exponentially higher. As someone who is deeply vested in your survival, let me assure you it's an important consideration."

He opened his mouth to reply, but she touched her finger to his lips.

"A wise person told me to sleep and then talk. I think what he meant to say is that everything looks and feels better after some rest," she said.

He nodded and then, smiling a little, licked her finger. She smiled, but the smile soon turned to more tears, gentle ones this time and, once again, he held her until she cried them both to sleep.

Chapter 23

Several hours later, Ridge woke first. He wanted to shower, but not as much as he wanted to stay and keep holding Maggie while she continued to sleep. Somehow it was as if neither of them had budged during their many hours of slumber, though they were usually both active sleepers. They were still facing each other and nestled together, her hands balled into fists at his chest, his arm slung over her waist. The temptation he had previously felt toward her had been snuffed out, probably by her grief for her dog. He found it nearly impossible to be turned on by a woman sobbing her eyes out for her lost pet. Instead he felt the usual warm affection as always, and a thankful appreciation for her continued presence in his life. What would he do without his sweet girl? He felt lost and alone at the prospect. In a little over six months, she had become the center of his universe, and not one part of him was tempted to stop and analyze why. It simply was. The same way the sun rose and set each day there was Maggie, at once his rock and soft place to fall.

A clump of hair tumbled over her face. He pushed it back and she shifted, scooting closer and pressing her face into his neck. *PING!* There it was, the physical attraction that had been miraculously absent returned with force. His hand slipped to her lower back and pressed her impossibly closer. She muttered his name, "Cam." Or was it "Sam?"

He froze. Was she awake or asleep? "Did you say something?"

Maggie rolled away from him and blinked, dazed. "What?"

"Did you say something?" he repeated.

"I don't know," she said. Rubbing her eyes, she sat up. "What time is it?"

"Four."

"AM or PM?"

"PM," he said. He missed her warmth, and he wanted an answer to his question. Had she said his name or Sam's? For that matter, what happened between her and her former fiancé in that house? He gave her the flash drive and told her he would help get her out. What else went down?

She drew her knees up to her chest and stared around the room, confused. He rested his palm on her lower back again. "Mags, honey, do you know where you are?"

"Yes, but my brain is sluggish. Do you mind if I shower first? That way I can try to wrangle together some food while you shower," she said, yawning and stretching.

"Fine. There are some clothes here, in the chest at the end of the bed." He used his toe to tap the chest.

She hopped off the bed and went to investigate, lifting the lid so she was hidden behind it. "Hey, there are no women's clothes in here," she complained.

"Yeah, not a lot of women have used this place. I'm fairly certain there are some new packages of underwear and toiletries in the closet," he said. He rolled to his back and stared at the ceiling while she rooted in the small closet. She withdrew and tossed him a four pack of unopened boxers.

"Apparently we're going to be sharing those," she said.

"At the same time?" he blurted, and she laughed.

"No, silly, it's not a three-legged race. Take which ones you want and toss me the other two," she said.

He held the underwear aloft. "I don't think women are allowed to wear boxers. Maybe I should keep all four. You'll have to go without, sorry. Not sorry."

She picked up a random shoe from the closet and tossed it at him. "Denying a hostage underwear is against the Geneva convention."

"That is not true, and you are not a hostage," he said.

"I was brought to a cabin in the woods in my pajamas with no clothes, no shoes, no makeup, and no form of communication. This is definitely a hostage situation."

"Would a kidnapper have brought you your purse?" he asked.

"For real, you did?" she asked.

"For real, along with your gun, but not your phone because it's traceable," he said.

"Hey, when are you going to tell me about the mole? How did you know there's a mole and who is it?"

"Shower first, talk later," he said.

She chucked the other shoe at him.

"What was that for?" he asked.

"You have a lot of stipulations on when we're allowed to talk. You're not the boss of me."

"Um," he began.

"Okay, you're the boss of me, but we're not at work," she said.

"Fine, we'll talk about the mole," he agreed.

"Wait, let me shower first," she said. "Toss me the undies, please."

He reached for his boxers.

"Not the ones you're wearing," she said.

"You didn't specify," he said.

She came over to him, took the package of underwear, smacked him on the head with it, and went to take her shower.

Ridge continued to lay on his back in the bed, trying hard not to picture what was happening in the room next door. Eventually the shower turned off and Maggie called out to him.

"Cam, are you ready for this?"

"Ready for what?" he asked.

"My debut. You're going to want to rip my clothes off when you see me, but don't do it."

He sat up on his elbows for a better view as she came back into the bedroom. He wolf whistled. "Sexy."

"I know, right?" she asked, turning in a circle so he could make a full inspection. She wore a too-big flannel shirt and too-long jeans that had been cuffed multiple times and cinched at the waist with an ill-fitting belt.

"I love your paper towels, Mr. Brawny," he said.

"Be right back, gotta go grab my axe and clear cut the forest," she called as she made her way out of the room and to the kitchen. He heard her begin her search through the cupboards. Smiling, he got up to take his turn in the bathroom.

Meanwhile Maggie began to search for food. What she found was not promising. The house contained zero fresh ingredients. All fruit, vegetables, and meats were canned. The good news was that she knew how to cook and was fairly adept at assembling something from nothing. The bad news was that, even with her best efforts, the resulting outcome would probably not be great. There was no way to get blood from a turnip and, in this case, she would be happy to have a fresh turnip to work with.

Ridge took long showers. Maggie had commented on it once because he was former military and taking short showers was kind of their thing. *That's why I do it,* he had replied. *Too many years being forced to take short, icy showers. Taking long, hot showers is one way I remind myself I'm out of the military and in charge of my own life.* Today she was glad for his prolonged absence because it gave her a chance to try and get her wayward emotions under control. Later, she would give in to her grief for Samson. Right now was not the time. Technically they were still on the job and needed to keep clear heads. Additionally, Ridge did not want to spend the next few days with a woman who couldn't stop weeping. She allowed a few, cleansing tears as she made her way around the kitchen and then ordered them back to their wells, to be retrieved at a later date when she was truly alone and could linger over her raw feelings.

"Smells good," Ridge said when he finally joined her in the kitchen.

"Hey, the ocean called. They want their water supply back," Maggie said, her back to him as she removed a dish from the microwave.

"The nineties called. They want that joke back," he retorted.

She turned and nearly dropped the hot dish in her hands. "You're wearing a hoodie."

"There wasn't a large selection in the box of miscellaneous clothing. Do you want to switch and I'll take the flannel?" he asked.

"No. It's, um, nice." It was more than nice; it was incredible. She was used to seeing him a certain way, in a well-tailored suit and tie. Even when he dressed down he usually wore a button down shirt, sans tie and jacket. She had never once seen him don a sweatshirt, let alone a faded gray hoodie. It made him seem so…attainable. No longer did he look like the Adonis who would only date supermodels. Now he looked like the boy next door, like someone she would have known and been friends with in high school, like someone she would have had an undying crush on.

"Maggie, you're staring at me," he said.

"I am, aren't I?" she asked as the hot dish began to burn her fingers. At last she set it on the table and shook out her hands.

"Would you like to tell me why?" he asked.

"Very much no," she said. She couldn't look at him. In addition to the hoodie, his usually perfect hair was wet and tousled. Perfection didn't tempt her. But this disheveled iteration of him was almost too much temptation. In her current emotionally vulnerable state, she began to genuinely fear what she might do. She sat on her hands and stared at her plate, determined not to make a pass at her best friend. Previously they had shared a fleeting physical temptation, but that was only natural. They were still male and female. So much time spent together would have that effect on almost anyone. Maggie had never found him as appealing as she did at this moment, and the realization couldn't have come at a worse time. *You will not make a fool of yourself; you will not mess everything up.* The pep talk helped some and she was able to raise her eyes when he spoke.

"What is this?" he asked. Thankfully he was motioning to the food and not her strange, new behavior.

"Chicken and rice and sweet and sour green beans," she said.

"Maggie, that's amazing. How do you do that? I know the kind of junk they keep on hand here."

"Food is my love language," she said.

"You're joking," he said, flicking her knuckles.

"No, it's true. It's a secret I've kept from you all these months," she said.

"What other secrets have you been keeping from me?"

He smiled, and whatever quip she was about to make died on her lips. *That I prefer men in hoodies and jeans rather than expensive Italian suits.* "I'm an expert marksman," she blurted, and he laughed.

"Cute," he said and dished himself a huge pile of casserole.

Yes, you are, Maggie wanted to say. He was a deadly handsome man and, strangely, that held zero appeal for her. She had seen him shirtless numerous times and stripped down to his boxers a handful more. She had appreciated his perfect physique, but in the same way she admired a statue at the museum. It was beautiful, flawless, and untouchable. But this unutterable cuteness might be her undoing. He was real and warm and adorable and she was in *so much trouble.* Her mind flailed about for something, anything to distract from her tumult.

"Tell me about the mole."

Chapter 24

"When you join the agency, you're afforded a certain level of protection and anonymity. For all intents and purposes, you don't really exist anymore. No one can Google you and find you on the web. You already know you're not permitted to have social media, but you probably don't realize the extent we go to in order to cover all traces of your life. There is no way, for instance, to find your address. Unless you work for the agency."

"You're saying the only way Sam's uncles were able to find me that night was because someone gave them my address," she said.

"That's what I'm saying," he said.

"What if they followed us home?"

He tilted his head at her, annoyed. "Maggie, it's not my first go round on this thing called espionage. We weren't followed."

"Don't get snappy. It *is* my first go round on this thing called espionage, and I don't know how it works. How was I to know you were keeping an eye out for a tail? I wasn't."

"I'm always keeping an eye out for a tail. It's written into my DNA now," he said, scooping another heaping helping of green beans. "The food is delicious, by the way. Thank you."

"You're welcome," she said absently. "Cam, it's no one on our team."

"It could be," he said.

"It's not," she assured him.

"How do you know?"

"Because I know," she insisted.

"Sweetheart, blind loyalty is nice, but it's not the kind of thing you can afford in this game. It could get you killed."

"It's not blind. I know the members of our team. None of them would ever, ever sell me out."

"Not for a million dollars?"

She blinked. "You think that's how much they paid?"

He shrugged. "No idea. Maybe it wasn't money. Maybe it was a threat to someone's child or mother or spouse. Would anyone choose you over their three year old daughter? My point is that you have no idea what made someone turn and, without that knowledge, you can't possibly know who it was."

She shook her head. "Not on our team, not possible. I refuse to believe it."

"I hope it's not from our team, but I don't have the luxury of ruling out suspects without evidence to the contrary," he said.

"Of course you do. It's your team. Stand up for them and say no one would do that," she said.

"I did, to the Colonel. But between you and me I'm admitting I'm not sure and I can't be sure until the mole is found. That's why I couldn't use any of them to come get you."

"Who were those guys?" she asked.

"Former SEAL team members," he said.

"Who is Ethan?"

He scowled. "A player."

"Easy there, Papa. I was asking out of curiosity, not because I want to have his babies."

"Good because he's not ready to settle down," Ridge said.

"Is that part of the SEAL training? Do they make you swear to be loyal to the country and emotionally unavailable to women?" she asked.

"I am not emotionally unavailable to women. Hello, I'm talking to a woman right now," he said.

"And if I were to say, 'Cam, I think we need to move our relationship to the next level,' how would you respond? Because I think you would leave a Ridge-shaped hole through that wall in your mad dash to escape my clutches," she said.

"Is that what you're saying?" he asked. "Because the way you've been looking at me since I stepped into this kitchen makes me wonder."

"I think if you review our history, you'll see I'm not the one who has ever stepped a toe over the line. In fact, I'm the one who reels us back when it happens," she said.

"What an interesting way of not answering my question," he said.

"What do you want me to say? That I find you attractive? You know I do. You're well aware of how you look," she said.

"Here's what's puzzling me: I've looked this way since you've known me, and for the last year you've studied me like I'm an interesting wallpaper in your grandmother's living room. And then tonight I step into the room and you're looking at me like you want to be the butter to my toast. That food analogy was for you, so you'd get what I'm saying."

They stared at each other over the small table. Maggie wished she were back in the gray dress with full makeup and jewelry. Instead she had scrounged whatever makeup she had in her purse and thrown her long, wet hair into a loose braid. Her ensemble looked like someone put a lumberjack in a shrinking machine, and now of all times he was asking her to declare herself, when she felt dowdy, insecure, and off-kilter.

190

"No words, chatty Cathy?" he taunted.

"Why do I have to be the one to talk?" she demanded at last. "You're possessive and jealous and sometimes you look at me like I'm the quarterback and you're the defensive end who desperately wants to go in for the sack. That's a sports analogy for you, so you'll get what I'm saying."

He blew out a breath. "You are the closest person in the world to me. The friendship we have is better than anything I've ever had with anyone else, and I'm including my entire dating history in there. I don't want to mess it up."

"Ditto." She thought that was the end of it, but he continued.

"So I think you should tread carefully."

Her eyes flew from the bean on the tip of her fork back to his face. "You think *I* should tread carefully? What about you?"

"Maggie, come on," he said, laughing a little.

She set down the fork. "What are you saying here? That you think I can't keep my hands off you?"

"Between us, who is more disciplined in every area of life?" he asked.

Her jaw dropped. "Are you aware of the words coming out of your mouth right now?"

"Settle down, I'm not trying to offend you. This is me being honest."

"First, never tell me to settle down. Ever. Second, you may be trying not to offend me, but you're failing heartily. Third, this is not you being honest. This is you being a self-righteous jerk."

Now it was his turn for shock. "You're calling me a jerk? You've never called me a jerk."

"You've never been a jerk before, at least not to me. Here's a word of warning for you: I'm like the Hulk. I may appear mild mannered and cheerful, but you do not want to see me angry."

He laughed again, another mistake. "You're being ridiculous. All I'm saying is that now is not the time to try and flip our relationship into something else."

"It's times like these I wish I were a man so I could punch you in the face and have done with it," she said.

"Maggie," he exclaimed, shocked again. He had never seen her like this, and he didn't get it. "What is your problem?"

"What is my problem? *What is my problem?* I'll tell you my problem. A man I was with for four years walked back into my life after a six-year absence, a man I thought I was going to marry. Now he's saying that, if we survive our current ordeal, he wants to get back together. And, in the middle of that, my best friend, the man I count on for everything, is telling me he thinks I can't keep my hands off him, that I'm such a pathetic loser I need a lecture about how it's 'not the right time for us' when, spoiler alert, I never said it was. Why do you have the delusion I'm so hot for your body, Cameron Ridge, when I have never once done anything to make you think that? Have I kissed you? Crawled naked into your bed? Begged you to touch me? No, never, not once. And yet you persist in treating me like a charity case who should be thankful for any scrap of your affection."

"Maggie…"

"Not done!" she yelled, standing. Then, "Okay, I actually am out of words. Never mind."

"What exactly did Din Chatti say to you when you were in that cell?" he demanded.

"His name is Sam, and it's really none of your concern," she said.

"Do I need to remind you he's a terrorist and I'm your boss?" he said.

192

"He's an American citizen who is innocent until proven guilty. And as far as needing to know what went down, let me assure you we were not discussing national security, *Mr. Ridge*."

"Are you still in love with him?" he demanded.

"Why do you care?"

"What do you mean why do I care? You're my friend, and he's a terrorist," he said, and now he was angry. "You are toeing the line dangerously close to insubordination."

"How's this for insubordination? I quit," she yelled, smacking her palm on the table.

"You can't quit. We're in the middle of an assignment. It doesn't work like that."

"Then I quit when this is over. You can't tell me what to do with my personal life," she said.

"I can when your personal life involves a terrorist," he yelled. He was standing now, too. Usually he towered over her, but today somehow they seemed to be the same height, as if anger had given her another foot of leverage.

"Stop saying that. He's not a terrorist! He's a good man who got mixed up in something he couldn't control."

"You don't know what was in his control," he yelled.

"Neither do you."

"Do you still love him?" he demanded.

"I don't know!" she hurled. He blinked at her, his anger morphing to hurt. "Cam…" she reached out a hand, but he backed away.

"Forget it. I'm doing a perimeter sweep." He turned and stalked outside, leaving Maggie to clean up the kitchen. She did so in short order and then had nothing left to do. There was no television, no internet, nothing to fill the long, empty hours ahead. She searched the drawers and came up with one paperback, an old spy thriller, probably someone's idea of a joke.

Ridge was outside for more than an hour. When he came back inside, neither of them spoke. He sat on the opposite end of the couch, crossed his arms over his chest, and stared at the wall. Maggie tried to make headway in the paperback, but she couldn't focus. They had never fought before, and certainly not said such awful things to each other and yelled and stormed away. She wanted to make amends, but she was still seething with anger. It was an odd feeling, to yearn for him and want to kick his teeth in at the same time.

"What's that?" he asked after an hour of silence, startling her so she jumped.

"What?" she asked, confused.

"In your hand. What is that?"

"A piece of chocolate I found in the drawer," she said.

"Is there more?" he asked.

"No."

"Then you have to share it," he said.

"Why? You don't like chocolate," she said.

"I like chocolate when it's the only dessert available," he said.

"You never even ate dessert before I started making you," she argued.

"And now I do. I love dessert, it's my favorite. Give me the chocolate."

"No. Finders, keepers."

"Are you really so selfish that you're going to hog all the chocolate for yourself?" he asked.

"What do you think?" she asked as she purposefully unwrapped the candy, making the wrapper crinkle as much as possible.

"Give me the chocolate," he demanded, extending his hand.

She shook her head and rushed to open the candy and jam it in her mouth. Before she could do so, he dove for her. She was ready for him. She sprang off the couch and darted away, running toward the safety of the bathroom.

Like usual, he easily caught her. Unlike usual, she put up a real struggle to get away, kicking, hitting, and biting any part of him that got in her way.

"Ouch," he exclaimed when she bit his wrist. He put her in a wrestling hold and took her to the ground, pinning her beneath him. "Give me the chocolate."

"Never," she said, still struggling to get away.

He flipped her onto her back and pinned her full beneath him, pressing her hard into the floor so she was rendered immobile. They were face-to-face now and panting with exertion.

"Maggie," he breathed.

"What?" she snapped, and then he kissed her.

Maggie responded immediately, dropping the chocolate to plunge her fingers in his messy, tousled hair. They kissed for a full four minutes before taking a breath and pulling back to stare at each other.

"Uh-oh," she whispered.

"Uh-oh we crossed the invisible line, or uh-oh this is a bad idea and we should stop?" he asked.

"Uh-oh, I never, ever want this to stop," she said.

He smiled. "The third option is always the best," he said and kissed her again.

Chapter 25

At first they were almost frantic, as if afraid someone might snatch the opportunity away from them. When they realized that wasn't going to happen, kissing became more a form of affectionate expression. It was relaxed, lingering, and no less enticing.

"Should we talk about this?" Maggie asked at some point.

"I think we've both proved we can't be trusted with talking," Ridge said. "Besides, we've done nothing but talk the last year. This is loads better."

"Good point," Maggie said and they resumed kissing.

"But should we be doing this?" she said a long time later.

"Yes," he replied, and the kissing continued.

"It's just that…" she tried again after another long interlude.

"What you're doing now, that's the opposite of not talking about it," he said. "Besides, it's innocent kissing. Friends can kiss." His lips migrated to her neck.

"Can they?" she asked.

"Yes," he decreed. "And the closer the friendship, the better the kissing. And you are, hands down, my closest friend."

"You're full of vital truths tonight," she agreed.

Approximately ninety minutes later she tried again, "But we're heading…"

He touched his finger to her lips. "We're not heading anywhere. We're lingering in the moment. We're being affectionate because it's been a rough few days, and we need each other. I need you. Don't you need me?" His hands captured hers where they rested face up on the carpet, pressing their palms together as he twined his fingers with hers.

"I need you," she agreed almost shyly. "But…" He stopped her again.

"Maggie, don't you have any idea how long I've wanted this?" he whispered.

"No," she said, shocked.

"By continually trying to stop what's happening here, you're prolonging my torture," he informed her.

"Can I ask you one last question? It's important, and it has to do with your past," she said, her tone suddenly serious.

"Anything," he said.

"Is this the first time you've ever made out with a miniature lumberjack?"

He burst into laughter and rested his forehead on her shoulder. "I can't get enough of you. Do you know that?"

"Please never stop trying," Maggie said.

"I…" he began, but almost immediately stopped talking. Abruptly, he sat up and cocked his head in the direction of the front window.

"What is it, Lassie?" she asked, sitting up beside him.

"A motor, a car."

"So?"

"So this place is designed to let us know when anyone approaches, and no one should be approaching," he said. He reached for his holster and gun and began to attach them.

"Maybe it's the Colonel," she suggested.

"The Colonel knows better than to come here. I'm supposed to make contact with him tomorrow. No one should be here. Get your gun, we're bugging out."

She reached for her purse and, by extension, her gun. "How do you do that?"

"Do what?" he asked as he stood and reached a hand to help her up.

"Go from that," she motioned to the spot they'd been, "to that." She waved her hand at him, now standing with gun in hand.

"With maximum effort and the prospect of picking up where we left off when this is over," he said, giving her hand a squeeze. "Stay behind me and do exactly as I say. Exactly."

"Really wish the magic box of ugly clothes had provided me with some shoes," she muttered. She was barefoot, and it was freezing outside.

He winced. "Great. Just power through the pain and don't think about it. Mind over matter."

"Remind me not to make you my labor coach when I have a baby," she said. He snapped on his helmet with the night vision attachment and reached for her, intending to put Kevlar vest on her.

"Absolutely not," she said, stepping out of reach.

"Absolutely yes," he argued, grasping her wrist and pulling her closer.

"Which one of us is the better target, the big agent with the gun or the tiny librarian without a clue? They're going to want to take you out to get to me. Don't let them," she said, shoving the vest back at him.

"We don't have time for a debate, and I'm your…"

"If you're about to remind me you're my boss, I'm going to quit again," she said.

"I'm the man who has to live with it if you get shot," he amended.

"So don't let me get shot," she said, shoving the vest into his hands and taking a step back.

"Holy geez, you're piece of work sometimes," he muttered as he attached the vest, grabbed her hand, and hauled her out the back door.

Outside the moon was full, but the night was cloudy. Maggie couldn't see anything, and her feet were already beginning to prickle with cold and soreness. Ridge affixed her hand to the back of his pants like a handle and led her into the woods. He moved in a zigzag, dodging piles of dried leaves so as not to make noise. Maggie did her best to walk lightly, but it was hard when she was stumbling blind and tethered. He led her to a sheltered spot beneath a large tree and pushed her to a crouch. He held up four fingers in front of her face. She nodded. There were four guards. His hands split apart, two fingers on each hand, indicating the guards had split into two groups of two. She nodded again. He pointed to his chest and then to the two fingers on his right hand. He was going after the two guards who had gone to the right. Reluctantly, she nodded, knowing what was coming next. He tapped her chest and pointed to the ground in front of her. *Stay here.* She nodded, wishing she could say more, knowing she couldn't. She had no idea how far away the men were, nor if they were close enough to overhear. Since Ridge wasn't using words, she guessed that was the case.

He took her right hand, the one grasping her gun, and put it in front of her, giving it a tap. *Use it if you need it,* he seemed to be saying. She nodded again, assuring him she would. His left palm, the one not holding a gun, pressed her cheek, and then he was gone. Maggie shrank back against the tree, feeling bereft and afraid. She could neither see nor hear anything. She would only be able to use her gun if someone walked right in front of her, practically begging to be shot.

She tried to make herself breathe slowly and deeply and then realized she probably sounded like a steam engine.

Abruptly she instead concentrated on breathing silently, on being as still and invisible as possible. Was anything on her body white or shiny enough to flash in the moonlight? Her skin and hair were the lightest parts of her. Turtle-like, she pulled the flannel over her head, covering her hair. Whoever wore it before her must have been gigantic because there was still enough sleeve left over to cover her hands. Would it be enough to disguise her? Did the guards have night vision? Probably.

Every snap of a twig or rustle of leaves sent her nerves into overdrive. What would she do if someone attacked? Could she actually shoot someone when threatened? It was one thing to learn new skills in theory and another entirely to put them into practice. The lifeless targets they'd used at Quantico were a far cry from living, breathing humans. Would she take a life to save her own? She might have to find out much sooner than she was ready for.

What if Ridge never came back? What if the worst happened and she was left all alone to defend herself? What if he got lost and couldn't find her again in the woods? Should she go look for him?

No, she discounted that possibility immediately. He had said to stay put, and he was big on having his orders followed, that much she knew for certain. She would stay until sunrise or until frostbite took her toes and they snapped off. The latter would probably happen first. Her feet were freezing and getting number by the minute. Though, now that she thought about it, the temperature was probably above freezing and her toes weren't in mortal danger. It only felt freezing to her because she had no coat, socks, or shoes. The temperature was probably somewhere in the forties.

Why are you contemplating the weather when trained men are trying to kill you? Her mind had zoned, as if she weren't surrounded by danger, as if she had all the time and mental energy in the world to ponder the thermometer. Maybe the mind reaches a limit of what it can handle; maybe she had reached hers. How long could a body stand in one spot, waves of fight-or-flight adrenaline crashing down?

A hand covered her mouth from behind. Before she could react, Ridge whispered in her ear. "It's me. I didn't want you to accidentally shoot me, so I came from behind."

The assailants could easily have done the same. Apparently she was fundamentally lacking when it came to surveillance. Her gun might as well be filled with confetti. What was the point of having it if she had no idea when anyone was coming for her?

"Two men are down, but the two who are left split and are flanking us. I'm going to go east and draw them out. I want you to walk due west through the woods for approximately one mile and then go north and follow the road but stay in the trees. In another half mile, you'll come to a gas station. Go there and call the agency. Ask to speak with the Colonel and only the Colonel. Use my clearance. He'll know what to do."

She clutched his vest and shook her head. What was he saying? He wanted them to split up and not just temporarily? Which way was west and which was north? She had no idea. The brief survival training she'd had at Quantico was nothing compared to the navigation training he'd had in the SEALs. What would become of him if she left him?

He pulled her into his arms and held her close. "Listen to me, it's going to be all right, but you have to go."

"Why? Why can't I wait here until you come back?" she asked.

"The other two men were hired hands with no training. They were easy. The two who are left...they're the uncles."

From all they'd been able to gather about the uncles, it appeared they'd had extensive training, both in the military and in the intelligence community. They knew what they were doing, and they were deadly at it.

Maggie felt cold with terror as reality set in. Without saying the words, he was telling her he didn't know if he could take them. He was trying to draw them out to save her. "Go now," he said, giving her a little shove away from him.

"No," she said. "I'm going with you. I'll be your backup."

"It's not up for discussion. It's an order," he said.

"I quit, remember? You can't give me orders," she said.

"Go," he said, angry now.

She shook her head. "Figure out a way to use me as backup or I'll be a tagalong liability."

He stared at her, completely flummoxed. No one had ever disobeyed an order before, and especially not in the field. He was used to SEAL members and fellow agents who did what he said. How was it possible that a librarian was the first to defy him?

"I think we both realize what needs to happen here," she said when he remained mute and mutinous.

"No, I don't think we do," he said.

"I need to draw them out, to be the bait, while you drop in and take them out."

"Out of the question," he said.

"Why? Because it's my idea?" she said.

"Because it's a bad idea, because so much can go wrong."

"It's the best idea. I'm the one they want. They have to know by now that Sam gave me the information and they probably believe I still have it. Why else would they go to the trouble of hunting us down?"

"Because they want revenge, because they want to make him pay by watching you be killed," he said.

"Either way it comes back to me. I'm the one they want, so let's pretend to give them what they want," she said.

He shook his head.

"If it were anyone besides me, what would you be saying right now?" she asked.

He refused to answer.

"You can't let your personal feelings get in the way of the job, Boss," she said, easing her arms around him. She stood on her toes and pressed her face to his neck. He squeezed her so tightly in return that it felt like her ribs might crack.

"If I agree to this, then you have to do exactly what I tell you."

"I will," she promised.

"If I tell you to run, then you run. Whatever I say, you have to do it as soon as I say it," he said.

"Yes, sir," she agreed.

"This is going to be dangerous," he told her. His hand was at the back of her neck, holding her ear close to his lips. She nodded. "If we don't make it…"

She shook her head. "I've never lost anyone on a mission before, and I don't plan to start now."

His lips at her ear curved into a smile. "I like the way you think, Agent Eldridge. All right, here's what we're going to do." He whispered the plan in her ear, and then it was time to go.

Chapter 26

They were tracking her. Even Maggie, inexperienced amateur that she was, could tell. Did they wonder where Ridge was? Did they know he was on the other side, tracking all of them? They could take her out at any time. That was the tricky part of the plan. Once she was in their sites, there was nothing to stop them from killing her. A shot to the heart, a shot to the head, and it would all be over.

"Don't be an easy target," Ridge had told her. "Zig, zag, never stop running and never run in a straight line. Very few people are good shots. They'll aim for your stomach because it's the easiest part of you to hit. So you have to keep moving, back and forth."

She had nodded, pretending she had any understanding of what it meant to be a human target. But it had been her idea to make herself one. There was no backing out now. And with her as the target, it freed Ridge to do what he did best; become the hunter's hunter. While the uncles traced her steps and followed, waiting for their shot, Ridge would be doing the same to them, waiting for the opportunity to take them down.

The problem, Maggie now realized, was that she was a woman and they were all men. As much as she wanted to pretend all things were equal, the reality was that they were faster with more staying power. Her energy was flagging, something neither she nor Ridge had factored into the plan. The farthest she had ever run was five miles, and that was on a paved track during the daytime. Now it was night, she was barefoot, cold, and numb, and almost at the limit of her endurance. Though she continued to dart, as Ridge had told her to do, her pace was getting slower, and the uncles were getting closer. She could hear them now, rustling behind her as they moved through the leaves. They were true hunters, waiting her out, waiting for her to drop from exhaustion. At the rate she was going, they wouldn't have to wait long.

She kept going, putting one foot in front of the other, until at last one bare toe caught on a root and she went down, down, down, landing hard on the cold, wet earth. *Move, move, move.* She could practically hear Ridge's voice in her head telling her not to be a target. So she rolled, ducking behind a tree as a bullet whizzed by her head. If they were close enough to take a shot, then they must be very nearby. One eye peered around the tree, searching the stillness.

"Maggie, stay," Ridge called from somewhere to her left. She spun in that direction but of course saw nothing until he stepped into the clearing, a gun to his head as one of the uncles frog marched him forward. Where was the other one? She had no idea. She stepped from behind her tree and raised her weapon, training it on the uncle who was holding on to Ridge. He continued forward as if she weren't armed, as if her gun were nothing more than a water pistol.

"Stop," Maggie said. He did, but probably more because he was already planning to do so.

"Where is the flash drive?" the uncle asked in Arabic.

"Let him go and I'll tell you," Maggie said, in English for Ridge's benefit.

"Tell me now or I'll shoot him in the head," the uncle replied. Maggie found it curious he hadn't told her to lower her weapon. He must believe her incompetent. It was time she showed him she wasn't. She took aim and fired, her bullet ripping through the hand that held the gun, mere inches from Ridge's temple. The uncle screamed and fell back. Ridge grabbed the fallen gun and spun toward the woods as the other uncle stepped into view.

Maggie wasn't quick enough to take the shot, but Ridge was. He fired, a belly shot that dropped the uncle where he stood. They remained silent, except for some adrenaline-fueled panting that might have come from either of them or maybe both. When it was clear the scene was secure and no one else was coming for them, Ridge spoke.

"You shot through his hand," he said, sounding half-awed and half-amused. "Do you have any idea how difficult it is to hit a target that precise from that far away?" Beside them, the uncle screamed in pain, hurling expletives at Maggie. Ridge took a zip tie from one of the pockets on his pants and secured the man, binding his whole hand to what was left of the one Maggie had disabled.

"At Quantico, I discovered a secret talent for shooting. I wasn't so good at running or fighting, but I could hit targets really, really well. And I told you I was an expert marksman," she reminded him. "Your amused reply was fairly misogynistic." She turned away from the uncle, not wanting to see the fruits of her handiwork. It was definitely different than shooting a target, but also easier when the life of someone she cared about was in danger.

"I wasn't being sexist. I've known plenty of women who can shoot. But you're so adorable. It's like believing a baby sea otter can shoot you. It doesn't add up," he said. He checked the second uncle and secured his weapon. Withdrawing a cell phone from the man's pocket, he turned it on and called the Colonel.

"Did you just call me a baby sea otter?" she asked. Exhaustion was beginning to creep in. She no longer had the capacity to decipher what was real and what was her imagination.

206

"Yes, but you should know that I love baby sea otters," he said. He rested his hands on her shoulders and peered into her face. "Are you all right?"

"My feet have seen better days, and it's likely I'll have some interesting nightmares after this, but yes, I'm all right. Are you all right?"

"Am I all right?" he echoed, and now he was back to sounding angry. "You disobeyed a series of orders, and then you saved my life."

"So it kind of balances out," she said.

"No, Maggie, it doesn't," he said. "When I am in the field, I have to be in charge of the situation."

"Look at it this way—how many more times do you think I'm going to be in the field with you?" she asked.

"I'm mad," he declared. "We're going to have to figure something out, if we're going to continue to work together."

"Of all the things we have to figure out right now, our work relationship is fairly low on my priority list," she said.

"It's foremost in my mind," he said.

She scowled. "Really?" Not the mixed up feelings between them? Not their friendship? Not romance? Did he really care about work more than any of those other, in her mind, more important things?

His thumbs began making little circles on her shoulders. "Maggie, when we're together, I need to know..." he began in a serious tone, but the whir of a helicopter interrupted him. The Colonel landed in the clearing by the cabin and stalked toward them, a team of people jogging to keep up. After that, they had no more time for conversation. Swarms of humanity descended on the cabin. Despite the fact that they had caught the uncles, and despite the fact that the information Sam gave Maggie prevented a sophisticated attack on Times Square that likely would have had ten thousand casualties or more, he was cranky.

"We found the mole," he announced to Ridge as soon as the uncles were safely secured. "You were right; it was none of your team." He sighed and forced out the words he obviously found painful. "It was my secretary. Woman's been with me for a decade. I fed a false location for you to several factions, your team included. I told my secretary the true address but failed to tell her about all the fakes. She was the only person besides me who knew the truth, and she sold the information just as quick." He shook his head, disgusted.

Maggie and Ridge made eye contact, and she smiled, relieved. She knew no one on their team had been the mole. They could go back to work as if nothing had happened. That is, if Ridge didn't fire her first. He was angry enough to do it, and she probably had it coming.

"Colonel, sir, where's Sam?" she asked when she could get a word in.

"Not sure yet. We're preparing a siege and search on the compound as we speak. I'll let you know when I hear something, little miss." He nodded toward the uncle with the damaged hand. "That your handiwork?"

"Yes, sir," she said.

He whistled appreciatively. "I don't suppose you'd consider becoming an assassin? Too few people are a good shot these days. A woman with those skills could be lethal."

She wasn't sure if he was joking. Previously she would have thought so, but half a year in the world of espionage had taught her nothing was ever too bizarre to be true. "I'll give it my full consideration," she said, making sure Ridge overheard. If he wanted to threaten her job, then she could let him know she was entertaining other offers.

Medics arrived on the scene and, when they had bandaged the wounded uncles, tended to her feet. They weren't too bad, considering. They cleaned and bandaged them, and she was able to put weight on them without pain, something she hadn't been able to say a half hour ago. When that was done, she sat on the periphery of the group, thinking. Not too long ago she had lived in a small college town and worked at a library. Tonight she shot a terrorist. She put her head to her knees and laughed until tears ran down her cheeks. If she ever did write a movie, everyone would find it too far fetched to believe.

Several hours later, another helicopter flew her and Ridge back to headquarters. Despite the fact that she had never flown in a helicopter before and didn't want to miss it, she fell asleep. When she woke, her head was on Ridge's shoulder, and he was holding her hand.

"Okay to do the debrief?" he asked.

She nodded, dazed. What time was it? For that matter, what day was it? She felt like she hadn't rested in ages and their last meal was only a memory. Had it been last night before they fought? Before they kissed?

She glanced at Ridge, the memory of his kisses still fresh on her lips. He was still wearing the hoodie, and her heart turned over. While he was dressed down, he felt like hers. Soon he would enter his office and put on a suit. Would the magic that had been between them disintegrate? Other people were in the helicopter with them. Ridge leaned in to whisper.

"You're going to have to stop looking at me like that."

"Or what?" she asked.

"Or I might do something that will get us both fired," he replied, his lips skimming her ear as he spoke.

Maggie shivered, and it had nothing to do with the icy air blowing through the chopper.

They landed on the helipad on top of the building. Anyone who was looking might wonder why a boring logistics company had a helipad, but then again this was DC, so maybe not.

"Duck your head," Ridge said, putting his hand on the top of Maggie's head and forcing it down as they disembarked the chopper. They took the elevator to the conference room and began the long debrief meeting, going over everything that had happened since the beginning of the party. Maggie couldn't allow herself to feel or even think too much. Every cell of her being felt drained and exhausted. She had no more left to give, but this was the nature of her new job. It didn't always keep regular hours, and it was no respecter of mental health or energy. Ridge wasn't complaining, and he'd had the same amount of sleep she'd had the last few days, which was to say hardly any. If he could do it, she could do it, and so she pushed on, answering deeply personal questions almost by rote as they came at her one after another after another.

"Din Chatti, the man you call Sam, came to see you in your cell when you were being held captive, is this correct?" A woman was asking the questions, someone from internal affairs who had seemingly been trained to remove all emotion from her voice. She didn't care about Maggie, didn't care about her answers. It was as if she were a robot that had been programed to get the truth, no matter the cost.

"That's correct," Maggie said.

"Relay the conversation to me in its entirety," the woman demanded.

Maggie rubbed at her forehead, trying to remember. It felt like it had been years, and yet it was only a day. "We talked about our former relationship a bit. He told me his uncles murdered his mother and threatened to do the same to me, that was why he went away, to keep me safe. He said he worked for them as their business liaison—he's tri-lingual, in addition to English and Arabic, he speaks Farsi, and I'm not sure if they are. I only ever heard them speak Arabic.

"Did you tell him you were an American agent?"

"I told him someone would be coming for me." Briefly, she made eye contact with Ridge who was watching her with an intensity that made her look away. "He drew his own conclusions from that statement."

"And that was why he gave you the flash drive?"

"I presume. He promised to help me get away, and then he gave me the information. Please, do you have any information on him? Is he safe?"

"I am not here to divulge information; I am here to ask questions and get answers," the robot woman answered.

"We don't know anything yet, Maggie," the Colonel said, surprisingly gently.

"What else happened?" this question came from Ridge.

"He kissed me. He told me he loved me, and he asked me to consider renewing our relationship, if we both survive."

"Did you kiss him in return?" he asked.

"Yes," she said.

"Did you tell him you would consider his proposal?" he asked.

"I told him survival was our primary objective and I couldn't think beyond that," she said.

"And what was his reaction to that?" Ridge asked. His tone was clinical; his gaze was anything but.

"He said I had always been good at playing hard to get," she said, and his lips twitched slightly.

They glossed over her time in the cabin with Ridge, for which she was thankful. She wasn't sure how truthful she was expected to be about the kisses they'd shared. Was that supposed to be public domain, too?

"You heard an engine approach the cabin," the interviewer said.

"I didn't. Agent Ridge did," Maggie clarified.

"What were you doing at the time of their arrival?" the woman asked, and Maggie bit the inside of her cheek to stop the inappropriate smile that began to spread.

"Enjoying a pleasant daydream," Maggie said. Ridge coughed and reached for a bottle of water. "There wasn't much else to do in the cabin."

"You left the cabin and took your service weapon with you," the robot woman prompted.

"No. It was my personal weapon, not my service weapon. The service weapon is too large for my hand. I prefer to carry my own gun."

"Where is your service weapon?" the woman asked.

"Secured in a safe in my bedroom closet, per agency regulations," Maggie said, and the woman nodded approvingly before continuing.

"What happened next?"

"We proceeded into the woods. Agent Ridge found a safe spot for me to stay while he went to, er, take care of the two guards." She had no idea what to call what he had done. It seemed callous to say he had disposed of two humans, but that was the outcome; the guards were dead. She glanced at him, wondering how he felt about taking two lives. Then she realized it was likely not the first time he had done so and he had probably long ago found a coping mechanism for the realities of his job. She added it to the long list of things they needed to discuss.

"He returned and suggested we split apart so he could draw the uncles to him, giving me a chance to escape through the woods."

"But that wasn't what happened," the woman deduced.

"I don't know which way is west," Maggie said and the Colonel surprised everyone by snickering.

"You refused a senior agent's orders because you didn't know which way is west," the woman clarified.

"No, I refused a senior agent's orders because they sounded like needless suicide in order to keep me safe. I'm an agent too, and a good shot. I knew I could provide adequate backup to give him a better chance of survival."

"What was Agent Ridge's reaction to your suggestion?"

She quirked an eyebrow in Ridge's direction. "He was not pleased."

"But apparently you won the argument," the woman said. Maggie was beginning to not like her at all. She seemed to be morphing from uninvolved spectator to instigator with an agenda.

"It was a split-second, tense environment, not given for a lot of back and forth debate. I pointed out to Agent Ridge that I could offer him backup and told him I refused to leave without him. He made the split second decision to change the plan and use me to draw their fire, since we both realized I was the intended target anyway."

"So you ran toward them and drew them out while Agent Ridge flanked from behind and provided cover."

"That's correct. Only they must have realized the plan because one of the uncles somehow got the drop on him," Maggie said, frowning. She had no idea what happened.

The woman paused and bestowed her attention on Ridge. "Agent Ridge?"

"The suspect had a clear shot of Maggie, and I had no clear shot of him, so I tackled him. We engaged in a hand-to-hand struggle until he was able to retrieve his weapon."

Maggie frowned, staring hard at the table while her heart thudded painfully with renewed adrenaline. Despite her best efforts, he had still offered himself up on a platter to save her. The uncle could easily have killed him. It was only by some miracle that he had decided to use Ridge as leverage instead of shoot him in the head and have done with it. She shivered, trying to push away the what-ifs.

When the woman was done grilling Maggie, she turned her attention to Ridge. They heard the entire story again from his point of view. While he didn't disclose what went on between them in the cabin, he also did nothing to disguise his frustration with Maggie over her disobedience. Dredging it up again seemed to renew his anger at her. He was practically seething by the time his interview was finished.

"Colonel, Agent Eldridge has had a rough few days. Can she be dismissed, sir?" he asked.

"Yes, I think we're done here," the Colonel said. "I've ordered a car for you, Maggie, to take you home."

"Thank you, sir. I need to check on my do…" she paused, remembering with sudden horror that Samson was no longer there, impatiently waiting for her return. To her embarrassment, she burst into tears and, despite her best efforts, couldn't get them to stop.

To her surprise, the Colonel stood and pulled her into a hug, gently pressing her face to the metal on his well-decorated uniform. "Now, there, little miss, you go ahead and cry. I'm a dog man myself, and I know what it is to lose one. It'll be all right," he soothed.

Ridge sat back trying not to let his jaw drop. He had known the Colonel for nearly a decade, since he was a young SEAL and the Colonel whispered in his ear, urging him toward espionage. During all of that time he had never seen one drop of softness from the man. He was old-school, the kind of career military guy who sprinkled nails on his morning cereal for the extra roughage. And now he was gently cuddling a woman while she cried over her lost dog. Ridge smiled and dropped his gaze to the table to hide it. Apparently he wasn't the only one susceptible to the magic that was Maggie.

At last Maggie's tears came to an end. The Colonel released her and she stepped back. "Thank you, sir."

"You're dismissed, Agent. Go get some rest."

"Yes, sir," she said. She crept tiredly from the room, not making eye contact with Ridge again.

Chapter 27

Home wasn't the same. It was no longer her safe space; she had been invaded. Worse, there was no Samson to greet her. The feeling of safety could be regained. The feeling of a cold, wet nose pressing on her hip could not.

The area where he'd fallen had been cleared of blood. The agency, most likely at Ridge's direction, had ordered the area thoroughly cleaned and restored. His body had been taken by the vet and would be returned after cremation, again at Ridge's direction. He had tried to think of everything to spare her pain, but there was no relief from the pressing emptiness of her house. Exhausted, she curled up in bed and cried herself to sleep.

When she woke, eleven hours later, she showered and ate a bowl of oatmeal. The house still felt empty and sad. She would grieve Samson for a long time, but the first brutal rush of emotion was over. Now life had to return to normal.

When she checked her phone, she had a text from Ridge asking her to call him when she woke up. With a fortifying breath, she pushed the button and waited for him to answer.

"How are you?" he said, in lieu of hello.

"I'm fine, how are you? Did you eat? Did you sleep?"

"Yes to both. I wanted to let you know that Din, ah, Sam was found safe in the house. They locked him in the cell they used for you. They beat him, but not fatally. He'll recover fine."

"What's going to happen to him?" she asked, her tone wary. Would he spend the rest of his life in federal prison?

"We flipped him," Ridge said.

Maggie gripped the phone. "You mean…"

"He's going to work for us, go back to the Saudis and pretend he's still working for the cause. No one knew about the family enmity that was going on there. He's going to be a treasure trove, if he works as well as he's promised he will."

"He could be killed," Maggie said.

"Better than prison," Ridge said. He sounded terse and she wondered why. Was it because he preferred Sam in prison? Or was it because of the personal drama between them? Probably the former; his mind always ran to work first.

"So I guess he's free now, free to pursue his former life," he said, his tone morphing from terse to bitter. Maggie smiled. Maybe his bad mood was a little about her.

"Hmm," she said, preferring to remain noncommittal in the face of his bad mood.

"There's something else," he said, and she gripped the phone again.

"What?"

"Ease up, it's a good thing, I hope. It's a SEAL team tradition to go out and celebrate the end of a successful mission. We're meeting tonight, and I want you there. I'm inviting the rest of the team from work, too."

"That's so nice," Maggie said.

"Will you be there?"

"Where and when?"

"Barney's at seven," he said.

"Yes," she said.

"I would pick you up, but I'm at work."

"Should I be at work? What day is it?" she asked, squinting as she tried to remember.

"You have a couple of days off, thanks to the Colonel and his newfound devotion to you," he said, and she could tell he was smiling.

"He's sweet, he reminds me of my grandpa," Maggie said.

"I once saw archived video of him breaking an operative's neck with his bare hands," Ridge said.

"Just like my grandpa," Maggie said.

He laughed. "If I'm late tonight, will you save me a seat?"

His tone gave her a shiver. "Yes."

"Good. And, Maggie, after this night is over, I think you and I need to have a long, productive conversation."

"Yes, sir," she said.

"Hold on to that deferential attitude. You're going to need it, Agent Eldridge," he said, and the call was over.

With nothing left to do for the next few hours, Maggie used to the time get ready. To say she was nervous to meet the other members of Ridge's former SEAL team would be an understatement. Besides her, they were the people he was closest to. They would be judging her, as she could tell Ethan had the night they met.

She wore the jeans her sister, Amelia, had convinced her to buy. It had been a big argument because Maggie couldn't imagine anywhere she would go that would be denim-appropriate.

"Sometimes you'll go out," Amelia had told her.

"If it's a date, I'll probably wear a dress," Maggie had argued.

"Trust me. Buy the jeans, they look amazing on you. Finding a pair of jeans that fits is a miraculous enough reason to buy them," Amelia had said. In the end, Maggie agreed, and now they were the perfect thing—not too casual, not too dressy. Amelia had picked a gray sweater for her, and Maggie wore that up top. She didn't want to look like she was trying too hard, though she spent a solid ninety minutes drying and curling her hair, more than she had spent getting ready for prom. Her makeup took forever as well, causing her to remember why she didn't usually put so much effort into her upkeep. She would never do this much work for every day. For tonight, everything had to be perfect.

When she arrived at Barney's, ten minutes early, Babs and Blue were already there. They greeted her like a returning dignitary who had been out of the country for months.

"Maggie, Maggie, Maggie," Blue said, picking her up and spinning her in a circle before setting her down and kissing both cheeks. "I was almost a work widower."

"We thought we might never see you again," Babs said, choking up near the end of her sentence.

"No, no, there will be no tears tonight. This is a celebration," Blue said, slipping his arm around Babs' neck.

"You're right," Babs said, pressing her fingers to her eyes. "I can't ruin my mascara when there are going to be eligible SEALs here."

"Did someone say SEALs?" Ethan asked. He led a group of four other men over whose brawny, crew-cut presence screamed "we're in the military!" "Maggie?" he asked, tipping his head and peering into her face. "I think it's you, but you looked different without clothes. Still completely adorable, though."

"For the record, I was wearing pajamas," Maggie said. "Ethan, this is Babs and Blue, the others should be along shortly."

"This is Ribs, Frog, Jones, and Shimmer," Ethan said, introducing the group of men behind him who were busy surveying the room. She recognized the gesture from Ridge.

He couldn't relax in a public setting until he had assessed the room for danger and made note of its exits, and even then he was never fully at ease.

"Shimmer?" Maggie echoed.

"He's iridescent with a flamethrower, long story," Ethan said. "Let's sit. Where's LT?"

"He said he might be late," Maggie informed him. She purposely left an open space between her and Ethan, but he moved closer and filled it.

"Cam asked me to save him a seat," she told him.

"He won't mind. We go back a long way," Ethan said. Smiling, he turned toward Maggie and draped his arm on the back of her chair. "So, you and LT. What's that about?"

"The eternal question," Blue interjected. On the other side of the table, Babs seemed to be hitting it off with Jones. LuAnn and Ellen arrived, saving Maggie from answering Ethan's query, or so she thought.

"I have a better question: Why does everyone else have a nickname and you're Ethan?" she asked.

"Ethan is my nickname," he said. "Ethan Allen, I'm from Vermont."

Maggie laughed, "That might be the most obscure nickname I have ever heard."

"I know, right?" he said, using the opportunity to ease in closer.

"You're in my seat, son," Ridge said from behind him and everyone turned to look at him.

"Ridge is wearing a hoodie," Blue announced.

"I didn't think he owned one," Ellen said.

"I thought he was born wearing a suit," Babs added.

Maggie had no words. She merely smiled at the sight of him in a faded sweatshirt, "Navy" emblazoned across the front in faded, gold letters.

"Here's a seat," Ethan said, grinning as he patted the free chair on the other side of him.

"Are you going to move or should I tip you out?" Ridge asked him.

"Maybe we should ask Maggie who she..." Ethan began, but Maggie cut him off.

"Cam," she said, making a little shooing motion at Ethan.

"Ooh, that burns," Jones said, and the other SEAL members laughed. Reluctantly, Ethan moved aside and Ridge sat down. But everyone was looking at them and they couldn't say a word. Maggie was afraid to look at him, afraid her eyes would reveal too much to the other members of the table. Ridge didn't say anything to her, but he did rest his hand on her thigh under the table and give it a squeeze.

"It's coincidental you arrived now, LT, because Maggie was about to tell us what's going on with you two," Ethan said.

"We've already been down this road," Blue interjected.

"What are you talking about?" Ridge asked him.

"With the whole little bit you guys have where you act like newlyweds and then insist you're only friends," Blue replied.

"Who said we're only friends?" Ridge asked.

"You did, a few days ago. You sat right there, same seat, and did the little cheek-to-cheek thing where you said, 'Love her, not in love with her. Best friends.'"

"Do you have any idea what he's talking about?" Ridge asked Maggie.

"It sounds like something he might have dreamed," Maggie said. "Doesn't ring a bell at all."

"No, no, no, we were making fun of you and you insisted there was nothing going on, that you were only friends," Blue said.

"That's crazy talk," Ridge said. "Why would I ever say that?"

"You guys, back me up here," Blue said, looking pleadingly at Babs and LuAnn.

"Are you sure we were here?" LuAnn said.

"Doesn't ring a bell," Babs said.

"It's been a stressful few days for all of us, Blue," Ridge said.

"I hate you all," Blue said. "Fine, back to Ethan's question. What is going on with you two?"

"What is going on is that I'm starving and tonight's on me," Ridge announced. The celebration that echoed around the table was enough to divert speculation from Ridge and Maggie, enough that Maggie was eventually able to lean closer and whisper in his ear.

"Am I fired?"

"I thought you quit," he said. "Twice, if I remember correctly."

"I had my fingers crossed," she said.

"These fingers?" he asked, picking up the hand closest to him and caressing it under the table.

"You're mad at me because I disobeyed," she said.

"I was," he amended.

"Not anymore?" she asked.

He sifted his fingers through the ends of her long hair as it rested on her back. "It occurred to me that I've been trying to run the office the same way I ran a SEAL team, but clearly they're not the same. You're not military, and neither is anyone else on the team. And I'm not anymore either, and I need to accept that and adapt. It needs to be more democracy and less dictatorship."

"How am I going to know when I'm allowed to disobey you and when I'm not?" she asked.

"How about if you obey me at all times, both in and out of the office?"

She laughed. "You're cute."

"Yeah?"

She nodded. "I like this." She plucked at his hoodie.

"I thought you might. I like this." He motioned to her jeans and sweater. "Another Amelia special?"

"Yes."

"I've never seen those jeans before," he said.

"First time wearing them," she said.

"They look good on you. They'd look even better off, though."

"Oh, my," she said, using her cold hands to try and cool her hot cheeks.

"Just when I think you could not be any cuter, you blush at innocent innuendo," he said.

"Suggesting I take off my pants, not so innocent," she informed him.

He leaned closer so he could whisper directly in her ear. "Do you remember that little scene in my office where I said you were playing with matches in a dry forest? I'm about to bring a blowtorch, and I guarantee you I won't be the one to break first."

"Have mercy," she said, turning away from him to fan her face. "What are you doing to me?"

"I don't know. What am I doing to you?" he asked.

"That's a discussion for a later time," she said.

"Check, please," he said.

"You know by offering to pick up the tab you've ensured we'll be the last ones to leave," she said.

He groaned. "I did not think this through."

"See, this is what I'm talking about," Blue said. "They're doing the newlywed thing, where they think they're alone in the room but really everyone is sitting here staring at them."

Maggie scanned the table and, as Blue said, everyone was now looking at them. How long they had been staring she couldn't say.

"We're friends. I told you that the other night," Ridge said.

"No, you said you…you just said…You're going to make me cry again," Blue said.

"Oh, he makes you guys cry, too?" Jones asked.

"What are you all talking about? I'm sweet and cuddly," Ridge said.

"None of us is buying what Maggie's been peddling," Ellen said.

"Of course he's nice to Maggie," Shimmer said. "Look at her, she looks like every baby animal from every Disney cartoon."

"Ever since you had a daughter, all your references are Disney," Frog complained.

"Yeah, that's why *we're* nice to Maggie. That's not why Ridge is nice to Maggie," LuAnn said.

"Did I mention you're all fired?" Ridge said.

"You can't fire us, you're not our lieutenant anymore," Ethan pointed out. "So go ahead and tell us what's going on here."

"What do you want from us?" Maggie asked.

"We want the truth," Blue said.

"You can't handle the truth," Maggie said.

"I like this one," Jones said. "She seems non-crazy. Remember Harlow?"

Ridge sat up. "No, no, no, no. Do not bring up Harlow."

"Who's Harlow?" Maggie asked.

"No one," Ridge said.

"You, shh," Maggie said. "Who's Harlow?"

"Ridge's former girlfriend, AKA Crazy Eyes. Show her the crazy eyes, Frog. You still have that picture of her from your wedding?" Jones said.

"Oh, yeah. Take me a sec to find it," Frog said and began scrolling.

"She doesn't need to see a picture," Ridge said.

"I think she does," Maggie countered. "What was crazy about her?"

"Psychotically clingy. The man couldn't breathe. She checked his phone, followed him around, and if he was late, she would start texting us, wondering where he was, as if we had a normal job with regular hours," Jones said.

"And she made out with Ethan," Frog added.

"You made out with his girlfriend?" Maggie said, leaning around Ridge to look accusingly at Ethan.

"It's a test we do, Maggie. Good news—you passed," Ethan said, tossing her a wink and a smile.

"Maybe I actually am a cheater, and I just don't find you attractive," Maggie suggested.

"Ooh, that's a burn that's going to linger," Shimmer said. "Yeah, I like this one."

"OK, here she is," Frog said. He turned his phone so Maggie could see it. She took it to get a better look at Harlow. She was pretty, but not the drop-dead knockout she had been expecting, and certainly not in the league with Ridge's sister-in-law, Isabel.

"You all look so young. When was this?" Maggie asked.

"Four years ago," Frog replied.

"What about the other girlfriends after Harlow?" Maggie asked.

"There haven't been any, to my knowledge," Ethan said.

"Me, neither," the others chimed in.

"Four years?" Maggie asked, giving Ridge a questioning look.

"I've been busy," Ridge said.

"No, LT, at four years, you've been in training for the priesthood," Ethan said, earning laughs from everyone but Maggie who was still too surprised to react.

Mercifully for Maggie and Ridge, the conversation moved on, and the evening ended up being fun.

"We're definitely going to have to do this again next time one of your team gets kidnapped by terrorists," Jones said.

"I think we're safe," Babs said. "Maggie's the only one of us who has dated a terrorist."

"Wait, what?" Shimmer demanded.

"We were so close to going the whole night without that fact being revealed," Maggie said.

"They didn't just date," Blue added, anxious to get in on the gossip as the group walked to the parking lot. "They were two months from the wedding."

"Wait, the guy she jumped in front of when I almost shot him is her fiancé?" Jones asked.

"Was, *was* my fiancé," Maggie clarified. "Six years ago."

"What is he now, Maggie?" Frog asked.

"Yeah, for LT's sake, we need to track the men in your life," Ethan said.

"I think, for the sake of the men in my life, I'm going to continue to remain mute when strangers ask me personal questions," Maggie said.

"We've seen you in your jammies. We're family now," Shimmer said.

"So are my brothers, and I don't give them details on my love life, either," Maggie said.

"All right, enough hazing of Maggie," Ridge said, putting his arm around her. She leaned into him a little. The SEAL members might have good intentions but, as a whole, they were overwhelming.

"We're joking, Maggie. You pass muster," Frog said, giving her a fist bump.

"If you're good enough for LT, you're good enough for us. But let's be honest, it's been four years. At this point we're willing to take anyone with long hair and feminine mannerisms," Ethan said.

"You guys are fun," Maggie said.

"Welcome to my nightmare," Ridge said.

Eventually everyone streamed away until only Ridge and Maggie were left. They turned to face each other, leaning on her car.

"Are you exhausted?" he asked.

"Is there any other state of being anymore?" she asked.

He rested his hand on her neck, his thumb skimming her jaw. "Still want to talk tonight?"

"Do you?" she countered.

He nodded. "Your place or mine?"

"You choose," she said.

"I'll follow you home," he said. "I'm out of food."

"How do you know I'm not?" she said.

"Good one," he said. She always had food on hand, and coffee and creamer, two things he was also usually out of.

They shared a smile. The tension went from a simmer to a boil.

"If we don't leave now, we might be stuck here forever staring at each other, waiting for the other to make the first move," she said.

"I volunteer to make the first move, but you're right. Home is more comfortable," he said. He opened her car door for her and closed it when she was safely inside before jogging to his car.

Chapter 28

The drive to Maggie's house seemed to take forever. Ridge had good intentions about talking first and taking things slowly. There was too much between them that needed to be hashed out. They would have a long conversation, all night, if needed. They would not let physical attraction get in the way of what needed to be said.

Maggie stood on the porch, searching for her key. Ridge parked in front of the house and jogged up the walk, stopping short behind her. She turned to smile at him and gave up looking for her key, instead reaching for him as he reached for her.

"I missed you," he said.

"It's been forever," she agreed, laughing.

He backed her against the door and cupped her face in his hands, "Maggie, I…"

The door behind her opened. Maggie screamed while Ridge reached for his gun.

"Surprise!" Maggie's little sister, Amelia, stood inside the house, beaming.

"Amelia," Maggie said, surreptitiously pushing down Ridge's gun hand in the hopes her sister wouldn't notice how close she'd come to getting shot. "What are you doing here?"

"The girl who rooms across the hall from me lives in DC. I hitched a ride with her for a couple of days. Oh, hello, pretty," she said, turning her attention to Ridge.

"Cam, this is my little sister, Amelia. Amelia, you apparently remember Ridge."

"So pretty, want to stare at his teeth," Amelia said as she did just that.

"Did I mention Amelia is twenty one? Very, very twenty one," Maggie said.

Ridge smiled and held out his hand to her, after having secretly secured his gun back in its holster. "Hi, Amelia. I've heard a lot of good things about you, and I'm already a fan of your work."

"My work?" she repeated, still staring at his freakishly perfect teeth.

"Maggie's wardrobe," Ridge said, motioning to the jeans Maggie was still wearing. Amelia looked down to see where he was pointing.

"I told you those were hot," Amelia said.

"You were right," Ridge agreed, pinching Maggie's thigh.

"Bosses are different in DC," Amelia said. "Are you guys coming in? And where's Samson?"

"Um," Maggie said, flailing about for an explanation as her throat grew thick and her eyes filled with tears.

"Samson died," Ridge said, clasping Maggie's hand and giving it a comforting squeeze. "There was an accident, and he had to be put down."

"Oh, no," Amelia said, covering her mouth. "That's awful."

Maggie nodded, sniffling.

"Hey, you guys have a lot of catching up and sister stuff to do. I'm going to take off," Ridge said. "Amelia, it was so great to meet you. Sometime when you come back, we'll all go out. Maggie and I will show you the town. Rather, Maggie will show you restaurants and I'll take you to a game."

"What game?" Amelia asked.

"Doesn't matter," Maggie said. "There's always a game somewhere."

Ridge put her in a headlock. "You love it. Admit it, woman."

"I love it," she agreed, hugging his waist. "I'll be in soon," she added to her sister who went back inside and closed the door.

"Thanks for the rescue. I didn't know how to tell her about the dog," Maggie said. She still couldn't bring herself to say Samson's name out loud; the pain was too raw.

"What are friends for?" Ridge asked.

"So much this," she said, standing on her toes to hug him as tightly as she could. "Whatever happens with us, however our conversation ends up, please know that you are the closest friend I have. I have no idea how I would do life without you. You mean the world to me."

"Same," he said, picking her up so she didn't have to stretch to reach him.

They hugged for a long time, until Maggie knew Amelia would probably open the door to check on her again. Reluctantly, she let him go. "Rain check on our conversation."

"The biggest rain check in the universe," he said. "Have fun with your sister."

"It's impossible not to have fun with Amelia."

"I sensed that," he said. "You two make me curious to meet the rest of your family."

"Come home with me for Thanksgiving in a few weeks."

"Hmm, what if I have a girlfriend by then?" he asked. His hands reached out and captured hers, unable to resist the temptation to touch her again.

"It's been four years. I think we're safe," she said.

"You were never supposed to hear that information," he said.

"Why four years?" she asked.

"I'm choosy," he said.

"I thought that only applied to selecting peanut butter," she said.

"Peanut butter and girlfriends," he said. "But you're one to talk. It's been six years for you."

"It's possible we know too much about each other," she said.

He shook his head. "Not possible."

"I seem unable to take the necessary steps to get to the door," Maggie said.

"Do you want me to carry you?" he offered.

"I think that would have the opposite effect of making me want to go inside," Maggie said.

Amelia jerked the door open and poked her head out. "I've been watching you through the curtain for like ten minutes. Are you going to kiss goodnight or what?"

"Perfection can't be rushed, Amelia," he said but then he leaned down and gave Maggie a sweet, gentle, perfect kiss. "See you, ladies." He turned and strode to his car.

"How much longer can your legs support you?" Amelia asked. "Because mine are weak, and it wasn't even my kiss."

"I'm waiting to collapse until he drives away," Maggie said, waving to Ridge as he got into his car.

"Holy mother of pearl, that man is intensely sexy," Amelia said. Then she clapped her hands over her mouth and grimaced. "Ew, am I saying things I'm going to regret about my future brother-in-law?"

"I have no idea," Maggie said, sagging against the side of the house as Ridge finally drove out of sight.

"But you are, like, together, right?" Amelia said.

"It's complicated," Maggie said.

Amelia put her arm around Maggie's shoulders and herded her inside. "Uncomplicate it for me."

"I can't, really."

"Why not?" Amelia asked. She closed and locked the front door behind them.

"He's my boss, and there are other factors involved."

"What other factors?" Amelia asked. "Get rid of them." For her, love was still black or white. Either you loved someone or you didn't.

"There's Sam," Maggie said.

Amelia rolled her eyes. "Maggie, I know you loved Sam, but that was, like, a million years ago. You have to let it go and move on."

Maggie sank onto the couch and covered her face with her hands. "Oh, Amelia, if only it were that easy."

"What's the problem? Do you feel guilty, like you're cheating on Sam? He would want you to be happy with Ridge."

"I'm not too sure about that," Maggie said, dropping her hands to bestow an amused smile her sister couldn't understand. "Do you remember Sam?"

"I was fifteen when he died, not a newborn. Of course I remember. I liked Sam, no, I loved him. He was a great guy, fun and sweet and gentle. He treated you well and you guys had a great relationship. But you can't mourn him forever."

"What if he came back?" Maggie asked.

"What?" Amelia asked, distracted by a text on her phone.

"What if Sam came back?"

Amelia looked up. "Are you having some kind of mental break or are you trying to tell me you believe in ghosts?"

"I'm being hypothetical. What if Sam came back and said it was all a big mistake?"

"First I think you should punch him in the face for going away," Amelia said.

"Let's say he had valid reasons," Maggie said.

"I remember what you were like after, Maggie. There's no reason valid enough for that," Amelia said.

"Play along, what if Sam came back?"

"Do you remember Wesley?"

"Your high school boyfriend?" Maggie said.

"Yes, we dated all of our junior and senior year."

"You were way too young for that," Maggie interjected.

"Not the time, Mom. The point is, I loved him, deeply and desperately, the kind of way you can only love a first love. My heart was shattered when we broke up. So this past summer, we were both home, and we got together and went out. I thought it would be so great, like we would pick up where we left off."

"That wasn't what happened?" Maggie guessed.

"It was awkward, and he's super into Japanese animation now. It was all he wanted to talk about. I found myself checking my phone the whole time, begging for an excuse to leave. I guess what I'm trying to say is that you're not the same person you were six years ago, and Sam wouldn't be, either, if he were here. If you had gotten married, you would have grown together. But being separate so many years, you grew apart. It wouldn't be the same."

Maggie hugged her. "You know you're the total package, both wise and beautiful."

"I know, right?" Amelia said, returning her hug. "And I learned it by watching you." Thanks to their oldest brother, Johnny, they had the habit of always saying the good things they felt, one of many benefits of having a special needs sibling.

"How much longer do I have to wait before you tell me what's going on with your boss?" Amelia asked, letting her go.

"Nothing, really."

"That, on the porch, was not nothing. That was a whole lot of something. And I can't help but wonder what might be happening right now if I weren't here." She nudged Maggie with her elbow.

"We were going to talk," Maggie said.

"Talk," Amelia repeated, putting the word in air quotes.

"Cam and I are sensible adults. We can have a full evening of conversation without giving in to our baser instincts," Maggie told her.

"Liar. I saw the way he was looking at you."

"How was that?" Maggie couldn't help but ask.

"Like it's a hundred degrees and you're the only popsicle for miles," Amelia said.

"You know other people don't make everything into food references," Maggie said.

"I know. Nobody ever knows what I'm talking about when I turn everything into food," Amelia said. "What's that about?"

"It's weird," Maggie said.

"As weird as pancakes with no butter," Amelia agreed, and the sisters dissolved into giggles.

Chapter 29

The next day Maggie spent with her sister. They went shopping and, to Amelia's delight, Maggie was much more open to all the clothing suggestions she made. She came away with a ridiculous amount of new sweaters, skirts, and dresses.

"This is too much," Maggie said, her arms loaded down with bags.

"It's a new season. You have to have different clothes," Amelia told her.

"But I also have to have food and mortgage payments," Maggie said.

Amelia rolled her eyes. "Right, Saver McSaverson, like you don't have money sitting in the bank, gathering dust."

"It's for emergencies," Maggie said.

Amelia picked up the new makeup she'd convinced Maggie to get. "I've seen your makeup stash. This lipstick is an emergency."

Maggie's phone beeped with a text from Ridge.

Having fun with your sis?

SO much, Maggie replied.

The office isn't the same without you. No one has tried to force feed me cake in days. Hurry back.

Tomorrow, Maggie typed.

Can't come soon enough, Ridge said, and Maggie smiled.

"That your boss?" Amelia guessed.

"Work stuff," Maggie said, tucking her phone back in her pocket.

"Work stuff," Amelia said, employing the air quotes again. "Is that what you kids are calling it these days? Speaking of which, I don't have to leave until noon tomorrow. Maybe I could go into work with you, check it out, say hi to the beautiful man in your life."

"Um," Maggie said, stalling. "It's kind of high security."

"Is it?" Amelia said. "Is it really? I thought you're a librarian."

"I am, but it's DC. Everything is high security here."

"Maggie, come on," Amelia said.

"Come on what?" Maggie asked, busying herself arranging her new clothes.

"How many librarians speak Arabic and go to Quantico for twenty weeks? I know your job isn't what you say it is."

"I can't talk about it, Amelia. Really and truly," Maggie said.

"I know, and I think that's so incredibly cool," Amelia said. "So, is your boss, like Bond, James Bond?"

Maggie shook her head. "I can't talk about it, and you can't either, I'm serious." She grasped Amelia's shoulders and looked in her eyes. "You can't talk about it with your friends, not even in a roundabout way. People could get killed, real people, people I know. Never, ever, ever talk about my job with anyone, please."

"Okay, chill," Amelia said, paling slightly. "I'm not a kid anymore, you know. I do realize these things, and I haven't talked about your job with anyone but Darren, and we both know our social recluse of a brother has no friends. He doesn't believe me that you're a, you know, a spy." She whispered the last word and looked frantically around.

Maggie smiled and released her. "I'm not, really. I am a librarian, I promise. Most of my day is spent compiling, cataloging, and dispersing information. It's just a different sort of information now."

"And Ridge?" Amelia asked, somewhat hopefully.

"Ridge is everything you think he is, and probably then some, hypothetically speaking because this conversation isn't happening. "

"Wow," Amelia mouthed. "Can I ask one more question?"

"Maybe," Maggie said.

"What happened to Samson, was it part of your job? And does it have anything to do with that massive bruise on your cheek you've been trying to hide with makeup?"

Maggie nodded. She had almost forgotten the bruise. It only hurt when she smiled, and her feet weren't sore at all anymore. It was as if her body had completely absorbed the trauma of the last few days.

Amelia's eyes widened. "Maggie, are you in danger?"

"Not anymore, and probably not ever again. It was a freak thing, but everything is OK now, I promise. And Ridge is, you know, pretty good at looking out for me. It's hard to think of anything happening when I'm with him."

Amelia nodded, a little dazed. Then her face cracked into a wide smile. "You are so in love with him."

"Amelia, don't mistake friendship for love," Maggie said.

"I'm not, you are," Amelia said. "Come on, Maggie, I see your face, I listen to your voice. I know the signs, and I know you. You're completely in love with him. I don't know how I didn't see it until now."

"Maybe there was nothing to see before. The last few days have been…extreme," Maggie said.

"No, this has been going on for a while. For months, your conversations have been peppered with stories about him. I thought it was because your job was intense that you were spending so much time together, but this has nothing to do with your job." She clapped her hands. "This is so exciting."

"Let's talk about literally anything else," Maggie said.

"How about your hair?" Amelia suggested.

Maggie laid a protective hand on her tresses. "What about it?"

"It's blah. You need something up here." She waved to Maggie's face.

"Like a mask?" Maggie suggested.

Amelia laughed. "No, like bangs."

"Bangs?" Maggie repeated, horrified.

"Not like the bangs Mom used to give us when we were kids, like those straight across the brow horror shows. I mean something side-swept and feminine. Let me do it, let me cut your hair." She clapped her hands together again.

"Let you cut my hair? Do you know how many ways that could go wrong?"

"Do you know how many ways it could go right?" Amelia countered. "Come on, trust me. I cut people's hair all the time at school. In fact, guys pay me to cut their hair for them. I have my own clippers and everything."

"Did you ever think that's maybe less about your skill with clippers and more about letting a pretty girl run her fingers through their scalp?" Maggie said.

"Yes, but I still make money off it, so it's good either way. Come on, I'm not going to take no for an answer. It's time for a change, and it's going to be totally perfect. Trust me."

"Famous last words," Maggie said, but she allowed Amelia to take her hand and lead her to the bathroom where she sat her on the commode and pulled out a pair of scissors and commenced cutting Maggie's hair. In the end, Maggie loved it. The side-swept bangs were exactly what her face had been missing. Amelia also trimmed the rest of her hair, something Maggie hadn't had time for since leaving for Quantico over a year ago. The trim was the perfect refresh she'd been hoping for and she smiled as she surveyed herself in the mirror.

"Maybe college was wrong for you. Maybe you should be a stylist," Maggie said.

"I'm thinking about it," Amelia admitted. "But I don't know how to tell Mom and Dad. I mean, I just spent four years getting a degree. How do I tell them it was a waste?"

"College is never a waste," Maggie said. "And good stylists can make a fortune. Your business degree could help you build an empire. You could open your own salon and franchise it."

"Maybe you should tell Mom and Dad for me," Amelia suggested.

"No, but I'll help you draft some talking points, if you want," Maggie agreed, still staring at herself in the mirror. She couldn't believe what a big change a few hairs could make. The new ones around her face framed it so much better. Her eyes looked bigger, her cheekbones higher. "This is perfect, Amelia."

"I know. You should always listen to me."

"I'm beginning to believe you," Maggie said.

"Let me pick your outfit for tomorrow and do your hair and makeup," Amelia said.

"All right," Maggie agreed.

"That was too easy," Amelia said, suspicious.

Maggie shrugged, too embarrassed to tell her that Ridge's wholehearted approval of everything Amelia had ever picked for her had been her deciding factor. "Hey, I found this awesome restaurant you'll love. I'm going to take you there, and then we're going to load up on cookies and binge watch *Gilmore Girls.*"

"In other words, a perfect night," Amelia agreed.

In the end, it was exactly the sort of restorative therapy Maggie didn't know she had needed. As much as she enjoyed spending time with Ridge, there was nothing like girl time with her sister to set things right.

"Maybe you should move here after you graduate," Maggie said.

"Do you think you'll stay here forever?" Amelia asked.

"At this point in my life, I don't know much," Maggie said. "But I do know that I love having you here."

"I'll give it serious consideration," Amelia promised her, and it was enough to fill Maggie's heart with a wondrous sort of hope. To have family in town would make her new life pretty close to perfect.

Chapter 30

The next morning, Amelia dragged herself out of bed, not bothering to complain about the unearthly hour Maggie had to rise in order to get ready and catch her train. As promised, she did Maggie's hair and makeup.

"Literally, I have never looked better," Maggie said, surveying herself in the mirror. "And I know how I usually look when I wake up, so believe me when I say you're talented at this, Amelia."

"I know," Amelia agreed. They hugged and kissed goodbye. Maggie grabbed her coffee and half jogged to make her train. It would not do to be late on her first day back after so many days away.

Arriving at work brought her a sense of comfort she hadn't expected. These were her people now, and this was her place. Everything and everyone were familiar, even her dumpy little cubicle felt homey and welcoming after a harrowing few days away.

Soon after she arrived, Ridge swept by, on the way to his office after a meeting. He didn't seem to look at her, but a couple of minutes later her phone buzzed with a text.

There are no words for how good you look.

Are there actions? she asked.

Great, now I'm going to be thinking about that while I talk to the president.

Are you joking with me? ARE YOU REALLY GOING TO MEET WITH THE PRESIDENT? Maggie was so excited, her fingers fumbled over the text.

Yes. Turns out the terror attack was even bigger than we first realized. He wants to personally thank the agency responsible for averting it, and the Colonel wants me to come along.

That is amazing. Take pictures and maybe some soap from the White House? She had no idea if the White House had special soap, but she assumed so.

I'm not sure stealing from the White House is the way to go right now, but I'll try to snap a photo. Also, you're coming with me.

Ha, good one, she texted, smiling.

"Not joking," he said, now standing in front of her desk. He gave it a tap. "Come with me, you've been summoned."

She stared up at him with a smile, still certain it was a joke. "That's not funny."

"That's because I'm not kidding. Come on, this isn't the kind of thing you want to be late for, Cinderella." He reached out a hand to her. When she failed to take it, he came around the desk, grasped her arm, hauled her to a standing position, grabbed her purse, and frog marched her toward the elevator.

"I can't meet the president," she said when they were in the elevator.

"Why not?" he asked.

"I haven't mentally prepared myself."

"You mean you haven't spent hours obsessing over everything that could go wrong," he said.

"Exactly."

"That's why I didn't tell you ahead of time." He tapped his temple. "I know you, and you're welcome."

She put her face in her hands then, remembering the perfect makeup job Amelia had done that morning, immediately dropped them. "I can't. I can't."

He didn't answer. They reached the ground floor. He took her hand and guided her through security. Once outside, a car was waiting for them, one of the ubiquitous black town cars used to transport government officials anywhere they needed to go. Apparently if you were important enough, the government began to doubt your ability to drive yourself places.

"Cam, I can't meet the president," she said once they were safely tucked inside the vehicle. Was she having a panic attack? Did a panic attack feel like a boa constrictor was giving her a hug?

"No choice now, baby, we're on our way." He rested his hand on her leg, nudging her dress up slightly so he was touching bare thigh.

"Have you ever met the president before?" she asked.

"Not this one, the last one, when I was a SEAL."

"Why would a SEAL meet the…Did you get a medal?"

He held up his thumb and first finger, pinched together. "A little one."

"What kind of crazy, mixed up world have you recruited me into, Cameron Ridge?"

"My world," he said, giving her leg a squeeze. He smiled in a way that made her forget the president, forget everything but him for a while. "I like your hair."

"I like your face," she returned, and he laughed.

"Does Amelia leave today?"

"As we speak, probably," she said.

"So maybe tonight would be a good time to talk," he suggested. "Want to go out?"

She shook her head. "I'll cook."

"I love it when you cook for me," he admitted.

"I know, that's why I do it," she said.

"You're very good at taking care of me," he noted.

"I could say the same about you."

"No, you go over and above. You make sure I'm fed and watered, bring me clothes at work, make real food for me when I've been eating takeout too many days to count."

"What about you? You check my doors and windows before you leave, take out my trash, bring me my favorite treats," she said.

"You're forgetting one important thing," he said. His thumb was making a little circle on the inside of her leg, making it hard to think of anything.

"What's that?" she whispered.

"I distract you from freaking out when it's most likely. We're here."

She looked around and saw they were under the portico at the White House. "Do I have time to throw up?"

"No. You'll do fine. Take a breath and enjoy it. Most of the time our job is thankless," he said.

"I think I prefer it that way," she said.

"Me too, but this is a blip. It may never happen again. And look on the bright side—if you totally blow it, no one outside this room will ever know. It's a closed meeting—no press."

"Thank you, Cameron. I'm completely comforted now," she said.

He kissed her hand and let it go. It wouldn't do to arrive at the White House holding hands and making googly eyes at each other like teenagers with a first crush.

A page greeted them at the door and led them to the Blue Room, the *actual Blue Room at the White House!* Maggie forced herself to stop thinking of everything that way, as if it should be in italics and end with an exclamation point. She was approximately three seconds from hyperventilating and overthinking everything wasn't helping.

The Colonel and a couple of senior members of the House Intelligence Committee were already waiting on them. They stood as Maggie and Ridge entered. Maggie belatedly realized this was for her benefit as a lady, and she smiled. Men of her generation and ilk didn't usually observe such quaint and chivalrous manners. The Colonel made the introductions, also for Maggie's benefit. Ridge apparently already knew the congressmen. Maggie shook hands, resisting the urge to curtsy. They made polite small talk for a few minutes, and then the door opened again. Everyone stood this time, including Maggie, to greet the president. *The actual President of the United States! Stop that,* Maggie reminded herself, taking a deep breath.

Again the Colonel made the introductions, and Maggie shook the president's hand. He was taller than he looked on television, and also nicer and more personable.

"Rumor has it you shot a man through the hand. That's quite a feat for a librarian," the president said, smiling.

"You should see what I do when someone's late with a book, sir," Maggie said without thinking, and the president laughed before moving on to speak with one of the congressmen.

Maggie tossed a glance at Ridge as if to say, *I did it!* He winked in return, a sly little maneuver no one else noticed. They had tea, complete with tasty, tiny sandwiches Maggie wanted to hoard in her purse and analyze later. *I'm having tea at the White House! Stop doing that,* she once again reminded herself, aiming for a casual expression, as if tea with the president and congressmen was something she did daily and not out of the ordinary for her boring life.

"Ride with me," the Colonel said when the meeting was over. Unlike the generic government-issue sedan Maggie and Ridge had arrived in, the Colonel's car had been fortified to be bullet and bombproof. It was also larger, with two long back seats that faced each other. The Colonel sat on one and Maggie and Ridge sat on the other.

"Maggie, have you given any more thought to my offer?" the Colonel asked.

"I'm sorry, sir, which offer?" Maggie asked, confused.

"To become an assassin," he replied.

Maggie couldn't help it, she laughed. "I'm sorry, sir. I didn't believe you were serious."

"I'm dead serious. Someone with your skill set, language capabilities, and charm would be invaluable."

"Thank you, sir, but I don't think I could kill a man," Maggie said.

"No one does until they do it the first time," he replied. "I know you like to travel, and it would be an interesting way to see the world. Of course you'd need more training, but we would provide that."

"Pardon me, sir, but Maggie's a valuable asset I'm not willing to part with," Ridge interrupted.

"Personally or professionally?" the Colonel asked.

"Both, sir," Ridge said, patting Maggie's knee as her cheeks flushed three shades of magenta.

"That part I can understand, but you know the lifespan of an assassin is short, metaphorically speaking. There are only a few good years before the vision begins to fade and the skills wane. You'd be back in plenty of time to settle down and have kids, if that's your plan," the Colonel said.

Maggie was certain she would never be part of such an unusual day or bizarre conversation if she lived to be a thousand. Was her boss really suggesting she should travel around killing people before coming home and having babies?

"Those are some wild oats I never imagined sewing," she said and winced at her own stupidity. Apparently today was her day for blurting ridiculous things to powerful men.

The Colonel laughed, a rusty sound like chains being dragged over a saw. "I want you to think about it and give it due consideration without any influence from your, uh, boss here. These are modern times, Maggie. A woman needs to decide things for herself."

"Yes, sir," Maggie agreed. *Dear diary, I'm having the weirdest day…*

They dropped Maggie at her floor before heading upstairs for a meeting. "Later," Ridge said, giving her behind a gentle pat as she stepped off the elevator. She swiveled to look at him, open-mouthed with shock.

"Cat's out of the bag now, hon," he said, motioning toward the Colonel who regarded her with mild amusement.

"My wife gives me that same look when I'm in trouble," the Colonel said, and then the doors closed.

The rest of the day was a wash for Maggie. She tried to be productive, but between the morning at the White House, the Colonel's offer to be an assassin, the upcoming dinner conversation with Ridge, and her coworkers pleas to hear details from her meeting with the president, she got nothing done.

Ridge was still in a meeting when it was time for her to leave. He texted that he might be awhile. She texted back and told him to take his time. She still needed to swing by the market for steaks. The upcoming conversation had the potential to be life changing; the meal should be equally epic.

She had just finished putting the potatoes in the oven and marinating the steaks when he knocked on the door. Maggie ran to answer it, laughing. "Why are you knocking when you have a key?"

"I don't have a key," Sam replied, smiling. "But I'd be happy to take one, if you like."

"Oh," Maggie said, her mouth going dry as her brain went blank.

"I was just released from federal custody, and this is my first stop. May I come in?" he asked.

She glanced at the street behind him. No sign of Ridge. As much as she needed to talk with Ridge, she also needed to talk with Sam. After a few seconds mental debate, she moved out of the way of the door, inviting him inside.

Chapter 31

"Are you all right?" Maggie asked. Ridge told her Sam had been beaten by the uncles, but it looked much worse than she imagined. His entire body looked bruised, swollen, cut, and one arm was in a sling.

"You should see the other guys," he said with some of his old self-deprecating humor. He had been a kind, warm, and funny man, able to laugh at himself and the world, equal parts tender and courageous. Maggie's heart pinged a little at the remembrance of who he had been and how much she'd loved him. "Maggie," he said, his tone now altogether different. What had her face revealed when she stared at him? More than she intended, that was for certain. He took a step toward her, but she put up a hand.

"I want to talk, Sam. Just talk."

"All right," he said, following her as she turned and led the way toward the sofa. They sat. "Are you okay?"

"Yes," she said. She felt fully recovered now. Between the rest she'd had and the visit with her sister, she felt ready to take on the world again.

"I'm sorry about your dog. Dogs aren't the same in my family, as you know, and I'm so sorry that my uncles…"

She put up a hand to interrupt him again. "It's not your fault, Sam, really."

"Isn't it?" he asked sadly. "It feels like everything is my fault; our broken engagement, your involvement in this whole affair. All because of me."

"Think of it this way: if we had never met, then I would never have learned Arabic, never have spent so much time in the Middle East, and never have gotten this job or the opportunities that have come with it," she said.

"I know, and that's why I'm apologizing to you," he said.

"No, I meant I'm happy about those things. I love my job, and I love my new life. It's more excitement and adventure than I ever dreamed possible. I mean, a year ago I was a college reference librarian. Today I…" she wasn't sure if she was allowed to tell him about meeting the president. "Today I realized how much this job means to me, how much it's changed me for the better."

"If I had never left, we would be six years married now. Are you also happy that didn't occur?"

"Don't be ridiculous, Sam. I would have loved being your wife. And you were correct; we would probably have two kids by now. At least two, maybe three because, with your big brown eyes, I wouldn't have been able to get enough of your babies."

He scooted closer to her and took her hand. "Would you still like to be my wife? Would you still like to have my babies?"

She blinked at him, her heart in her throat. "A part of me still wants those things," she admitted.

Outside, Ridge reached for his keys and then realized Maggie had probably left the door unlocked for him. He reached for the handle, pushed open the door, and saw Maggie and Sam sitting close together on the couch, her hand in his, their eyes on each other. Silently, he backed out of the house and closed the door. He stood on the porch for a while, debating with himself. On the one hand, he wanted to go inside and physically toss the terrorist scum from her presence. On the other hand, Maggie needed to find her own closure on the man. Again.

He went back to his car and drove down the block to wait, refusing to let his mind dwell on any other possibility than Maggie finding closure in the situation. There was too much water under the bridge, much too much. Besides, Maggie was no longer available. She knew that, didn't she? That was the point that stuck in his craw, that maybe he hadn't been clear enough for her. Maybe by giving her space and trying not to rush her, he had left room for doubt. What if that space opened a place for the next in line? For Sam?

Ridge white knuckled the steering wheel. He would give them an hour. After that, he was going in, ready or not.

"Sam, I loved you. Until you faked your death and ran out on our wedding, you were a wonderful boyfriend and fiancé, so kind, thoughtful, attentive, and romantic. I could not have wanted anyone better. You cared for me with no pretense, no games. That was why it was so difficult when you were gone, because what we'd had together had been so good. A year ago, if we'd had this conversation, I probably would have said yes, let's try to pick up where we left off. But this year has changed me irrevocably and in ways I can't begin to describe. I've discovered I'm more than who I thought I was."

"That's what's so heartbreaking, Maggie. You're becoming the person I always believed you were. You are larger than life to me, and I don't think I will ever get over you," he said.

"I think you will. No, I know you will. You will find someone to fill up all the empty places and make you whole again, I know it in every fiber of my being because you're too good to go to waste."

"How can you say that, after all that has happened?" he said.

"Because, despite circumstances beyond your control, I still know the man you are. I still believe in you."

252

"Is that what happened to you? You found someone to make you whole again?" he asked.

"Yes," she said.

"The cowboy from the party?" he guessed.

She smiled.

"He had better be worthy," Sam said.

"He is," Maggie replied.

They talked for a while longer, putting off the inevitable and painful goodbye. At last she walked him to the door and stepped onto the porch, hugging him impossibly tightly.

"I do love you, you know that," she said.

"I do. Not in the way that I'd hoped, but I do. And I love you, far more than you could imagine," he said.

"Be happy, and be at peace," she said, kissing him gently on the lips. It wasn't a romantic kiss, but a kiss of goodbye, of release.

"And you as well. I wish you every happiness," he said in Arabic.

"And you as well," she replied, also in Arabic. They gave each other one last hug, and then he went away, back to the rental car, back to a new job as a spy and a life that would be dangerous and fraught with peril for as long as he lived. Maggie swiped a few tears as she watched him go and then, almost as soon as Sam pulled away, Ridge pulled up. It occurred to her that he had probably been waiting and watching her goodbye with Sam.

"Oh, hey, um, Sam stopped by, and…"

"Nope, no more words from you. Now is the time to listen as I speak. I'm not taking the chance on one more minute going by before I say what I need to say," he said.

"I'm listening," she said. She tucked her arms behind her back and stood at attention.

He picked her up and carried her inside.

"I thought you were going to talk," she said.

"You're barefoot and not wearing a coat. It's thirty degrees out. Have some self-preservation, woman." He set her down and closed the door.

"Now I'm ready. Here's the thing, Maggie. I always believed that when I found the woman I wanted to spend the rest of my life with, I would know immediately. There would be some kind of sign from heaven, a thunderbolt that struck me numb and proved I had found the one. Everything would go so smoothly that I would have no doubts she and I were perfect for each other. I would fall in love at first sight, and we would live happily ever after forever. And, as it turns out, I was right because, from the first moment I met you, I haven't been able to get you off my mind. I told myself I hired you because you were competent and good at what you do, but that was only a bonus. The real reason was because I loved you. From the moment you licked a piece of muffin off your palm to the moment you smacked my hand for attempting to touch your cookies, somewhere in between there, I was gone. And I have never been the same, and I have never regretted one second my decision to bring you here under false pretenses or woo you under the guise of friendship. Because you're also my best friend. You are my everything, my entire world, and I want to be the same for you. I want to be your best friend, your lover, your partner, and the father of your children. And if you say you're going to take the Colonel's job and become an assassin, then I'll say I'll be your caddy, follow you around the world, and carry your ammo because I'm not going another minute with things up in the air and unsettled between us. I love you, I adore you, and I need you in my life in every way completely."

She blinked at him, trying to absorb the mad rush of words. "Wow, you are really good at making speeches. I'm not, so I'll just say that six years ago, I thought my life was over. When I began putting it back together, bit by bit, it stretched out in front of me, a long, lonely, boring road. Then you showed up with an unbelievable job offer and a chance to start over in a new city. And you believed in me, you encouraged me every step of the way as I took an impossible leap. When I fell down, you were there to pick me up. I wasn't looking for love, ever again, but you made yourself so lovable I couldn't help but fall in love with you. And it happened so seamlessly I didn't even realize until it was too late."

"That was a good speech, Maggie," he said, brushing her newly shorn bangs out of her face.

"Yeah?"

"One of the best," he said.

She slipped her arms around him, and he returned the favor. "Did you really love me from the beginning?"

"Yes."

"Why did you wait so long to tell me?"

"Denial isn't just a river in Egypt. This former SEAL was terrified. I was afraid of my feelings, and I was afraid of messing up the perfect thing we had going. I was so delusional, I believed we could be platonic roommates and nothing would happen, that if I just kept stuffing down and ignoring my attraction to you, it would go away."

"When did you first realize?" she asked.

"I think sometime around that trip to London. When you drove me to the airport. I began to suspect, but I wouldn't let myself look too closely at what was going on."

"London?" she exclaimed. "That was forever ago."

"It took me a bit to figure out why every parting was more painful and why it seemed like my heart was only beating when we were together, why I couldn't stop touching you and had no desire to even try."

"Oh, Cam, that's so mushy and romantic. I love it," she said.

"There's one more thing, while we're getting it all out. I'm not certain I want to stay in DC forever. I miss being from a small town. I don't want our kids to grow up in the city. Maybe someday I'll go into the private sector or teach somewhere."

"I don't care where we go or what we do or how we live, as long as we're together. It's a sad, tired cliché, but it's true," she said.

"Not to ruin this perfect moment, but I'm starving. The last food I had was the tiny sandwiches at the White House," he said.

"Good because I am cooking your favorite meal, including a rib eye steak that cost more than my first car. I was going to bake your favorite pie, but I ran out of time. No dessert, sorry."

He picked her up to bring her eye level. "You're in luck because I stopped by your favorite bakery and bought the cupcakes you love."

"You really do love me," she said.

"Was there any doubt?" he asked.

"No." She kissed him, and it was a long time until supper.

Printed in Great Britain
by Amazon

69734453R00156